Poor Dear Esme by A.M. Burrage

Alfred McLelland Burrage was born in Hillingdon, Middlesex on 1st July, 1889. His father and uncle were both writers, primarily of boy's fiction, and by age 16 AM Burrage had joined them. The young man had ambitions to write for the adult market too. The money was better and so was his writing.

From 1890 to 1914, prior to the mainstream appeal of cinema and radio the printed word, mainly in magazines, was the foremost mass entertainment. AM Burrage quickly became a master of the market publishing his stories regularly across a number of publications.

By the start of the Great War Burrage was well established but in 1916 he was conscripted to fight on the Western Front. He continued to write during these years documenting his experiences in the classic book War is War by Ex-Private X.

For the remainder of his life Burrage was rarely printed in book form but continued to write and be published on a prodigious scale in magazines and newspapers. In this volume we concentrate on his supernatural stories which are, by common consent, some of the best ever written. Succinct yet full of character each reveals a twist and a flavour that is unsettling.....sometimes menacing....always disturbing.

There are many other volumes available in this series together with a number of audiobooks. All are available from iTunes, Amazon and other fine digital stores.

Index Of Contents

CHAPTER I

Having reached the dregs of his second cup of breakfast coffee, Esme arose, folded up his table napkin, helped himself to a cigarette from the packet of "Player's" lying open at Uncle Dick's elbow, and crossed the room to examine himself in the gilt-framed mirror which overhung the fireplace.

It was not for the purpose of admiring his own good looks that he approached the mirror. He was as healthily free from that kind of vanity as any other average boy of sixteen. Nature had cast his features in a girlish mould, and had completed the job by giving him a girl's rosy cheeks and sensitive small mouth. Against the compulsory acceptance of these gifts Master Esme was forever in rebellion. He spent much of his time trying to make his face look hard and weather beaten, and he scowled now at the thin veneer of bronze which only served to make him look like one of those aggressively healthy modern maidens.

"All truly handsome men," he remarked, quoting from an advertisement and speaking at the reflection of Uncle Dick, "are slightly sunburnt. I've grilled myself for the last week and I still look like an advertisement for Somebody's face cream. I'm going to try walnut juice."
The mirror which reflected Esme and Uncle Dick also reflected most of the typical "sitting room" of a seaside apartments house. The window framed a view of a forest of masts clustered in the harbour of the little Cornish port, with a green hill scarred by rocks rising beyond. Esme's gaze in the mirror roved over the room and the view through the window, and finally focused itself upon Uncle Dick, who had neither stirred nor made any reply to his last remark.

Something was the matter with Uncle Dick this morning. He had received a letter which had obviously cast the shadow which clouded his face, for he had read it through at least a dozen times. Something of his evident anxiety communicated itself to Esme, who stood watching him through the mirror with a vague foreboding of coming trouble.

Uncle Dick was Esme's Uncle Dick only by courtesy, and by token of his being the boy's guardian, for they were not related. He was a man of fifty, without a grey hair in his head or a pound of fat on his great carcass which turned the scale at fifteen stone. Dick Farman was a curious mixture of the sportsman and the *dilettante,* but nobody who had not heard him talk would have suspected this good-natured athletic giant of a line of poetry or a sympathetic water-colour study of a landscape. But some of the music and the yearning of Keats were in the verses which he contributed to the reviews, and he painted English scenery—sometimes getting as much as ten guineas for a water-colour sketch—with the feeling and the understanding of a true lover. For the rest, he eked out a precarious livelihood by backing horses, at which, being an admirable judge of racing, he made a small but fairly steady income. His trophies as a rowing man and cross-country runner —when they were not in pawn—were more than sufficient to cover the sideboard at his little home in Surrey. Utterly lovable, with the heart of a child beating under the chest of a giant, generous to the verge of madness, irresponsible as a boy, every man's friend and no man's enemy—these are but the most necessary lines in a rough verbal sketch of Uncle Dick. One more touch and then this narrative shall be left to reveal more of him. Esme had once seen him weeping for sheer joy at the glory of a sunset; within an hour he was drinking beer and studying "form" in Ruff's Guide, before going to bed he caused his ward to read aloud to him six of his favourite odes of Horace. This was the man responsible for the upbringing of young Esme Geering.

Esme turned suddenly from the mirror, crossed the room and thumped Uncle Dick heavily and heartily upon his broad shoulders. It was like smiting the base of a cliff.

"I wish you wouldn't smoke, you young devil," said the other, looking around and noticing the cigarette.

"It stunts the growth and stultifies the brain," said Esme equably. "Good word, stultifies. Uncle, you're pipped. You don't look a bit like the chap who takes the morning Kruschen. I'll go and tell Joe to get the boat ready and see if I can get hold of some bait. You want a good blow on the sea."

Uncle Dick seemed not to hear all of this cheerful speech. His eyes still roved up and down the sheet of notepaper lying before him on the table.

"It's rather decent of me," said Esme, a little piqued, "to want to cheer you up. I was just going off by myself for an hour to have my hair cut. It must be done. I'm beginning to look like a spring poet."

Then it was that Uncle Dick seemed thoroughly to rouse himself. He half turned in his chair and scrutinised the boy thoughtfully and with approval, as if he were proving a sum in mental arithmetic.

"Leave your hair alone," he said, with a sharpness which was very unusual with him. "For God's sake don't have it touched! I mean it, Esme."

The boy was puzzled and fell back upon the heavy sarcasm in which youth indulges.

"All right, uncle. But hadn't I better take violin lessons, so as to live up to it?"

Uncle Dick smiled and regarded the boy with sudden affection.

"Esme," he said, "you're a young devil. I've done my best for you. I've brought you up to be a sportsman, I've tried to make you a decent Christian J. I've taught you to love Keats; and I've sent you to a damned good school—my own old shop. But I don't know that you're a credit to me. You're a precocious little devil in every way. You know as much about racing as I do—and that's more than is good for any man. What would your father say if he knew that you smoked cigarettes and drank beer at your time of life?" Esme's sensitive mouth curled at the corners. It always did when his father was mentioned.

"He takes such a lot of trouble about me, doesn't he? You're the only father I've ever known, and I don't want another or a better."

"You young devil!" said Uncle Dick, but as softly as a mother speaks to her first baby. While he was actually a mass of sentiment he firmly believed that he hated and despised it.

"What's the matter, uncle?" Esme asked. "There's something queer about you this morning. You haven't been losing money, have you?"

Uncle Dick shook his head and picked up the *Western Morning News* from the floor.

"Aunt Ducky won the Bishopboume Handicap," he said. "She was returned at seven to one. Didn't I *prove* to you yesterday that she *must* win at seven stone six? Miserable poverty reduced my stake to two pounds, Esme, but—"

"Well, that's fourteen. Better than a smack in the eye with a wet jellyfish. I thought you'd dropped more than you could afford. Is it something in that letter you're worrying about? "

"Yes." Uncle Dick glanced at the sheet of paper again. "Esme, we're in the soup—both of us. Your father is coming home from Africa in the autumn."

The boy uttered a little sound of dismay, and Uncle Dick looked up at him once more.

"Will he—will he want to take me away from you?" Esme faltered.

"No, old chap. He's only coming home for about a month. But—but he'll want to see you."

"I'm sure I don't want to see *him*. He's never written to me or wanted me to write to him. He's simply treated me as if I didn't exist. But I don't see why his coming need bother you."

"Don't you? Well, of course, you wouldn't see.

I'm an old man to go to prison, Esme"

"Prison!"

"I never meant to be dishonest, old boy. It seemed to me at the time to be the right thing to do. I'm not sure that it wasn't now. But I've sinned grievously according to the law, though I did it for your sake. I've always been a silly casual, absent-minded chap, making my own laws, according to the angle from which I look on life. And it doesn't do. It doesn't do, Esme!"

The boy was staring at him in open-mouthed amazement by the time he had finished speaking.

"Golly, uncle!" he ejaculated. "What *have* you been up to?"

"It's only right that you should know," said Uncle Dick with something like a groan. "I've always meant to tell you. For sixteen years your father's lawyers have been sending me fifteen pounds a quarter for your maintenance and education—"

"And it isn't half enough," the boy protested hotly. "Why, I must be costing you two hundred a year at Wryvern."

"But as soon as he sets eyes on you your father will know that I have swindled him out of nine hundred and sixty pounds. I suppose in a sense I have, although I never looked at it in that light. I did it all for the best, Esme. Good intentions and the way to hell, you know, old chap."

Esme, puzzled, impatient, and perturbed, made a tempestuous gesture to illustrate his feelings.

"Uncle! For the love of Mike, what does it all mean? ''

"It means just this, my boy," said Uncle Dick. "You're a fine, sound, healthy boy, getting on towards being a young man. Well, when your father entrusted you to me before leaving England you were a perfectly charming baby *girl.*"

Esme fell back a step. He had never before suspected Uncle Dick of being mad, except after that pleasant and harmless fashion peculiar to the artistic temperament. But this sounded like sheer raving.

"A baby *what?*" he shouted.

"Hush, Esme! A baby girl. So you see your father will naturally—"

"But it's not *sense!* It's impossible! Uncle, you're pulling my leg."

"I wish to goodness I was, my boy. It's a long story. Come out for a stroll on the cliff and I'll get it all off my chest. Perhaps you can help. There might be a way out yet. You wouldn't like to see your poor old uncle in prison or in a lunatic asylum, Esme, and if I escape the one, the worry of it will drive me to the other."

"If I were having a bet on it," said Esme with the cruelty of youth, "I should back the lunatic asylum every time. Come out and get some fresh air, Uncle Dick. Me a baby *girl!* 'Struth!"

CHAPTER II

On the slippery cliff path hewn out of the rocks, with the sea beneath them on the one side, and on the other the harbour, river mouth, and the clustered white houses deep in the hollow, Uncle Dick's fine eyes were dashed with sudden bright tears.

"All that beauty, Esme," he said, laying a hand on the boy's arm. "I've loved Nature so desperately, Esme. Green hills and blue sea and the wind in my ears—it makes me bleed verses. How shall I endure the four walls of a prison cell for two years?

They'll give me at least two years. I shan't live through it. Fancy coming out of prison and not knowing the names of the three-year-olds! Esme, I've been a good sportsman to you. I never thought to ask you to repay me; but the time is coming when I shall have to throw myself upon your generosity."

Esme was a little moved, but continued not to show it.

"Of course, I'll repay you if I can, Uncle Dick," he said. "But do tell me what it's all about." Uncle Dick pointed to a slab of rock, convenient for two to sit upon, and greatly favoured o' nights by young men and maidens, generations of whom were responsible for its smoothness and its polish.

"Come and sit down," he said. "It's a long story, and a hard story to tell. Look here, old chap, you're not your father's son. I mean you're not his daughter. No, dash it, I mean Esme Geering was a girl, and you're no relation at all to old Tom Geering."

Esme sat down on the rock more violently than he had intended.

"What *are* you saying?" he asked with an air of weary, but saintly, pathos.

Uncle Dick sat beside him and slowly filled a pipe, while his gaze fingered on a flock of gulls wheeling and screaming over a shoal of mackerel.

"Esme," he said, when the pipe was alight, "I'll have to tell you something about my younger days and the man you've always thought was your father. He wasn't a great friend of mine. In fact, I don't think I liked him much. But we were at school and Cambridge together, and we saw each other pretty often; and that sort of thing passes for friendship. In our different ways we both came a mucker. The girl I wanted to marry threw me over, and I married a woman who was none the worse for being a barmaid. Geering came to a financial crash, and at about the same time his young wife died in giving birth to a girl, whom he called Esme. Esme is a name that will do for either sex.

"Well, my poor wife was living then, and when Geering went out to South Africa to make a fresh start he dumped the child upon us, and arranged for a quarterly sum to be paid us through his lawyers. Well, I couldn't refuse to take the kid, and I couldn't afford to refuse to take the money, for I was even more hard up than I am now. I liked the kid well enough, but wished it had been a boy. Poor little soul!—we only had her a month."

"What happened to her, then?" Esme demanded. "And where do I come in? Who am I, anyhow?"

"I'm coming to that," said Uncle Dick. "You must let me tell the story in my own way. Where was I? Oh, yes! Well, the poor kiddy brought us luck. Hardly did she come into our hands than I sold two pictures, three sets of verses, and backed Cicero, the winner of that year's Derby. So my poor wife and I decided to take the child to Margate for two or three weeks.

"Well, we arrived in the evening, and I went to look for rooms while my wife went shopping. We arranged to meet in an hour's time outside the jetty. I took little Esme with me, found suitable accommodation, and handed her over to the landlady to be looked Rafter while I went down to the jetty to meet my wife. That was the last time I ever saw Tom Geering's daughter."

Esme interrupted with a low whistle.

"Jove!" he exclaimed. "What became of her? Was she lost or kidnapped?"

"I don't know which to call it." Uncle Dick took ₜhis pipe from his mouth and assumed an air of melancholy befitting the subject. "You know," he continued, "how absent-minded and forgetful I've always been. Temperament, my dear boy, and it's no use trying to fight against it. Do you know, on my solemn oath, by the time I met my wife I'd forgotten the address of the lodgings where I'd left the kid, and I hadn't more than a dim idea of where the road was."

A muffled sound came from Esme, and Uncle Dick glanced sidelong at his - *protege.*

"Esme, you little devil," he exclaimed, "you're laughing!"

"Laughing! Oh!" The boy writhed like a hooked eel. "It's enough to make a cat laugh. You are the outside limit, Uncle Dick. Well, go on."

"We searched Margate, my boy," said Uncle Dick. "I went literally from door to door. I got the police to help me. I advertised in the local papers. It was all no good. Little Esme had vanished."

"What about this little Esme?" the boy asked, pointing to himself.

"Well, by an extraordinary coincidence, having just lost one kid we found another."

"You were born lucky, Uncle Dick. Who were my people? "

"I don't know."

"*What?* You don't mean to say that you actually *found* me?"

"Yes—on the beach."

"Good Lord!" The boy heaved himself up and then collapsed. "It's a bit of a knock to find that oneself was an unwanted kid, and that one hasn't a right to any sort of name, so far as one knows. And Margate beach of all places! I hope it was at the Cliftonville end."

"Little snob! No, Esme, I am sorry to wound you, but you had better know the whole truth. You were found under a whelk-stall near the jetty."

The boy's only reply was a faint gasp, as if he had almost lost consciousness.

"Dear boy," Uncle Dick continued, a rich note of sympathy in his voice, "I would have kept it from you, if I could. I should like now to hold out some hope that your parents were honest, reputable folk from whom you had somehow strayed. But honesty compels me to confess that your clothes—a single and scanty garment of pink flannelette, no cleaner than it ought to have been—could only lead one to suppose that your mother could not face the prospect of support-ing you. One would like, of course, to encourage the poetic thought that you were a child of magical lineage brought ashore by a wave like King Arthur. But your single garment had evidently never been near the water; and, moreover, the whelk merchants are careful to keep their stalls beyond the reach of the tide."

"For the love of Mike, don't rub it in!" Esme pleaded faintly. "I may not be a gentleman, but I have my feelings."

"Your father," said Uncle Dick judiciously, "was very likely a man of good family. There is breed in you, my boy. My knowledge of the world compels me to be pessimistic about your mother."

"All right," Esme interrupted. "Get on with the story, Uncle Dick. So you adopted me instead of the kid you'd lost. I'm just beginning to realise how grateful I ought to be. But I don't feel like gushing just now."

Uncle Dick stooped and knocked out his pipe on the rocky surface of the path.

"Yes, dear boy, we adopted you. The guardians made no difficulties, and even hinted that there were a few dozen more to be had if we could do with a quantity. You were a dear little chap, Esme, and we hadn't the heart to let you go into an orphanage. My poor wife and I both took to you on the spot.

"Well, there were two or three reasons why we called you after the kid we'd mislaid. We had to find a name for you, and Esme's a boy's name as well as a girl's. Then I somehow couldn't bring myself to write and tell Tom Geering what had happened. It might have broken him up. And after, I couldn't have afforded to clothe and keep you without his allowance. Also, I couldn't have stopped the allowance without confessing that the real Esme had disappeared.
You see what a mess I was in? So I took the line of least resistance; I always do. Thus you became Esme Geering, and if you were only a girl instead of a boy everything would be all right forever and ever, amen." Esme roused himself and smiled feebly.

"Crimes of Paris!" he ejaculated. "You *have* made a mess of things, Uncle Dick. Didn't you know all along that it must be found out? It's a wonder it wasn't all discovered years ago."

"I never bother about to-morrow," said Uncle Dick. "I've always been an improvident old fool. It's my temperament, you know, Esme. And things drifted along so comfortably! Your father—I mean Geering— didn't take the slightest interest in you. The firm of lawyers in Leeds who sent the money regularly every quarter-day contented themselves with a curt inquiry after your health, to which I was nearly always able to reply that it was excellent. As time passed I got so used to the idea that everything was safe. And now your father—I mean Tom Geering—is coming home!"

"Wow!" said Esme. "In fact, two wows!"

He was sorry for Uncle Dick and very sorry indeed for himself, but he was becoming more and more conscious of the humours of the situation.

"It's no laughing matter, Esme! It means prison for me unless you help."

"Help? I'll help if I can. I owe you such a lot, Uncle Dick. If it weren't for you I'd have been at Barnardo's, I suppose?"

"Barnardo's? You'd have been at Borstal by this time, you young devil!"

"Well, what can I do? I can't change myself into a girl, can I?"

Uncle Dick leaned towards him. There was something ingratiating in the gesture, and there was a wheedling, humorous light in his eyes.

"Couldn't you, Esme?" he asked pleadingly. "Not just for a month or two? Perhaps even less? Just to save your poor old Uncle Dick from prison?"

Esme stared at his guardian, rolling his eyes.

"Forgive me, Uncle Dick," he said, "but this is sheer babble."

"It isn't, Esme! I could take you away from Wryvern for a term. You'd make a beautiful girl dressed up in girl's clothes. You—"

"*What?*"

"In another month your hair will be long enough for us to have it—er—bobbed. We—"

He was interrupted by an explosion from Esme, who suddenly went off into a fit of hysterical laughter.

"What a priceless rag!" he burst out. "What a jewel of a rag! Some girl, by George! Run away, you boys! Wow, wow! *Two* wow-wows! Uncle Dick, you're a blithering genius!"

"I do get ideas sometimes," Uncle Dick said modestly. "I can write to your house-master and tell him that I propose taking you to Switzerland."

"Eh?" Esme grew serious. "Careful, Uncle Dick! When I go back I shall be expected to speak French like a Geneva watch, and describe the edelweiss leaping from cataract to cataract over the measureless Alps, and how the Swiss peasant yodels of a morning on his way to the condensed milk factory. You'll get us caught out that way."

"I *will* take you to Switzerland—afterwards—for the Christmas holidays. I'll manage it somehow. Oh, Esme, my dear boy, you've taken such a weight off my mind! "

"Well, I don't mind doing it. It'll be a howling rag. Then I shall be getting a term's holiday "

Uncle Dick interrupted with a little cough.

"Well, not exactly a term's holiday, Esme. Of course, I don't expect you to do any work. You'll be just marking time at a girls' school, but—"

This time Esme shrieked aloud. It was a shrill soprano scream, for his voice had not yet broken, and it made Uncle Dick jump as if he had been stung.

"Girls' school! Girls' school!" There was a frantic ring in the voice. " I say, Uncle Dick, I'm not going to fall for that!"

"Very well," said Uncle Dick, with a martyred air. "I'll go to prison. You need not say another word."

"But why in the name of—of common sense need I go to a girls' school? Why can't I dress up as a girl, and go about with you?"

"Because," said Uncle Dick, "I'm an absent-minded man, and I'd be certain to give the show away. For another thing, if you're at school, you may only see your fa—Tom Geering, I mean—once or twice. If you're not at school, you'll be with him more or less all the time he's over here, and you'd find it a strain. Besides, you'd probably give yourself away, or make him suspicious. But in a nice quiet girls' school—"

"Oh, hell!"

"A small school I know of, Esme. It's kept by a friend of the woman I ought to have married. I shall be able to get for you a lot of little comforts and attentions that would be impossible in a school run more or less on public school lines. I can get you a private bedroom, for instance—"

"That wouldn't be a comfort," commented Esme; " it would be a necessity."

"And I could get you *off* gym. And I'd arrange for you to take private studies, so that you wouldn't have to mix too much with the other girls. Besides, think what a rag it would be, Esme!"

"Oh, splendid! But I prefer a rag to last only for an hour or two, instead of for months. Besides, I believe they'd be able to quod me for it if they caught me. And what about my second fifteen colours? I was a cert for them. Might even have got a show in the first."

Uncle Dick reassumed his look of imminent martyrdom.

"Say no more, Esme!" he exclaimed. "I have sacrificed much for you already. I will sacrifice more. I will go to prison."

But Esme laid a hand affectionately upon Uncle Dick's arm.

"No, you won't!" he cried. "I may have been found under a whelk-stall, but I've been brought up among gentlemen, and I won't allow it. I'll go to your perishing girls' school and see it through."

CHAPTER III

Purlingdon, as everybody knows, or ought to know, is a suburb on the outskirts of south-west London, twelve good miles from Charing Cross. On three sides it is bordered by other suburbs; on the fourth there is what the estate agents still describe as the glorious open country.

Motoring along the Great West Road, which is as straight as a spear striking at the heart of London, one certainly leaves the suburbs behind at Purlingdon. But for miles the glorious open country is as flat as a man's hand, dreary fields on either side advertise themselves as eligible building sites, dingy hedges, dust laden in the summer, line the way, and on nearly every bam and fence is a glaring poster advertising the week's attractions at the Purlingdon Hippodrome. Most of the Purlingdon houses are very new, and by standing up in all weathers seem to be continually defying some law of Nature, but there is an older part of the suburb, reminding one that the place was once a village, and that green fields once lay between it and London. Sumphill Road is part of old Purlingdon, and consists of a single row of houses which faces the back gardens of a terrace of new villas.

Sumphill Road had once been pretentious. The merchants and retired tradesmen, who wore side whiskers, and their wives, who wore crinolines, considered it a good address. The houses were built in pairs, semi-detached, four storeys high, and each had a garden of nearly an acre; but tall trees in the front gardens shut out the light, and grimy overgrown shrubs and evergreens kept the cellars damp even in the dryest summer. For the houses in Sumphill Road, having been built before suburbs were properly invented, had each a basement. They were a sad-looking dreary row, built of slate-coloured stone, and seemed mutely to be pleading that they had seen better days. Partly because no high- spirited servant girl will stand a basement, and partly because of their dreariness of aspect, the rents of these good-sized houses were smaller than that of their bright cheeky little neighbours.

To this road came Mrs. Hannah Toy, B.A., Lond., in the days when it was possible to rent a house, and estate agents were civil. She then proceeded to found a school for the daughters of gentlefolk by the simple process of knocking two of the houses into one and putting up a board. She called it St. Mildred's College, because a saint sounds very well in the name of a school. She did not herself believe in saints, and did not intend, if she could help it, to place her establishment under the patronage of one; but as she had never heard of a St. Mildred she satisfied her conscience without doing possible harm to her business.

Mrs. Toy was a widow who had spent most of her life in various schools. After considerable experience as an assistant mistress, she had married the late Gabriel Toy, a traveller in tyres for bath chairs. After only a few months of married life, a damp bed in a temperance hotel ushered him into the unknown, and left his widow to collect the £2,000 for which he had very prudently insured his life. This enabled her to realise an old ambition and start a school of her own.

Mrs. Toy did not take day-girls. The County School and other monstrously efficient and disgracefully cheap secondary schools had ruined the business. Besides, there was little money in it, and she was short of accommodation. Into the two converted houses she squeezed herself, four assistant mistresses, fifty daughters of gentlefolk, and a skeleton staff of servants. By keeping a "good, plain, wholesome diet," very plain indeed, and charging an inclusive fee of £70 a year, she out-thrived any ordinary green bay tree. Her methods, like herself, were a little old-fashioned, but the girls who left her care had a reputation for being "nice," and it was seldom that she had to advertise for pupils.

It was on the 28th of September, ten days after the school had reassembled after the summer holidays, that Cuthbert received orders to be at the station and attend to the luggage of Miss Esme Geering, who was to arrive at 5.10. Cuthbert inhabited a small dungeon close to the scullery, and spent most of his days, and a very fair proportion of some of his nights, in cleaning boots. Fancy shoes that required no polishing were not allowed at St. Mildred's, and it was by the sweat of his brow, by elbow grease and honest spittle that Cuthbert earned his daily bread. He was a short, stout youth of sixteen, prematurely muscular through his labours, and a confirmed hater of women. Familiarity with their footwear had bred contempt for them.
He received his instructions about the new girl's box with an air of weariness. It meant another pair of boots a day; and, with the winter and the bad weather approaching, he would have liked to see St. Mildred's a far less thriving concern.

Tea at St. Mildred's was at half-past four; and at ten minutes to five when the procession of girls came clattering out of the great dining room—two rooms knocked into one—Miss Chadpole was waiting outside, with the air of one who had kept an appointment and arrived first. She beckoned to four girls in turn, and they responded to the signal with alacrity.

"Eleanor, Margaret, Caroline, Christine," she said, calling them all by name, "I want you. Will you go up to my room and wait for me?"

Miss Chadpole was the only mistress at St. Mildred's with any pretensions to good looks. Most of the girls had conceived a romantic adoration for her. And for the one or two who were singled out by her for anything particular, it was considered a heavy "score" over the others.

Caroline was the first to arrive in Miss Chad- pole's bed-sitting-room—although the others made a close race of it—and bagged one of the two basket chairs, the one which Miss Chadpole did not herself use.

"What's the row?" she asked.

She was a girl of about sixteen—all four were approximately of that age—and she was the only one of the four who could not be called pretty.

She had straight, mouse-coloured hair, a face too pale and too broad, and she was never short of a few pimples. Possibly on this account she was not very popular in the school.

"Is it a row?" asked Christine.

Margaret was peeping inside a copy of Browning's Poems to see if the pressed rose, which she had surreptitiously laid there, still remained.

"I thought," she said, "that the darling was looking troubled."

"Not troubled," corrected Eleanor. "I should say, sweetly serious."

"It's all the same," said Margaret.

"Of course it isn't!" ejaculated Caroline. "It is quite different. You're sweetly serious when you're in church, but you are not troubled—so sucks!"

"Miss Chaddy wasn't in church, so sucks to *you!*"

They were all four more or less rivals, and hardly ever met without squabbling and argument. All four of them immediately began to talk at once, but the sound of Miss Chadpole's step outside acted upon them like a Hindoo charm, and the assistant mistress entered a silent room.

"You can sit down, girls, and make yourselves comfortable," she said, as she closed the door.

"Mrs. Toy has asked me to select four of you whom I can trust. I have chosen you."

"Oh, Miss Chadpole!"

"Oh, how lovely!"

"What is it, Miss Chadpole?"

Miss Chadpole seated herself in the basket chair which had been reserved for her, and bestowed upon them all that smile which she found useful in getting people to do things.

"I dare say," she said, "you've heard that there's a new girl coming to-day?"

"Yes, Miss Chadpole," Caroline broke in. "I heard Mrs. Toy tell Cuthbert he must go to the station."

"You shouldn't listen to what Mrs. Toy tells Cuthbert."

"But Cuthbert was singing a song called 'Boiled beef and carrots,' and I thought Mrs. Toy was going to reprove him. She did, too, she said it was disgusting. I rather like boiled beef myself." The other three girls were all frowning at Caroline for talking so much. She contrived to make a face at Christine without being observed by Miss Chadpole, who said: "You should not listen to Cuthbert's songs, Caroline.

Mrs. Toy more than suspects him of going to the Purlingdon Hippodrome and other shameful resorts. But I want to tell you about this new girl, who will be here very soon, because I want you all to look after her, and be nice to her, so that she doesn't feel strange here."

There was an enthusiastic chorus of assent, which Miss Chadpole quelled by a gesture. "Her name," she said, "is Esme Geering."

"Esme," said Margaret. "What a sweet name!"

"You must be very, very kind to her," said Miss Chadpole, "because the poor dear girl is an invalid, and has been brought up in a very strange way by an old bachelor uncle, who doesn't believe in doctors."

"I know!" exclaimed Caroline. "I had an uncle who was a Christian Scientist, until they came and told him that he only thought that he had broken his leg. But he thinks he's dead now."

"Shut up!" whispered Margaret. "You and your relations!"

"Oh, poor thing!" cried Eleanor. "What's the matter with her?"

"I think it is some nervous complaint," said Miss Chadpole vaguely, " but I don't quite know. She isn't allowed to do gym., because her uncle does not believe in it. And no matter how ill she is, she is never to have a doctor."

"Oh, what a shame!" cried Christine. "Never mind. When she's taken ill we will all nurse her." Miss Chadpole smiled benignly.

"She will be very strange to school life," she said. "I gather that so far she has hardly mixed amongst girls. What education she's had she's had from her uncle. As she is so delicate you mustn't be jealous if she has certain privileges. Mrs. Toy has allowed her to have a room to herself."

"Lucky bargee!" murmured Caroline.

"She won't be allowed to play hockey?" murmured Christine, who was an enthusiastic centre forward.

"I don't expect so. We shall find out from her in time. By the way, I don't suppose any of you girls are very anxious to do prep, to-night?"

There was no mistaking the enthusiasm in the chorus of voices which responded.

"Because," added Miss Chadpole, with a gracious smile, "I've begged you all off. Mrs. Toy is just going, or has already gone, to the station to meet her. She's going to bring her up to my room. You can sit here talking to her as long as you like. I do so hope you will get on with her. Now, tell me what you all did with yourselves during the holidays. I've hardly had time to have a chat with any of you."

They were still talking when the sound of a cab outside sent Miss Chadpole to the door, and the four girls to the windows. The assistant mistress waved them back, and then vanished. As Miss Chadpole descended the stairs she heard the hall door open and Mrs. Toy's voice, grimly cheerful, exclaim:

"Well, here we are, Esme. This is your new home." There was a pause, and then: "Oh, wipe your feet, child! Good gracious, I did not know there was so much mud about!"

Going within view of the hall, Miss Chadpole beheld a tall slim girl attacking the mat with the energy of a terrier. Mrs. Toy stood by watching, with a rather j strained and puzzled expression on her thin lined face. Her rimless glasses were a little askew, and the gloved hand which still clung to her skirt looked tightly clenched.

"This is the hall," she said with the air of one imparting information. "That is the big schoolroom on the right—but I think some of the girls are going to show you round. You'd better go up to Miss Chadpole's room and take off your shoes. Somebody will lend you some slippers until your box arrives. Oh, here is Miss Chadpole! Miss Chadpole, this is Esme Geering, our latest arrival, of whom I have already told you. Miss Chadpole will take you in the modem and in the dead languages, Esme."

The new girl was certainly rather pretty. She had a shy boyish grin, which was somehow attractive and disarming. Her voice, when she spoke, was deep, but rather pleasing.

"How do you do?" she said, in a rather louder tone than girls generally use.

"How do you do, Esme?" said Miss Chadpole. "I have already heard a great deal about you. I hope you will be very happy here. Do you know what class she'll be in, Mrs. Toy?"

"Of course I don't!" the headmistress retorted with some asperity. "I have hardly exchanged a dozen words with the child. Are you well up in French, Esme?"

"Pretty well, thank you. I have read Zola in the original."

Miss Chadpole coughed and nearly smiled in spite of herself, for Mrs. Toy's expression was comically awful. Mrs. Toy bit her lip and contented herself with saying: "Yes, you should have come to school before, child. No man can bring a girl up properly. Miss Chadpole's room is upstairs. Run up, and Miss Chadpole will follow."

Esme gave the mat a final kick, smiled, and crossed the hall to the foot of the stairs. Directly his back was turned Mrs. Toy's mouth was close to Miss Chadpole's ear.

"A most extraordinary person," she murmured in one flurried breath. "I only hope I have not made a mistake in accepting her. I found her having an argument with a porter. Such language! Most unseemly! Do you know what a yahoo is?"

Miss Chadpole looked as if she had been asked a conundrum.

"No, I don't," she replied. "What is it?"

"I don't know, but she said the porter was one. She said he was a yellow dog-faced one. I don't know what to do about it. It may be an improper word for all I know."

"She's been badly brought up," Miss Chadpole answered. "The refining influence of St. Mildred's will soon have its effect upon her."

"I don't think she is quite a lady," Mrs. Toy whispered nervously, and most astonishingly close to the truth. Then, seeing that Esme was half-way upstairs and disposed to linger, she gave the assistant mistress a little push.

"There, Miss Chadpole," she added," go and look after her for a few minutes. I declare I feel quite shaken."

Four eager girls awaited the appearance of Esme in Miss Chadpole's room. The assistant mistress introduced them in turn, and they shook hands self-consciously.

"This is Caroline Bax, Eleanor Hartopp, Christine Richards, and Margaret Buddery. They are going to show you round and tell you the rules of the school. Sit down, Esme. I wonder whether one of you would lend Esme a pair of slippers?"

All four said that they could, and all four made a rush for the door. Miss Chadpole laughingly called them back.

"One pair will do," she said. "Christine, will you go and get yours?"

"I'm not," said Esme, with a good-humoured smile, a bally centipede!"

Miss Chadpole flinched at the adjective, and there was a sound of suppressed giggles in the room.

"Esme, that isn't a very nice word. You mustn't use it here."

Esme sighed, let himself sink into a chair, and coughed vigorously behind his hand. He was conscious of having made an inauspicious beginning. But he felt safe.

The mirror told him what a splendid girl he made. Even although his hands and feet were of nobler proportions than one generally finds in a young girl, detection seemed almost impossible.

"Did you have a nice journey?" asked Caroline, while Christine was out of the room.

"Oh, pretty fair, thanks! It isn't very far, is it? but I hate trains. And they hadn't got a *Sporting Life* fat the bookstall at Waterloo. My Uncle Dick told me to read the article by the Newmarket man. He says that the winner of the Caesarewitch . . ."

He checked himself suddenly, seeing more horror dawning in the eyes of Miss Chadpole.

"And," he went on, transferring himself from the frying-pan into the fire, "there was a porter down at the station here who seemed to be looking for a thick ear."

The three girls bounced in their seats. Miss Chadpole positively twittered.

"A thick ear!" she repeated. "What in the name of gracious is that?"

'It is what a porter sometimes gets for taking no notice when a gentleman—I mean a lady—tells him to do something."

Miss Chadpole looked appalled, even abashed. She had met many sorts of girls and had dealt with many cases vaguely described as difficult. But the new girl, Esme Geering, was altogether outside her experience. If this was a sample of her speech and conduct, then discipline at St. Mildred's would go to the four winds of heaven. Yet it seemed so much easier to laugh at this cheerful little hoyden than to rebuke her. Indeed, she could think of no terms of reproof, and salved her conscience with the thought that Esme was to be pitied for an unholy upbringing. As she said to the four girls she had selected as Esme's mentors, "We must all be sorry for poor dear Esme."

Christine, arriving with her slippers, found electricity in the atmosphere of the room.

"You'd better take off your boots?" said Miss Chadpole.

Esme sighed as he proceeded to unfasten the laces of a pair of boots which went half-way up his muscular young calf. He had protested bitterly at his having such a pair made for him, but Uncle Dick had been adamant on the subject.

"It will be a joy," he remarked, "to get rid of these bally heels. It's like walking on stilts."

Whilst another invisible ripple went round the room, Caroline raised her voice. She never missed an opportunity of mentioning her ultra-fashionable appearance during the holidays.

"Oh, but those heels aren't *high I*" she exclaimed. "I have a pair of grey suede shoes—of course, I can't wear them here—made in Paris. You can get them at Scavenger and Tubbs at Streatham for twenty-nine and eleven, and the heels are inches and inches!"

Esme interrupted her with a shudder.

"My Uncle Dick would read the Riot Act if I wore anything like that," he said.

Miss Chadpole thought she knew the type of man. "I suppose," she said, "he doesn't like you to wear corsets?"

"Crimes of Paris! No!" exclaimed Esme in holy horror. He had got his boots off by now and picked up the slippers. "Thank you very much—er—Christine," he added.

A moment later there was a little ripple of laughter, in which Miss Chadpole reluctantly joined.

"I think I can find you a shoehorn," she said.

"Twenty shoehorns wouldn't help," said Esme, looking ruefully at his feet. "I am an 'also ran ' in the Cinderella business. I am going to put my boots |on again. I had to have *these* made for me. The man at the shop said that his sister had married a policeman, and their daughter had just the same sort of feet."

Miss Chadpole, however, had an inspiration. Two terms ago one of the girls had suffered badly from chilblains, and an enormous pair of bath slippers, big enough to allow for heavy bandages, had been procured for her. These were fetched; and Esme's boots passed early into the care of Cuthbert. They were the first objects his eyes alighted on when he lit the gas in the boot-room at eight o'clock.

"Gawd blimey!" he said from the bottom of his heart.

CHAPTER IV

"Where did you spend your holidays, Esme?" Margaret asked.

Miss Chadpole had departed, leaving the four tried and trusted pupils to make the new girl feel at home. It was not their fault that they were unable to accomplish this.

"Cornwall," said Esme shortly.

He was beginning to be a little bored by his company. He had not, as he expressed it to himself, "much time for girls." That Christine Richards was rather nice—pretty too—but she was only a flapper after all. Eleanor and Margaret he found himself liking a little less, whilst Caroline, whom he had already christened the "Spotted Wonder," he positively detested.

"Cornwall!" exclaimed the chorus. "Oh, how lovely! I have never been there, but they say it is too thrilling and romantic for words. What did you do down there, Esme?"

"We did a bit of fishing," said Esme indifferently.

He was suddenly conscious that all four were admiring him, and this irritated more than it pleased him.

"Fishing," said'Christine, "how lovely. My aunt would never let me fish. It must be lovely fun."

"Oh, it's all right at times. Makes you swear like a trooper, though. You ought to have heard my Uncle Dick when he sat down on the head of a conger that wasn't dead!"

There were more titters, and Christine said: "Oh, Esme, you are priceless! But we thought you were an invalid!"

"Me an invalid!" Esme exclaimed, and then, remembering himself, added in an altered tone: "Yes, of course I am."

Caroline crept closer to him, and Esme edged away. He liked Caroline rather less than any other girl he had ever seen.

"Poor Esme," she said softly. "What's the matter with you?"

"You wouldn't understand if I told you," he answered impatiently.

He did not want to spend the whole evening talking to these girls. He knew that he had a private room to go to somewhere, and foresaw possibilities of smoking a quiet cigarette out of the window.

"Oh, but we should!" said Caroline. "There are so many new complaints nowadays, aren't there? I had a cousin who died of nervous eczema."

"Mine's a nervous complaint," said Esme, recollecting some of Uncle Dick's instructions, "and indigestion, and anaemia, and a touch of hereditary gout. It's a great wonder I am still alive."

"It is if you won't see a doctor," said Eleanor, who was the most practical of the four.

"Doctors are all humbugs," said Esme, remembering more of what Uncle Dick had told him to say. "They know less about healing than the African medicine-man I who tries to cure diphtheria by cooking one of his nephews. I will die before I see a doctor!"

"I think it's very unfair of you," said Eleanor. "If anything were to happen to you, think how unpleasant it would be for Mrs. Toy."

"Yes," said Caroline, "you've got a room in one of the attics. They'll never manage to get a coffin down those stairs."

"I think I would like to see my room," said Esme rising, grateful for the opportunity given to him. "Would one of you please mind telling me where it is?"

"We'll show you," said Christine rising. "Poor Esme, I expect you are tired after your journey. Supper is at half-past seven, but you'll hear the bell."

They led the way up to the top of the house, and pushed open the door of an attic, whose window overlooked the bare back-garden. It was furnished to accommodate a servant, with illuminated texts on the walls, which pointed out the benefits of early rising. There was one strip of threadbare carpet, two china dogs of desolating hideousness, and a small home-made bookshelf, containing such literary treasures as: "Blind Betty's Text," and "Jessica's Old Organ."

"Healthy reading for the young!" said Esme, transferring his attention to the small bed, which had been designed to make early rising a luxury. "I wonder," he added, "if they would mind my having the room repapered. I can't live in a room of blue church bells and red grapes. I've been gently nurtured, and, besides, I'm delicate. I must speak to Mrs. Toy about it."

A snigger caused him to look round at his four companions, who were all on the verge of hysterics. Poor little blighters, he thought suddenly, they couldn't help being girls! It would be rather low-down on his part not to respond to their overtures of friendship. He wished that there was some hospitality that he could offer them, but his box had not yet arrived. "Won't you sit down?" he asked graciously. "There is one chair, and there's room for three to sit on this beastly book-shelf, if we can get it down. This room isn't exactly luxurious, but I suppose it will have to do."

It was, in fact, a long way behind the study he shared at Wryvern in the matter of comfort. But it was a haven of sorts, and infinitely better than none at all. A thought struck him, and he pulled a packet of cigarettes from his skirt pocket.

"Any of you girls smoke?" he asked casually.

There was another sensation.

"You mustn't smoke here!" Margaret exclaimed. "You'd be expelled, really you would!"

"I have to," said Esme, "it does my nerves good."

"I'm sure," said Eleanor, "that Mrs. Toy would *never* allow it."

"Well, she's not going to know."

An awful thought struck him. Did girls sneak on one another? He did not suppose they did, but he was not quite sure on the point. He decided, however, to risk it.

"Well, I'm going to have one now," he said. "You girls had better join me. We can open the window and blow the smoke out into the air. Come on! You've all smoked before, haven't you?"

They all confessed to an occasional surreptitious, cigarette during the holidays, but they had not hitherto ventured it at school. Nothing so desperate and daring had entered their heads before. But this strange new | girl seemed to have brought with her an infectious kind, of lawlessness. They all looked at each other.

"I hope," said Esme carelessly, "they won't make you ill."

Adam and Eve are beguiled with different wiles. They are alike, however, in being unable to withstand a temptation artistically presented. If Adam had ' found the apple first and shown it to Eve, there would still have been work for the angel with the flaming sword.

"Of course, a cigarette won't make us ill!" said Eleanor indignantly, taking one.

The packet passed around. There was what the late Mr. Browning described as "the blue spurt of a lighted match." The five gathered around the window and blew little smoke clouds out in the damp, dismal evening air. Christine took only two puffs.

"They're rather strong," she said, "and I haven't smoked very much before. Do you mind if I throw mine away?"

Esme nodded. He rather admired her for not Smoking for sheer "side."

"I'll throw it out of the window, then," said Christine. "It'll fall just outside the boot-room, and Mrs. Toy will put it down to Cuthbert. He's allowed to smoke."

"Pooh!" said Caroline, inhaling with the noise and power of a steam vacuum cleaner. "They're only just ordinary."

But they were not. Esme was forever trying experiments in cigarettes when his means allowed of it. They allowed of it now, for Uncle Dick, in a great burst of gratitude, had done the right thing in the matter of pocket money. He had recently had a big slice of luck, having put the proceeds of seven poems and two watercolour sketches on the winner of the St. Leger, and no Vanderbilt had ever felt himself so wealthy. Wherefore Esme had abandoned for once the mild and fairly harmless Virginian cigarettes and invested in a packet of Smelloni's Imperial Havana Blend. The tobacco of them was as black as the inside of Jonah's whale, and the odour of them was as pungent as a pound of raw camphor.

Esme suddenly found himself smiling. He felt more friendly disposed to these girls—all except Caroline— now that he had got them smoking. He was going to wake up St. Mildred's College during his brief stay!

"Have a good time during the holidays?" he asked them all affably.

Caroline and Margaret had both been to Brighton, Eleanor to Bexhill, and Christine to Eastbourne. They had all enjoyed themselves.

"Meet plenty of nice boys?" Esme inquired.

They did not take much notice of boys, and said so. They were all of an age to take more notice of girls older than themselves, or men rising thirty.

"I don't care for girls very much," said Esme, tapping the lighted end of his cigarette on the windowsill. "I much prefer boys. There's some sense in them. I wish I was one."

"Are you going to be a Moth or a Beetle?" Margaret asked him suddenly.

"Neither. I have had enough changes lately. I feel more like a sick pigeon up in this beastly attic!"

"You'd better be a Moth," said Caroline. "We are all Moths—all four of us."

"Meaning," he asked hopefully, "that you go out at night? Rather sporting!"

"No, of course we don't. Don't be silly! The Moths and the Beetles are two rival societies. The Moths all adore Miss Chadpole, and the Beetles are all in love with Mr. Tonkin, the drawing-master."

Esme shuddered visibly. If anything were needed to show him that between him and these girls there was a great gulf fixed, this alone would have done it.

"Ugh," he exclaimed, blowing smoke violently, "this sort of stuff makes me ill!"

"Talking about being ill," said Christine gently, "you don't look a bit well, Caroline."

Caroline certainly did not. Her face seemed to have attained the impossible in turning a shade more sallow, and little beads of moisture shone on it. She failed dismally in trying to smile.

"I've not been...very well... all day," she muttered. "I said... there was something wrong... with the cheese ...we had last night..."

"I didn't have any," Eleanor faltered, "but I'm not feeling well myself. I have suddenly turned quite queer."

"I think," faltered Margaret, "that I am ... I am going to be sick..."

Eleanor flung her cigarette from the window as if it had suddenly come to life and bitten her. "It's these beastly things!" she cried.

Margaret's cigarette followed, and Caroline tossed hers into the grate, whence Esme had subsequently to retrieve it.

"I'm going to be sick, too," Eleanor announced miserably.

"And I'm going to be . . . very sick indeed . . ." Caroline faltered.

Esme tossed his own cigarette out of the window and sprang to the door, which he threw open.

"For the love of Mike," he implored, "not here!" One upon the other's heels three maidens tottered out and blundered to the stairs. They broke suddenly into a scrambling run. Esme and Christine stared at one another in mingled perturbation and amusement.

"They'll be all right in a minute," said Esme, hopefully. "I don't mind telling you that I was taken that way once myself. They'll be as fresh as paint after." There was a noise on the landing below—that sound with which the cross-channel stewards are so familiar. "Murder!" said Esme. "Now we're for it!"

"I'll go and see," said Christine, and, tearing past him, fled down the stairs.

She was back again in hardly more than a minute.

"It was Caroline," she said. "She couldn't get any further! Now we're in for it! We shall all be expelled."

"You won't," said Esme. "You didn't smoke."

"Yes, I did; I had two puffs, and I shall have to admit it."

"But they needn't find out. I don't suppose the room smells of tobacco."

"No, but Mrs. Toy will find out they had been ill, and want to dose them. She has got a nose like a hawk's."

"So I have noticed."

"I mean, like a bloodhound's."

Esme did some hard thinking for a moment or two. He didn't much care what he did at St. Mildred's, but, on the other hand, he was there for a purpose, and it would never do if he got himself "bunked" even before he had started properly on his career as a schoolgirl. Besides, he had the four girls to consider. It was going to be a serious matter for them.

"I know," he said. "I'll nip out and get some peppermints."

"You can't. The house is always shut after five o'clock. It's like a prison."

"What about the maids? Wouldn't one of them run out and get something if they could earn an odd bob?"

Christine shook her head hopelessly.

"I don't think so," she said. "One of them is under notice to leave for running an errand without permission. She's doing her best to stay on, and wouldn't risk going again. The others are all grumpy old things."

Esme did some more thinking.

"Isn't there any window from which I could hop out? Although I'm rather an invalid, I'm as agile as a young hart on the mountains of Gilboa."

In spite of herself Christine could not help laughing. Then, mingled with the sound, came the trudge of heavy footfalls on the stairs, suggestive of somebody mounting them under a burden. A few minutes later the door was pushed wide open and Esme's trunk entered the room with Cuthbert somewhere underneath! it. He shed it with a loud crash, puffed, gasped, and turned around to find that the room was already occupied.

"Saved!" said Esme.

"Sorry, miss. I didn't know you was in."

"Don't mention it, fair youth! How do they call you?"

"Cuthbert, miss."

"And a right gentle name. Don't dream of apologising, Cuthbert. If I were on a sinking ship, I shouldn't | want the captain of the lifeboat to apologise for butting in. What have you done with my Gladstone, Cuthbert, which contains among other necessities a game of Ludo, a set of Halma, and eleven new embroidered nighties?"

Cuthbert looked aghast.

"I didn't know there was any more luggage!" he said.

"I'm not sure of it myself, but nobody can say anything to you if you go down to the station and look. Can you run, Cuthbert?"

"Sometimes, miss," said Cuthbert, looking profoundly mystified.

"Well, then, run as you've never run before, and return here with all despatch, and with half a pound of the most powerful peppermints that money can buy. If anybody sees you going or returning, you've been to the station to look for my Gladstone which may not be there. Do you understand, Cuthbert?"

He groped for where his trouser pockets used to be, suddenly recollected himself, and took out a lady's purse—to him an abomination—and handed five shillings to the boot boy.

"You may keep the change," he said.

Cuthbert grinned broadly.

"Thank you, miss. I beg pardon, miss—per'aps I oughtn't to mention it, but there's an 'uddled figger lying on the floor of the bathroom below, making a noise like the moaning of a dying 'en. "That's Caroline," said Christine to Esme.

"Never you mind about dying hens," said Esme, still addressing Cuthbert. "You get those peppermints *tout de suite.* Oh, and Cuthbert—did you happen to notice the smell of tobacco smoke when you came into the room?"

Cuthbert grinned with sudden comprehension.

"You aren't 'arf a nib, miss!" he exclaimed admiringly. "No, the smell's all gone now."

"You'd better imitate the smell, then. Only get back as soon as you can I"

And so it happened that late that night Mrs. Toy held forth to Miss Budging, the chief assistant-mistress, on the adulteration of foodstuffs.

"Even," she said, " those boiled sweets, those bull's- eyes which we had hitherto thought to be so harmless, are dangerous to eat. I've just had to dose three of the girls who had been taken ill; and the smell of peppermint about them made me feel quite faint. They all admitted they had been eating bull's-eyes. That new girl, Esme Geering, seems to have brought them with her."

"Ah," said Miss Budging. "What do you think of her?"

Mrs. Toy frowned and narrowed her eyes like a scientist trying to study microbes through a defective glass.

"I hardly know," she said, " I hardly know. You haven't seen her yet?"

"Oh, yes, I have!" said Miss Budging, somewhat acidly. "I was going to talk to you about her. I entered her room after supper, and she"—here her voice trembled—"she told me to knock the next time I wanted to come in. She said that masters at a boys' school never dreamt of entering a boy's study without knocking. I never heard such insolence in my life!"

"Tut!" said Mrs. Toy, her frown deepening. "Tut, tut, tut!"

"And that isn't all," added Miss Budging in a voice that gathered gloom as she continued. "As I entered the room the wretched girl was posturing in front of the looking-glass, and I heard her saying very distinctly, 'Chase me, boys!' "

CHAPTER V

For obvious reasons, Uncle Dick had temporarily given up his artistic little home in Surrey. When Geering returned from Africa it would never do for him to be moving in a locality where Esme was well known as a boy. He had taken a small and fairly comfortable furnished flat in Wandle Street, Bloomsbury, and spurred himself to earn sufficient money to keep his two establishments going and Esme supplied with an inordinate amount of pocket-money. Towards this end he got himself to work on one of the sporting papers, and wrote reminiscent articles about his old athletic days—days just before and just after he had won the Diamond Sculls. He also continued to extract good-sized weekly sums from various bookmakers. He was an admirable judge of a two-year-old, and the nursery season was his harvest-time.

Very anxiously indeed did Uncle Dick await Esme's first letter from St. Mildred's College. He breathed a deep sigh of relief when, after three days, a letter arrived in the boy's handwriting, the contents of the letter, however, caused him some trepidation. It was as follows:

"My dear Nuncs:

"Here I still am, you see, although I nearly managed to get bunked the first night. And I shouldn't have minded if I had, except for your sake. How I am going to stick this out for a whole term is more than I know. All I can say is,

'Thank Heaven that I'm not really a girl.' It's a hades of a life!

"The girls here don't know what on earth to make of me. None of them have ever met a girl before with so much sense in her. On the whole I think I am pretty popular with them and I wish I wasn't. One of them, named Caroline, who has a face like somebody's first attempt at a blancmange, has been messing around me, asking me to be her 'best friend.' Always the little gentleman, in spite of my skirts, I put up with the attentions of this Nature's error until this morning, when I had to tell her off for good and all. She hates the sight of me now, and has gone about whispering to everybody about the way I go on, and telling them she's sure that I'm not a lady—which is the surest thing I know. Mrs. Toy and all the mistresses loathe the sight of me. Everything I do seems to be wrong, and they keep on correcting me, and hinting that I've been badly, brought up. I never knew before how differently girls are supposed to behave from boys.

I am in the Upper Fifth Form, where they have crawled as far as the First Book of Caesar. The First Book of Caesar in the Upper Fifth! I ask you! And the fair charmer who takes us in Latin falls over ablative absolutes as if they were trip-wires, and has to dig every other word out of the 'die.' Thank goodness, I haven't got to do any work!

"I never appreciated Wryvern so much till now. I see by the notes in the *Sportsman* that the fifteen is very weak this year, so I could have had a chance if I had been there. Just my luck!

"Cuthbert, the boot-boy, brings me the *Sportsman* every day, and I hide it under my mattress. Without Cuthbert life would be impossible. He takes in a ' blood,' called the *9 Pirates' Own,'* and he thinks I am just like Fearless Freda, the Maiden Orchid Hunter. So I get him to bring me home comforts in the way of cigarettes and so forth. I lower a string out of my window at night, and Cuthbert does the rest. We nearly got caught the other night when he was sending me up a bottle of Bass and the string slipped off. You wouldn't believe a bottle could make such a row.

"Well, uncle, I'm doing my best, and I shall keep the flag flying as long as possible. One of these days something inside my head will snap, and I shall return to you in a blaze of glory, so the sooner my alleged Papa arrives the better.

"Hoping you are fit and well,

"Your affectionate nephew—no, niece,

"Esme."

Uncle Dick laid down the letter with a little sigh.

"The boy's badly brought up," he reflected. "All my fault! I've been too weak with him. Always let him do as he liked. Not that there's an ounce of real vice in him. Oughtn't to smoke, though, and drink beer. Only does it for devilment. Perhaps it's as well he's away from Wryvern for a bit; and from what he tells me the House must be abominably slack. No discipline. Half a mind to take him away altogether. Bring him up myself. Be firm with him."

The train of thought completed the circle and came back to Uncle Dick himself, and suddenly he bowed his head.

"How can I preach to the boy?" he asked himself aloud. "Who am I to preach to anybody? I'm not fit to have charge of a wheelbarrow, let alone a boy! I'm a weak and wicked old fool!"
He rose to his feet, his eyes shining with real tears. Uncle Dick was always able to produce tears of self-pity at a moment's notice.

"I'm a miserable and a lonely old fool, too," he thought. "What might not Edith have made of me if she had married me! What wouldn't she have made of that boy if she had helped me to rear him? We both needed her—Esme and I. But I will be firm with him! I'll start being firm with him for his own sake! If he gets himself expelled from St. Mildred's, I'll—I'll hit him!"

Uncle Dick began being firm by sending Esme two pounds and imploring him to be careful. His pen would not write the word which his conscience dictated. It was not in him to be firm with anybody, least of all with Esme. The boy was to him what a toy dog is to a childless woman. When the letter was stamped and sealed, he lingered at the desk, and after long minutes of hesitation proceeded to write another, which he addressed to Miss Edith Cheville.

She was the woman whom Uncle Dick should have married nearly twenty years before. They were so suited to each other that, when she persistently refused him, it seemed to him that she was trying to baulk Providence. Edith Cheville was one of those women with an inherent fear of marriage. This she might have overcome if she had not also been afraid of Uncle Dick. She knew all his shiftlessness, all his weaknesses and follies and while, perhaps, she loved him the more because of them, she dared not trust him to be her partner in life.

It was many years now since Uncle Dick had seen; her, and although they had agreed to be "friends," they seldom exchanged letters. Occasionally he heard of her. Once he had heard a woman say that she had met a Miss Cheville at the house of a Mrs. Toy, who kept the girls' school at Purlingdon. It was that casual remark which was primarily responsible for Esme being where he now was.

This is what Uncle Dick now wrote to his old sweetheart
"My dear Edith:

"Thanks to your recommendation and the trouble you took on my behalf, my niece Esme is now at St. Mildred's College, and, I hope, not doing her poor old uncle too much discredit. But, reading between the lines of her letter, I feel she is something of a handful.

"You might guess what a muddle I have made of bringing up the girl. I am the last man in the world, as you would agree, who ought to have undertaken such a task. Esme is just like a boy, and not a very good boy at that; and I fear her father will be disappointed when he sees her.

"I hear that you have a niece at the school—one of your sister's children, I suppose, as her name is Christine Richards. I wonder whether you would do me a favour for old sake's sake, and get your niece to take a friendly interest in mine? There's nothing like the refining influence of the friendship of a nice girl, such as a niece of yours could not help being. If you would drop her a line.

He wrote more, pages more, all in the same formal vein. Uncle Dick dared not trust himself to write otherwise, for his pen ran away with him like an Irishman's tongue. But the love lyrics under his name, which appeared in the magazines, and were afterwards wailed to music in suburban drawing-rooms, were all secretly dedicated to her.

Having finished the letter he proceeded to write one such, but only got as far as—

"Oh, you've stolen the honey right out of my heart. Little brown bee in the April garden" when the muse deserted him. He sighed and, after a mental struggle, postponed his task. Five minutes later he was studying a column in the evening paper headed, "To-morrow's Programme at Newmarket."

"It looks to me," he murmured, "as if The Little Captain has seven pounds in hand of everything else in that two-thirty race."

Uncle Dick's letter to Edith Cheville bore fruit at St. Mildred's College two days later, and it were best to lift the curtain on Esme during morning school, while Miss Chadpole was taking the Upper Fifth in Latin.

Esme had a seat in the back row of desks, and sat, with a pile of superfluous books in front of him, writing rapidly with a pencil while the rest of the form blundered through half a chapter of Caesar's adventures among the Gallic tribes.

Caroline, now Esme's sworn enemy, sat in front, immediately opposite the chair and table occupied by Miss Chadpole. A glance round at the back of the form was sufficient to assure the practised eye of Caroline that Esme was engaged upon private business behind the screen of books.

"Esme *does* work hard," she whispered to her neighbour, loud enough for Miss Chadpole to hear.

Miss Chadpole took the hint, and focused suspicious eyes upon the back bench.

"Esme!" she cried suddenly.

Esme jumped.

"Begin construing at *His rebus cognitis.* And stand up when I speak to you."

Esme got slowly and unwillingly upon his legs.

"*His rebus cognitis,*" he said, "—er—these things having been learned—er—these things having been learned—er—er—these things having "

"Just as I thought!" snapped Miss Chadpole. "You have not been attending. You can't find the place."

"Who's the old boy scrappin' with now?" asked Esme, scanning the book. "Still the Nervii? Troublesome lot of fellows, the Nervii.'

Miss Chadpole bit her lip. The class tittered.

"Silence!" she cried. "There is nothing to laugh at! Esme, how dare you answer me in such a way! And what's that you've got behind that pile of books?"

"This?" asked Esme, holding aloft an exercise book. "This is the Minerva Theme Book, for the use of schools. On the front we have space for the name of the young pupil. On the back we have the weights and measures—all except the ale or beer measure, which is hardly fit for a young girl to read. Also the multiplication''

"No!" cried Miss Chadpole, finding her voice after a momentary loss, "what's that piece of paper you've got there?"

"This? Oh, this is a cricket match between Middlesex and Surrey. You play it with a code—a equals one run, b equals four, c equals caught, and so forth. Then you read straight out of a book and stick down the score."

Miss Chadpole edged forward and took the offending piece of paper, which she tore across and across again.

"Lucky for Surrey," Esme commented. "They were in for a fearful hiding. Now they can call it a draw."

The class tittered again, but there were those who looked displeased. Miss Chadpole was the adored of the mistresses, with the reputation of being a " darling," and ragging her was a breach of unwritten law.

"Take that sweet out of your mouth!" fumed Miss Chadpole. "It is insulting to speak to me with a sweet in your mouth. Throw it out of the window."

Esme obeyed.

"Have you got any more?"

"Afraid I haven't, Miss Chadpole, but I could soon get you some."

Miss Chadpole went from pink to white.

"If I have any more such impertinence," she said, "I shall send you up to Mrs. Toy. You must stay in this afternoon, and write out"

She paused, trying to think of something babyish which would throw ridicule on Esme.

"You must write out five hundred times 'I must learn to be a good girl.'"

"I was—till I met you," Esme murmured.

He was sullen throughout the remainder of morning school, angry with himself for having behaved badly, and directing his anger at Miss Chadpole and at the school. A mistaken sense of dignity galled him for being under the authority of women, taught—punished, and nagged at by them. By dinner-time he was ripe for rebellion, and had made up his mind to refuse to do the lines. This meant certain expulsion.

But the boy, for all his precocity and bad manners, was good at heart. He had a sound schoolboy code which would not admit of his "letting down" Uncle Dick. He realised at the back of his disgruntled mind all that Uncle Dick had done for him, and made new resolutions to see the adventure through. As he had predicted, his impersonation of a girl had soon ceased to be a joke. It was now an affliction.

After the mid-day dinner, when the girls went to disport themselves in one of the two playrooms or the bedraggled garden, Esme strode moodily into the empty classroom, took out paper, pen and ink, and glowered at the map of England hanging opposite. If any of the fellows at Wryvern could see him now! The mighty indeed was fallen.

He had been sitting thus a minute when the door opened and Christine Richards looked in.

"Hallo!" she said, and entered, closing the door.

"Hullo!" said Esme ungraciously. "Come to gloat?"

"Don't be so horrible, Esme! I'm very sorry for you."

"If you're half so sorry as I am," he said, grinning wryly, "you'd be in tears."

"No, but I am!" Christine insisted.

"Oh, rot! You're one of the Moths. You can't understand anybody who doesn't go snuffling around that overgrown board-school teacher."

"The Moths have passed a vote of censure on you."

"Thanks. I'll have it for breakfast."

"But I wouldn't agree to the vote. I've left the Moths."

He regarded her with a sudden interest.

"I always thought you weren't quite such an idiot as the others," he said grudgingly.

As he looked at her he realised for the first time how deep and vividly blue were her eyes. She had that soft fair hair which caught all the coloured rays of the sun, delicate little features, a faultless colouring of skin. No doubt, he thought, she would be considered pretty. He had never taken count of such things before. Now her prettiness and the look of friendship in her eyes stirred in him some dormant emotion, like one of Uncle Dick's poems or a stave of music.

Suddenly he felt himself flushing and made a little petulant movement.

"Well," he said, "I suppose I must get on with this. What have I got to write out? 'I try to be good, but the girls won't let me'?"

"No, Esme, don't be silly! You'll be expelled if you play any tricks. You know perfectly well what you've got to write. *I* do, anyhow, and I've come to help you." Esme stared at her in real amazement. He would not have believed any of the girls capable of such a sporting offer. That this was an overture of friendship he was well aware, but somehow he did not resent it as he had resented the overtures of Caroline Bax.

"I say, that's decent of you!" he exclaimed. "But it can't be done, thanks all the same. Our hand-writing's a bit different, you know."

"Yes, but you can show what you've done to Miss Chadpole, and you can show what I've done to Miss Budging, who'll be in charge after prep, to-night." Esme nodded his head several times.

"There's something in it," he said. "But I don't see why you should trouble. *You* haven't been playing the goat, you know."

"I don't mind writing a bit."

"Jolly good of you. But why? You don't like me, do you?"

Christine was beside him now. She laid a hand as light as a feather upon his shoulder.

"Of course I do! You're such a funny old thing. You're quite, quite different from any other girl. Of course, you've been brought up by a man, and that makes such a difference. I should like to meet your Uncle Dick. He must be a dear!"

Esme stared at her.

"What do you know about my Uncle Dick?" he demanded.

"My Aunt Edith used to know him. Her name's Miss Cheville."

The name was only too familiar to Esme. He dropped his pen.

"She's the woman," he said, "who ruined my uncle's life."

"She didn't! She wouldn't ruin anybody's life!"

"She wouldn't marry him, and that put the lid on it. I'm never going to get married myself. I don't know a -girl—I mean a boy—who—anyhow, my Uncle Dick took the count because of her."

"A count's a man, silly!"

"I mean he—he—well, he sort of wasted away in his inside. And it was all Miss Cheville's fault."

"My Aunt Edith loved him very much, although she wouldn't marry him. I believe she still loves him. She's never married anybody. She wrote to me asking after you."

"Oh!" said Esme. "It's to please your aunt, then, that you want to be decent to me; not for myself?"

Christine's slim arm slid around Esme's shoulder.

"Don't be an old stupid! Of course, I like you awfully. I *want* to be friends."

Esme allowed himself to melt a little more.

"I don't mind being friends," he said, "but I can't go wandering about hand-in-hand with you all day long, or any of that sort of thing. I'm different from other girls."

Christine was a little puzzled. She felt rebuffed, but would not let him see.

"All right," she said cheerfully. "Now let's get on with some of these lines. Oh, have you got a secret, Esme?"

He jumped at the abruptness of the question.

"Holy smoke! I should just think I have!"

"So have I. I've never told anybody yet. But someday I'll tell you. It's an *awful* secret."

Esme smiled politely and began to write. For the next twenty minutes the scratching of the two pens alone broke the silence of the room.

CHAPTER VI

From that time onwards Christine and Esme became friends, but the friendship, on Esme's side, was not a violent one. He felt a curious shyness about displaying his liking for Christine, and seemed to endure rather than enjoy her worship.

Secretly, though, he became so fond of her that he came to ask himself if this was not what is sometimes called "falling in love." He was aghast and ashamed of the discovery, as if it were some sort of shameful accident, and his own mind, which accused him, turned and hotly denied the accusation.

He had never had a sister, he told himself, and Christine, like Somebody's Cocoa, supplied a long-felt want. Other fellows had sisters, and were fond of them. He would pretend to himself that Christine was his sister.

Thus the two became friends without being inseparable. Esme's perverted sense of dignity saw to that; and to others, even to Christine herself, the friendship seemed a somewhat one-sided affair.

Since Esme's quarrel with Caroline Bax, and his passage of arms with Miss Chadpole, his popularity with the other girls had fallen like the glass before a storm. Caroline found it easy to convince the rest of the Upper Fifth that any girl who could be rude to dear Miss Chadpole deserved to be a social outcast. Esme's aloofness was taken to be "side" and a girl with "side," who was also definitely "not a lady," was unendurable.

Christine shared some of his unpopularity by joining the outcast, and as Esme would not spend all his spare time with her they both had spells of loneliness.

Esme preferred the very little girls to the girls of his own age. They were jolly and babyish, and their silliness was not irritating to him because they were not of an age to know any better. He rather enjoyed romping with them.

Three or four days after he and Miss Chadpole had declared war upon each other he earned for himself the nickname of "Whelkie," and it came about in this way.

Four or five little girls chattering in the garden hailed Esme as a friend, and asked him, disconcertingly, how he came to visit the world.

The stork, it seemed, was responsible for little Freda Mason's appearance in this vale of tears.

"The doctor brought me in a black bag," said Mary Porter.

"My mother found me under a gooseberry bush," added Beryl Smith.

Esme's sense of humour could not resist the temptation to blurt out the literal truth about himself.

"I," he said, "was found under a whelk stall."

The screams of laughter which greeted this sally attracted Miss Budging, who descended upon the group like a large black vulture, demanding to know the cause of the merriment. Five hysterical little girls all told her at once, and Miss Budging frowned.

"I think," she said, "that you might spend more of your time with girls of your own age, Esme."

The story spread throughout the school in a few minutes, and Caroline Bax sniffed and said that "what Esme Geering said about herself was very likely true." Thereafter Esme was always spoken of as "Whelkie" behind his back, and often called it to his face. He was, however, quite indifferent about it.

Need of masculine companionship often drove Esme to the boot-room to hold converse with Cuthbert. He did not like Cuthbert, but Cuthbert was useful to him, and, anyhow, he was a boy.
Cuthbert's ambition in life was well-defined, pointed, and simple. Very soon he was going to bequeath the boot cleaning at St. Mildred's to some unfortunate successor and join a trade. After a little while he intended to be a trade union official and go into Parliament, and have a big house and servants and a lot of money without doing any work.

"What do you do with yourself on Saturday afternoons?" Esme asked him, almost wistfully. "Play football?"

"No, miss, I don't *play,* but I follers the Kennington Ghurkas. They're in the League, you know."

"Oh, soccer!" said Esme scornfully. "Professional soccer!"

"Lor', miss, it ain't 'arf all right. You ought to come and watch 'em play sometimes. Old Alf Tcks, the centre-forward, he's a fair treat. The way 'e can get 'is elbow in a feller's ribs, or just tap the ball down with 'is 'and,.-without the referee spottin', is a fair wonder. Gets nearly all their goals, 'e does. The Ghurkas nearly always wins at 'ome because of us supporters. We boo the visitin' team from the moment they comes on the field to the moment they goes orf. We shouts ' Foul! ' or ' Dirty dog! ' whenever they touches the ball. And when one of 'em gets knocked out we shouts, ' Get up, yer lazy 'og, don't lie there shammin'! ' Talk about sport!"

"Sport isn't in it," said Esme, resisting a strong temptation to rub Cuthbert's nose in the blacking.

Cuthbert spat enthusiastically on the toe of a boot.

"Yes," he said, "it's us supporters that wins 'arf the matches, so it's just the same as playin'. I spoke to Alf Tcks once. The players was cornin' out of the dressin'-room and I shouted out,' 'Ullo, Alf! ' And do you know, miss, 'e nodded at me. Straight 'e did!"

"These great public men," said Esme, tongue in cheek, "often haven't got any side. A mere private gentleman might be quite stand-offish. But soccer's a rotten game. Now rugger—" "Gar!" exclaimed Cuthbert. " *Rugger's* a rotten gyme! It ain't no sport to watch. It's a gentleman's gyme. Soccer is the gyme of the people—the free-born British prolytairiat. Rugger! Why, if you was to go to a rugger match and boo the visitin' team, the *'ome* team wouldn't like it. Besides, it's so rough!"

Esme warmed up to the argument.

"Well," he said, "isn't there sometliing to be said for that? When I used to play rugger—"

Cuthbcrt dropped the blacking brushes.

"You, miss!" he ejaculated. "Strewth!"

Esme saw his mistake and sought to cover it.

"Oh, not very often," he said, "and not proper Rugby, as I'm only a girl. But what I was going to say—"

"Well, miss," said Cuthbcrt, recovering the dropped brush, "you'll excuse me, won't you? when I calls you a nib. Because I says it from the bottom of my heart. And if I may say so, miss, you've got a useful pair of feet for playin' football."

"I've scored from a place kick very nearly on the touch," Esme said modestly.

"Well, durin' my time 'ere, I've cleaned the boots of all sorts of girls. I remember Molly Flummery, who used to think she was a 'ot cross bun, and used to dread Easter because of bein' cut open and buttered. She's now in a private 'ome for the afflicted, miss, on account of 'er usin' a croquet mallet on 'er own ma durin' the 'olidays. I've met some queer girls, upon my life, miss, but never one like you. More like a boy, you are."

"There are more things in heaven and earth, Cuth- bertio, than are dreamed of in your philosophy."

"I thought you was more than ordinary a bit of a nib when you got me to get you them cigarettes. But you could ha' knocked me down with a worm-cake when you asked me to get you that bottle o' Bass the other night. Straight, you could!"

A sound of loud breathing outside warned Esme of the approach of the headmistress. Mrs. Toy, when she hurried, respirated like a pearl-diver after a tussle with a shark, and thus gave notice of her approach.

"And the next time," Esme said in a loud tone, for her benefit, "just put on a little less blacking and a little more shine."

The half-open door opened fully, and Mrs. Toy appeared. She bestowed upon Esme a steady glare, like that of the man whose portrait is in the advertisement pages of the magazines, to whom you are invited to send nine penny stamps and the date of your birth.

"What are you doing here, Esme?" she asked. ("Get on with your work, Cuthbert.")

"I've come to see Cuthbert about my boots."

"Well, you had better go to the playroom or out in the garden."

Esme turned away, and Mrs. Toy followed him out. "Come here, Esme," she said, "I want to speak to you."

Esme went there.

"Since you have been here," said Mrs. Toy, seizing Esme's elbow and leading him slowly down the garden, "your conduct has been anything but good. I hear nothing but complaints of you. Among them is that you spend too much time gossiping to Cuthbert."

"Does Cuthbert mind it?"

Mrs. Toy ground her teeth.

"How dare you say such a thing! Do you not know that no lady ought to speak to a servant at all, except to give orders? Familiarity with servants is most detestable. It—it—"

"It breeds contempt," suggested Esme, blandly and helpfully.

"Yes, it breeds contempt, and while I am headmistress of St. Mildred's I am not going to have any of my girls looking contemptible. Now, Esme, I do not want to have to ask your uncle to take you away, but I warn you that I may have to resort to such a step unless your conduct improves. Your Uncle Richard would, I know, be cut to the heart. Your father, now hastening across the ocean to see the daughter he only remembers as a baby, might well wish that the ship had sunk with him, if he landed to hear you had been expelled."

"*Je ne pense pas,*" Esme murmured below his breath.

"So," said Mrs. Toy, "if you persist in your undisciplined conduct, you see what misery you will, bring upon yourself and upon others. Now, will you promise me to try to do better?"

Esme promised, but with the hopelessness of the repentant sinner who is morally certain that he will fall again. Mrs. Toy displayed her gold teeth in a grimace which did duty for a smile.

"That is good, Esme," she said. "And now your friend Christine has an invitation for you this afternoon to meet a most charming lady. Your conduct has been so bad that I did not intend to allow you to accept it, but, on second thoughts, I think it would do you good to meet her, since you have been brought up so much among men. And now you had better go and find Christine."

Esme found her in the class-room and slapped her boyishly across the shoulders.

"Many thanks, old thing, for asking me out this afternoon," he said. "Mrs. Toy's just broken the news to me. What's it all about, and who's the sweet womanly woman Pm to meet?"

Christine bit her lip and then smiled.

"Oh, what a shame!" she exclaimed. "I meant it to be a secret until the time came. My aunt, who is your uncle's old friend, Miss Cheville, is coming down to see me. She is going to take us both out to tea. Tea, and cream buns, and chocolate eclairs. Won't it be scrummy? "

CHAPTER VII

Christine was an orphan and had been brought up by Miss Cheville, just as Esme had been brought up by Uncle Dick. Partly because of that, and partly because they had once been such great friends, the boy visualised her as a sort of female copy of his guardian.

But Edith Cheville was nothing of the sort. At half past three Esme was hauled into Mrs. Toy's stiff little drawing-room to meet a neatly dressed little gentlewoman who carried her forty years as if they were twenty-five.

Edith Cheville's figure, in a well-tailored suit of blue serge, was like that of a young girl. There was none of the sharp lines of spinsterhood about it. Her face, a little too broad for technical beauty, was stamped with the seal of human kindness. She was one who seemed made to be confided in, trusted and loved, and gave strangers to think that she must be the youthful mother of many babies.

"Aunt Edith," said Christine, "this is Esme."

And before Esme could realise what was happening, this charming woman had risen and kissed him.

"I am so delighted to meet you, Esme," she said. "I have known about your existence for years. Why, what a big girl you are! And pretty! Your Uncle Dick must be very proud of you. How is he?"

"He's very well, thank you," Esme said, and added for a purpose: "But he isn't happy."

The charming lady's eyes softened.

"Poor old chap!" she said. "Give him my love when you see him or ^vrite to him." She took Esme by the shoulders and stared, smiling, into his face. "So it is really *you!*" she exclaimed.

Strange to relate, Esme did not resent this treatment. One thing which he had never understood before was made clear to him. He had often wondered at Uncle Dick's infatuation, had been secretly a little impatient with him for allowing a woman, or rather the memory of one, to cast a shadow over his life. Now, having come in the least degree under the same spell himself, he could partly understand.

But he hardened his heart, determining not to treat her with unmixed cordiality. She seemed very nice, and she was Christine's aunt, and she was going to take him out and stand him a tea. But, on the other hand, she had "done Uncle Dick down," and his sense of loyalty forbade his feeling too friendly.

"So," said Edith Cheville, "you're Chrissie's great chum? I'm so glad."

Christine laughed.

"Don't say that, Aunt Edith, or Esme'll curl up at once."

"Oh, we're very good pals!" said Esme uncomfortably, staring out of the window.
The word "chum" was loathsome to him. It was a word which, he held, girls and women used when they thought they were borrowing from the vocabulary of the sterner sex. Among boys it occurred only in antiquated school stories and, he supposed, in certain schools of the baser sort.

Christine took Miss Cheville's arm.

"Come on, Auntie dear," she said, " let's get out of this prison."

"Hear, hear!" said Esme, and Edith Cheville laughed.

"Yes, let's go out," she said. "Chrissie always calls the school a prison, but I know she's very happy here. I hope you are, too, Esme."

Esme was silent, and Miss Cheville repeated the last remark when they were all outside the gate.

"Of all the piffling, putrid, palsied institutions I've ever been in, heard of, or dreamed of," said
Esme, "St. Mildred's gets away with the bun every time."

Miss Cheville laughed, and thought she heard an echo of Uncle Dick in this little outburst.

"Why, what's the matter with it?" she asked.

Esme sighed hopelessly.

"What *isn't* the matter with it!" he exclaimed.

"Esme's so funny," Christine explained. "She doesn't like girls."

Here, again, Edith Cheville thought she could detect the result of Uncle Dick's upbringing. She had made a mysogynist of him, she thought, a despiser of women, and he, in turn, had brought up this girl child with a contempt for her own sex. Her own responsibility in the matter confronted and frightened her. She could not help liking and being amused by this mannish little hoyden. With proper care, she believed that Esme might yet be an ornament to the nation's budding womanhood. But as she was, with her appallingly masculine manner and inelegant choice of phrases, this Esme was quite impossible.

"Of course," she said thoughtfully, "this is your first school?"

"Oh, no! I mean—yes. Yes, of course it is," said Esme blunderingly.

"So your Uncle Dick brought you up and educated you all by himself? Yes, I daresay it's a bit tiresome to start going to school at your age."

"It won't be for long," said Esme, with a set look. "My—er—father's coming home, you know. As soon as he goes back to Rhodesia I shall make Uncle Dick take me away."

Miss Cheville smiled to herself. She prided herself on having been able to read between the lines of Uncle Dick's letters to her. The news of Geering's intended return had awakened in him a sudden sense of responsibility. Naturally, Tom Geering would not like to find a daughter like Esme awaiting him, and might ask why she hadn't been sent to school.

"I used to know your father," she remarked.

Esme started and regarded her in momentary trepidation.

"Did you, Miss Cheville?" he stammered.

"It was some time before you were thought of," she continued, smiling.

"What was he like?" Esme asked.

"He was—very nice."

"That means you didn't like him," said Esme shrewdly. "When anybody says ' Very nice ' in that tone, they generally mean 'N.D.G.'"

Miss Cheville laughed.

"Really, Esme! Your expressions!"

"Sorry! But what was he like?"

"I must own that I thought him rather self-centred."

"Take it from me, Miss Cheville, he's self-centred!" Esme cried hotly. "Do you know, he's never once written to me or asked for me to write to him. And he's got bags of money now, and he's left Uncle Dick to bear nearly all the expenses of my education."

Miss Cheville regarded Esme with a puzzled frown.

"But," she objected, "you told me you hadn't been to school before."

"Murder!" said Esme below his breath. He was beginning to think that his was a simple nature, too essentially honest for conspiracies. He coughed hard to gain time.

"Well," he said, "*he* doesn't know that I haven't been to school before, and if I had, Uncle Dick would have been frightfully out of pocket. As far as he's concerned it's all the same. You see what I mean, Miss Cheville."

The kind lady patted his shoulder.

"Don't think too harshly of your father, my dear." She was remembering that Tom Geering had lost his wife when the child was born. "Perhaps there are reasons, through no fault of yours, why he cannot love you as a father ought."

"You're right there!" said Esme vivaciously.

"Anyhow, it doesn't matter. There's no love lost between us on either side. I'm sticking to Uncle Dick."

"That's right, my dear. Poor Uncle Dick! You owe him a great deal. What are you going to do when you grow up?"

"Oh, Esme'll marry, of course!" Christine laughed. "I thought about the merchant service,"

Esme murmured, caught napping again.

"The merchant service!" Miss Cheville almost screamed.

Esme, realising what he had said, looked aside and rolled his eyes in horror.

"As a stewardess, of course," he amended hastily. Christine's aunt laughed outright.

"You're making fun of me, Esme," she said, "and it's very naughty of you."

"Oh, Esme's always saying things like that," said Christine. "She's a regular terror, Auntie dear."
The danger had passed, and Esme puffed out his cheeks and sighed noisily with relief. "But," he reflected, "if I make any more floaters she'll smoke me for a certainty."

Miss Cheville took them to tea at a pastry-cook's with a small room at the back. They sat down to thin bread and butter, strawberry jam, cream buns, and *Eclairs*. Christine and Esme were both able to do considerable execution among these delicacies, and conversation languished accordingly. It was not until tea was nearly over, and they were both eating under the pressure of their hostess, when Miss Cheville quite innocently dropped a bombshell on Esme's head.

"Do you know," she said, smiling, "that until I heard from your uncle a short while ago I was always under the impression that you were a boy. . . .Why, what's the matter, Esme?"

Esme had promptly gone purple in the face and choked. It was a good hearty choke. Christine arose and rendered first aid in a manner which suggested congratulation for some athletic achievement. Miss Cheville hastily poured him out another cup of tea and made him drink it.
Eventually peace was restored.

"Are you better now, dear?" Miss Cheville asked anxiously. "You're not looking a bit well."
"It's these cream buns," Esme explained. "They put boracic ointment in 'em instead of cream. Talking of boracic ointment—"

"Auntie was saying that she always thought you were a boy," Christine interrupted. "How funny! What made you think that, Auntie?"

Esme shot her a poisonous glance, and then stared hard at the pattern on his plate.

"Years ago, when I first heard of you, my dear," Miss Cheville said, renewing the topic with a smile, " I'm almost sure your Uncle Dick wrote to me saying that he was looking after Tom Geering's little *boy*. Or perhaps it was because Esme is a boy's name, too, that I had that impression.

"That must have been it," said Esme.

"And yet I'm sure he referred to you as a he."

Esme felt the moisture gathering on his brow.

"Oh, that's very likely!" he said with a hollow laugh. "After all, all kids look much alike, don't they? and I don't suppose Uncle Dick bothered about what I was. You always speak of a dog as a he, don't you? I wish I *were* a boy."

Both his hearers laughed.

"Well, I'm almost sure," said the elder, "your Uncle Dick referred to you as one. I've still got his letter somewhere. I must try to find it."

Esme devoutly hoped she wouldn't. Just at present she was inclined to think that her memory had been at fault, or that Uncle Dick had carelessly written the pronoun "he" instead of "she." But if she saw the word "boy" in Uncle Dick's handwriting it would set her thinking. Esme was aware that he was regarded by everybody as a very odd sort of girl. The letter, if Miss Cheville found it, might give rise to certain suspicions. He wrinkled his brows as he tried to think of what might follow. She seemed what he called a " good sportsman," but one couldn't be sure.

His thoughts were interrupted by a discussion between Christine and her aunt. A visit to one of the local cinemas was suggested, and Esme applauded it. Not that he cared for the cinema, but it was preferable to his prison-house, and he would not be compelled to carry on a conversation. He had already realised that it was not safe for him to talk too much.

Accordingly they went to see a film version of the life of Titus Oates, and afterwards he and Christine accompanied Miss Cheville to the station to see her off. Esme submitted to being kissed again, and breathed relief when the train slid out of the station. On the whole he had had a very good afternoon, and although he had skated rather clumsily over some thin ice, he felt that he had done no particular harm. Another day at St. Mildred's was almost over.

Poor dear Esme! Just when he felt surest of his temporary security the Fates were arranging for him to suffer forthwith one of the shocks of his young life. The past, in the person of young Cedric Bingham, was hurrying to confront him.

CHAPTER VIII

It was already dark when they left the station. Purlingdon, which slept during the day, awoke to some activity in the mornings and evenings. Now the shops were bright with electric light, and the stout sons of Purlingdon were returning home from their City offices. All the youth and beauty were abroad. Beautiful young girls gazed into shop windows, asking each other in awed voices if what they saw could be real silk at one and eleven-three. Dashing young men in soft felt hats and shooting jackets passed forth and back, twirling their canes and trying to catch glances from the aforementioned maidens. All the cheaper seats in the cinemas were rapidly filling up. Yes, Purlingdon was broad awake, and had some of the gaiety and sparkle of a casino town. Some—but not much.

Esme turned to Christine.

"Well," he said, "what are we going to do?"

"Go back to the school, of course," Christine said.

"It's an original suggestion. I hadn't thought of that. Because the cage is open, I don't see why the birds should be in such a hurry to fly back."

Christine stared at him.

"What did you think of doing?" she demanded.

"Getting a decent supper for one thing. I'd heard the expression ' Hard cheese ' before I came to St. Mildred's, but I didn't know what it really meant. It's my considered opinion that the old geyser puts it through some secret process of ossification. You come along with me, old thing. I've got some money." Christine, who was hungry again by now, thought yearningly of poached eggs and cocoa, but she shook her head.

"We should get into a frightful row," she said. "Mrs. Toy knows that Aunt Edith wouldn't keep us out so that we were late for supper."

"We might put it to her so that she thought "

"She'd only write to Aunt Edith, and Aunt Edith would write back. And then the fat would be in the fire, and very likely I shouldn't be allowed to go out with her any more during term. But if you want to stay out, I'll stay."

Quite unconsciously she had hit the only safe way of managing Esme. Immediately he was anxious to show her that he, too, could be generous.

"No," he said; "I know you hate rows, and that wouldn't be fair. We'll cut back now. But we may as well buy some grub on the way, and I want some cigarettes."

Christine clicked her tongue.

"Esme! You're sure to be caught smoking sooner or later."

"Not now that I've arranged for my bedroom door to stick. It takes any of those females about five minutes to shove it open, so I get plenty of warning, and, as I'm always careful to smoke out of the window, the room doesn't smell. The dear old girl is too mean to have the door seen to, and she doesn't know I had it off the hinges the other night and nailed some cardboard underneath it to make it hang."

Christine bent double and began to laugh hysterically. "You really are the limit, Esme," she said. "I don't believe there ever was another girl in the world like you! I don't know what I should do without you." The boy's heart softened to her. A little flood of emotion, which he suspected of being unmanly, suffused him. It was decent of her to like him as much as she did. Where the others sneered and avoided him her loyalty held her fast. For his sake she had been willing to risk staying out late. She would sink or swim with him whatever happened. A good sort, Christine. Dash it all, why couldn't she have been a boy?

"Well, we've had a jolly good time," he said awkwardly. "And I haven't thanked you yet. Thanks most awfully, old thing."

"Don't mench. Besides, it wasn't my doing, and you've already thanked Auntie. Of course I should have asked to bring you if she hadn't suggested it. You're rather a dear, aren't you, Esme? ''

" A beauteous creature!" said Esme, admiring his own reflection in a shop window. "But you rather put me in the shade, you know."

"I believe," Christine murmured a little plaintively, "you *do* like me a bit."

Esme began to wriggle uncomfortably.

"I regard you," he said, "as the prop of my declining years."

"There you go," Christine complained. "You always turn off and say something silly. I don't believe you like to be liked. I've often wanted to kiss you, but you've never wanted to kiss me."

"Kissing's awful rot," said Esme, looking hard into the distance. "Germs and all that," he added.

Esme was just then suffering agonies of bashfulness and praying hard for something to intervene. His prayer was answered, but not as he would have wished. It was just then, full in the glare of a street lamp, that he came face to face with Cedric Bingham.

You must know Cedric Bingham, and it were well to state immediately, without any beating about the bush, that Cedric was a fool. In appearance he was a tall, apple-cheeked youth of twenty, with pale yellow hair parted in the middle, a rabbit mouth and prominent front teeth. Esme had reason to know him, for Cedric had been gone from Wryvern for only about a year, and although the disparity in their ages prevented them from knowing one another very well, they were both from the same house.

Cedric Bingham was the son of a rich man in the Midlands, who manufactured household utensils from the baser metals somewhere in the neighbourhood of Birmingham. Cedric had been destined for the Army, and, being a fool, had been duly ploughed at the entrance examination to Sandhurst. Something then had to be done about him, and his father, being unwilling to allow him to eat the bread of idleness, had used some influence to get him a berth in the London and Suburban Bank. That he should be sent to the Purlingdon branch was a piece of sheer chance which looked like being a dire misfortune for Esme.

In the year since he had left school, Cedric had grown into a somewhat exquisite youth, always much too well dressed, and having a subtle taste in ties and socks. Already he was discovering that he had a keen eye for a pretty girl. He had a taste for romance, a confirmed belief in the power of his fascinations, and knew the Christian name of every good-looking barmaid in Purlingdon. He was a survival of a type which, thirty years before, was to be seen waiting outside every stage door, sucking the handle of a whangee cane.

He started and stared when he saw Esme. Esme too started, and then looked hurriedly away, choking back a quick exclamation. Christine glanced at him and saw the strained expression on his face.

"Why, what's the matter, Esme?" she whispered. "You look ill."

"Those infernal cream buns," began Esme miserably.

"Miss Geering! Miss Geering!"

Esme was aware of the step behind him and the low insinuating voice. He hurried on. Christine glanced quickly and fearfully over her shoulder.

"Esme," she whispered, "there's a man following us!"

"Is there?" hissed back the goaded Esme. "Then—then let's hurry. Don't let's have anything to do with him. Cheek, I call it! Remember, we're—we're *ladies.*"

"Of course!" said Christine primly.

But Cedric Bingham was not lightly to be shaken off. He followed a yard in the rear, smiling all over his simple glowing face, coughing, and uttering little apologetic chuckles. This girl was the image of the Esme Geering he had known at school. A thousand to one she was his sister. He must certainly speak to her.

"I say! Miss Geering!" murmured the voice winningly.

"Why," exclaimed Christine, vastly thrilled, "he knows you!"

"This," said Esme, in a letter describing the incident to Uncle Dick, "was like the last straw to the cornered rat. I had to do *something!*"

"Look here," he whispered hastily to Christine, hardly knowing what he said, "I shall have to speak to him. D'you mind walking on a yard or two? I—I won't be a minute."

With that he faced his tormentor, and was within an ace of planting a workmanlike left straight in the smiling, ingratiating countenance which beamed upon him from under a champagne-coloured velour hat. The hat came off promptly, and Cedric stood, bowed to the shape of a note of interrogation, fondling it between his hands.

"Er—excuse me," said the swain in a beautifully modulated voice, "but—er—aren't you Miss Geering?"

Esme growled at him like a terrier.

"What the blazes has that got to do with you?" he demanded in a tone which almost caused Cedric to overbalance.

"Oh, quite! Oh, yes, of course—quite!" he stammered.

"I am only a poor defenceless schoolgirl," continued Esme, almost pathetically, "but," he added, with sudden fire, "I could give you such a jolt in the jaw, my lad."

"Oh—er—quite!" agreed Cedric politely. "Yes, quite! I don't think you—ah!—quite grasp me, though."

"I shall in a minute, if you don't buzz off!"

"Hadn't you a brother at Wryvern?"

Esme's troubled brow and still more troubled mind cleared together. He saw immediately the error under which Cedric laboured. So long as his disguise had not been penetrated he could breathe again.

"Yes," he said.

"I knew it. You're the image of him. The likeness is really—really—well, it's a real likeness. The moment I saw you, I said to myself, "That must be Esme Geering's sister.' How is he, Miss Geering?"

"Dead!" said Esme in a hollow voice. .

"Dead!" echoed Cedric, also in a hollow voice.

The moment after Esme had said it, he realised his mistake. It had seemed to him the easiest way of disposing of his other self. Then it occurred to him that Cedric was probably a member of the Society of Old Wryvernians, and a regular recipient of the magazine. He would look in vain for the obituary notice and probably write to somebody at the school.

"Dead to us," he amended. "He got himself—er— bunked. You will oblige me by not speaking of him again."

"Oh, quite I Got himself bunked, did he? What for? I had a letter only the other day from a fellow named Vince, saying he hadn't come back this term, but he didn't say—"

"He was sacked privately at the end of last term," said Esme, trying to assume the air of a sorrowing sister. "Please don't ask any questions or speak of him again. Father's grey hairs, and the grave and all that," he added vaguely.

"Oh, quite! I'm sorry. What's he doing now?"

"Time," said Esme promptly, and the young man drew back abashed.

"Oh—ah—really. Er—isn't it remarkable meeting you here, and my recognising you? Your name's Esme too, isn't it? I heard that other girl call you—"

"Yes," Esme returned glibly, "his is Esme George, and mine's Esme Claribel. We caught it off the same grandmother."

Although Esme had shown himself to be no ordinary young girl, it was plain that Cedric Bingham was attracted. Esme, who could never resist playing with fire, was not averse from dallying with him, now that he judged his secret to be safe. Finding himself at a loss for a second feminine Christian name he had borrowed Miss Budging's.

"I'm in the bank here," volunteered Cedric.

"What, the one where the wild thyme grows?"

"No, the one where the wild manager grumbles. Ha, ha, that's rather good. And you're at St. Mildred's, aren't you? Splendid! I know one of the mistresses there. She used to be governess to my kiddy sister." Esme's jaw dropped.

"Which one?" he demanded.

"Miss Budging. Funny old gazeeka, what? I go and see her sometimes."

"Well, don't for goodness' sake say you've spoken to me".

"A pukka sahib," said Cedric with dignity, '* would never dream of such a thing."

"And—don't mention my brother to her."

"Oh, quite!" murmured Cedric, looking unutterable things. "I'd do anything you asked me, Miss Geering," he added in a low, thrilling whisper. "May I—may I call you Esme?"

Esme looked away from him, squinting horribly.

"I'd sooner you called me Claribel," he said softly, "since my brother has disgraced—"

"Oh, quite—er—Claribel. And will you call me Cedric?"

"I shall always think of you as something else," murmured Esme, bearing in mind an opprobrious nickname which Cedric had been called at school.

"Really? I say, what?"

"Never mind!" said Esme. "I must run now."

"Must you? Must you really? We shall meet again."

"Not if I know it, you rabbit-faced freak," Esme thought.

"I'm afraid—" he began aloud.

"I've a premonition that we shall meet again quite soon, and Pm a wonderful chap for premonitions."

"Good night,   Cedric," Esme said softly, with downcast eyes, and hurried away from him. Christine was awaiting him, a picture of anxiety.

"What a time you've been, Esme!" she exclaimed. "Who is that man, and how did he know you?"

"He—er—knew me," Esme muttered.

"Of course he did, silly! Why wouldn't you speak to him at first?"

Esme was bubbling over with suppressed mirth. He would have given much just then to take Christine into his entire confidence. But, as he could not do that he found himself compelled to invent some acceptable story.

"I never wanted to set eyes on him again!" he said tragically.

Christine turned and stared at her companion.

"He broke my heart, and I hate him, curse him!" said Esme, drawing on what remained in his memory of something in a book which he had been reading. Christine uttered a little squeal of delight.

"Esme! *Darling!* Is this a real romance? Oh, *do* tell me. Esme, you don't mean to say you were in *love* with him?"

"He was handsome and dashing," Esme murmured pathetically, "and I was young and inexperienced. Can you blame me?"

"I didn't think he was very good-looking," said Christine decisively.

"Nobody asked you to," Esme returned.

"Pm sorry, dear, I didn't mean to offend you."

"You haven't! I hate the sight of the blighter."

"No, you don't," gurgled Christine. "Deep down in your heart you still adore him. Do tell me all about it. Oh, Esme, I think you're simply wonderful!"

"I met him down in Cornwall," said Esme glibly, "while I was there this summer with Uncle Dick. He was staying at the same hotel. He was handsome and brave and dashing, and before I had time to look into my girlish heart—er—before I had time to look into my girlish heart—"

"Yes, yes, you were in love with him," prompted Christine hastily.

"A true bill!" said Esme, with a chesty sigh. "At first he showed me—er—marked attentions. Used to bring me shrimps and things. How was I to know that he meant nothing by it? "

"Of course you weren't to know—not if he brought you shrimps," Christine exclaimed sympathetically. Poor dear Esme! "

"Chrissie," said Esme solemnly, "I put it to you as—er—woman to woman. Would you ever forgive a man who threw you over for a ginger-headed wench? "

"Never!" said Christine decisively. "Not ginger!"

"That," said Esme, "is exactly how I feel. I could have forgiven him a common or garden blonde. I might have sympathised with him if he had been enslaved by blue-black hair and the snapping fiery eyes of Spain. But ginger, and with green eyes! And thirty if she was a day!"

"I wonder you didn't die," murmured Christine, "and then perhaps he'd have been sorry, and starved himself to death on your grave."

"I thought of that," said Esme, "only my Uncle Dick wouldn't have liked it. And now, Chrissie, you—you understand, don't you?"

Christine inclined her head and, reaching for Esme's arm, gave it a squeeze.

"Perhaps," she said softly, "he really loved you all the while, and only flirted with the other girl to make you jealous. Of course, I know just how you feel. Pride is a dreadful thing! But you really do love him still, Esme, and I'm sure it will all come right. Why was he sent here to meet you? It was Fate that did it."

"Yes," said Esme with a heavy sigh, "Fate has done it on me! Don't let on to the other girls for goodness' sake."

Christine's eyes were dim with awe and sympathy. Esme's stock had risen about five hundred per cent, in her estimation.

"My dear," she exclaimed, "need you ask? But oh, Esme, if I can ever do anything to make you happy by bringing you together again—"

Esme interrupted hastily.

"I shouldn't bother too much about that," he said with a cough. "I don't know how I feel about it myself. I—er—I must look into my girlish heart again."

By this time they had reached St. Mildred's, and went in in silence, both busy with their respective thoughts.

CHAPTER IX

It is here necessary to desert Esme for a little while and follow Cedric Bingham. We left him in the bright lights of the main street of Purlingdon. Let us accompany him through some glass swing doors and into the still brighter lights of the saloon lounge of the "King and Keys."

Cedric was both excited and elated. He had met a girl and a half, by Jove! A little spitfire, by gad! A girl with some zip and sting and spirit about her!

For some while now he had been thinking it time that he had a serious love affair, but until now he had failed to encounter a situation sufficiently romantic to intrigue him. True, Esme Claribel—or Claribel as he must call her—was very young, seventeen at the most, but extreme youth was a fault she would soon outgrow. Besides, he had just been reading an historical romance, of which the heroine was no older, and bearded men had drunk to her, and said " Zounds," and stabbed each other's vitals for her. Cedric wished he had lived in that age, when a man could *be* a man.

Cedric was already weaving a romance about himself. Handsome young devil-may-care fellow meets sister of an old schoolfellow. Learns that old schoolfellow is in disgrace, been expelled and all that, and now in prison. Innocent, of course, and dashing young hero sets himself to prove it and win beautiful heroine's love and eternal gratitude. Meanwhile beautiful heroine is at school, cut off from him. Sweet stolen meetings, smuggled notes, both of them using wit and cunning and ingenuity to establish a line of communication and arrange little secret heart-to-heart talks. Golly, life was going to be worth living!

"Good evening, Nellie," said Cedric, swaggering up to the counter. "A small port, please." Let your gross materialist bloat himself with beer, let your stricken wretch seek to forget his sorrows in whisky; wine, red wine, is the stuff for heroes and lovers. He was served with a small glass of a decoction which a man of more experience might easily have mistaken for cough mixture, and retired to a comer seat, where he resumed the pleasant occupation of weaving dreams.

But Cedric was not long left alone. At the end of a few minutes Reggie Wardle arrived upon the scene and saluted Cedric by lifting two fingers to the brim of his hat. Young Wardle was one of the few young men in Purlingdon whom Cedric condescended to know. He was about two years older than Cedric, a fatuous good-natured youth, who worked in the office of his father, a local lawyer. He ordered a Bass and came to sit beside the brooding romantic.

"How's it going, old top?" he inquired.

"Fine, thanks," said Cedric absently.

"You're looking all right. What's the matter? Somebody left you a fortune?"

Cedric looked at once astonished and pleased.

"What!" he exclaimed. "Do you notice something unusual about me?"

"You look as if you had backed a good winner, or is it only that Kruschen feeling?"

"As a matter of fact," Cedric remarked slowly and impressively, "I believe Pm in love."

"What, again?" Reggie inquired blandly.

"Don't say that." Cedric looked a little hurt. "All my other affairs have been—"

"Just so. They have been. The tense will do. What are you drinking? Some more of that red ink? Lucky you haven't got my ancestors, my boy."

On an ordinary occasion Cedric would have stoutly affirmed that his ancestors were just as scandalous a lot as Reggie's. But he was not going to quarrel with Reggie. Just then he needed a confidant.

Reggie went up to the counter, and returned with another Bass and another glass of port.

"Well," he said, "here's to her! May she never grow old and ugly. Tell us all about this latest spasm of yours, Cedric."

Cedric needed no second bidding.

"Come and sit close, then," he said. "One can't shout ladies' names about a place like this. To begin with, she's quite a flapper—not a day over seventeen. Matter of fact, she's still at school here."

"What, at old Mother Toy's?"

"Yes. I recognised the hat ribbon."

"H'm. I like 'em a bit older than that myself. Still, they get older, don't they? And they don't get younger."

"Oh, quite! Well, perhaps you wouldn't like her, Reggie. She's pretty enough, but she's got rather big hands and feet. And she's a regular little spitfire. Still, I like a girl to have a bit of *sting* in her."

"All very well," conceded Reggie, "so long as it doesn't get worse as she gets older. Being in a bank, you ought to know all about compound interest."

"She was out with another girl from the school. I walked into 'em only a few minutes ago. I was at school with her brother, and I spotted the likeness at once. We stopped and had quite a little chat. I'm not one of those chaps who boast about these things, but I couldn't help feeling I had made a bit of an impression."

"It's a good start for you," Reggie observed, "if you were at school with her brother. What sort of lad was he? "

"Oh, quite a decent kid," said Cedric tolerantly, forgetting how intensely he had once disliked Esme. "Younger than me, of course, but I saw a great deal of him, being in the same house. Reggie, there's a mystery about that kid. He got himself sacked for something, and now he's in prison. Family even don't mention his name, and all that. Fact! She told me so herself."

Reggie uttered a low soft whistle.

"I should think it was a pretty useful sort of family to steer clear of," he remarked.

Cedric tapped the little table in front of him with the bottom of his glass.

"Do you know," he said slowly, "I can't help believing that the boy is innocent."

"H'm! What's he been up to?" Reggie inquired, immediately assuming a semi-legal manner.

"I don't know."

"Then my dear old fruit, how can you possibly—"

"Because he wasn't the sort of kid to go off the deep end. Plenty of high spirits, you know, and all that, but nothing really wrong about him. Do you know what I've been thinking, Reggie? I've always fancied myself a bit of a Sherlock Holmes. If I could only find out what he'd done, and then prove his innocence, it would help me no end with the girl."

"Rather!" his friend agreed cordially. "Of course, it would. Wouldn't she tell you what he had been up to?"

"No. Shut up like an oyster. Asked me never to mention his name again. It looks to me as if he was supposed to have been stealing something hefty. Anyhow, I can soon find out."

"How?"

"By writing to one of the chaps at the school. It must have happened there if he got sacked for it, mustn't it?"

Reggie stared at him almost admiringly over the rim of his glass.

"Good old Sherlock!" he exclaimed. "But there's one thing against you. How are you going to act the sleuth when you're shut up in that bank all day?"

"I've got a holiday due to me, and coming off shortly. Besides, if necessary, I can get myself sacked. I don't want to be there. Then I should have a good long holiday while my governor was getting me another job."

Reggie nodded thoughtfully.

"Well, good luck, old thing. Have you made any arrangements to meet the girl again?"

"Can't very well while she's shut up in that beastly school. I know a bit about it, as my sister's old governess is there as a mistress. They keep a pretty sharp look out on the fillies there. Don't know how she managed to get out with that other girl to-night. Very likely been to see somebody off, as they were coming from the station. Of course, I shall try to smuggle notes to her, but it's going to be pretty difficult."

"It is!" Reggie agreed dryly. "Can't you make this old governess of your sister's useful?"

"Oh, Lord, no! She's made of solidified vinegar. Looks like a piece of over-ripe Stilton. But, of course, I shall go and see her pretty often now in the hope of getting a squint of Claribel."

"That your divinity's name?" Reggie asked, lifting an eyebrow.

"Esme Claribel Geering. Pretty name, don't you think? Sort of name you want to go on repeating to yourself. Well, Reggie, if you can only think of a way of smuggling notes to her, I'll be eternally grateful."

"I'm your man, guv'nor!"

It was not Reggie who spoke. Both he and Cedric started, and looked sharply around them. The bar was empty save for themselves and the girl behind the counter, who was knitting a jumper with an air of intense preoccupation.

"Did you—hear anything?" Cedric demanded in a low voice of awe.

"I thought I heard—"

"So did I!"

"It's me speakin', guv'nor," said the Voice. "Hold on! I'll be round in 'arf a tick."

"Great Scott!" cried Cedric, horrified. "It's somebody in the other bar."

"So it is!" Reggie reached out and rapped at the partition with his knuckles.

"Matchboarding," he announced. "Disgraceful!"

While they were staring at one another in dismay the door opened, and a stocky, sharp-featured youth sidled into the room. He was a stranger to them both, but not to the reader, who has already been introduced to Cuthbert. His coat was buttoned up tightly, and beneath it something bulky was imprisoned against his chest. He approached the two young men with a nervous grin which tried to appear ingratiating.

"Was it you that spoke to us just now?" Cedric demanded.

Cuthbert nodded and came nearer.

"Then what do you mean by listening to a conversation between gentlemen?" demanded Cedric in quite a swash-buckling tone. "Who the devil are you, anyway? "

"I couldn't 'elp 'earing somethin' wot you were sayin'," Cuthbert said huskily.

"How much did you hear?" Reggie inquired sharply.

"I 'eard that gentleman say a lady's name, and as 'ow 'e wanted to send 'er notes on the sly, like."

"And that's all?" Cedric demanded.

"That's all, sir, and as I told you through the partition, sir—I'm your man."

"Behold," said Reggie, "Gupid's messenger."

"But how can you take notes from me?" asked Cedric, not knowing whether to be angry or delighted.

"I'm the boot boy at St. Mildred's, sir. I does a lot of little jobs for Miss Geering, sir. She ain't 'arf a nut!" He might have added that the bottle of Bass which was buttoned up under his coat was intended for that eccentric young lady's consumption, but instinct told him that beer would immediately give the affair an unromantic flavour. His not to spoil romance—particularly a romance which looked like being profitable to himself.

Cedric grinned broadly at his friend before turning to Cuthbert.

"Then you *can* take notes between us!" he exclaimed.

"Bags of them, sir," said Cuthbert, grinning.

"Where am I to find you when I want you?"

"I'm in 'ere at this time every night—in the next bar, sir."

"And I can trust you to deliver them safely, and not be caught carrying them?"

"You can trust me all right, sir. Miss Geering does, any'ow."

Cedric considered a moment. This sudden piece of good fortune would almost have turned his head had he not concentrated on keeping his faculties clear.

"Look here," he said, "you look an honest sort of fellow, and I'm disposed to trust you. I'll give you two shillings for every note from me which falls safely into Miss Geering's hands, and a shilling for every one you bring me back from her. How will that suit you?"

Cuthbert nodded briefly. He too kept his head, but it was difficult for him to quell his excitement when he reflected that if the romance got into good working order it would be worth a guinea a week to him, besides what he got out of Esme for other commissions.

"By George, old man," Reggie Wardle remarked to Cedric, "this is a slice of luck for you."

"Wot about writing a note this evenin'?" Cuthbert suggested, his palm itching.

Cedric immediately felt for his pocket book.

"That's a bright idea," he said. "You're a very intelligent young fellow. You ought to make your way in the world."

It was a happy Cuthbert who stole back to St. Mildred's a quarter of an hour later. "Blimey!" he reflected. "If this isn't a slice of luck! Twenty-one bob a week, if they writes regular, Sundays included. And when love's young dream is o'er I think I sees a way of getting a bit of dough out of that sportin' young lady. She's got a brother in chokee, 'as she? I bet she don't want everybody to know *that*. Ha, they may scorn me for me 'umble birth, but it's brains wot counts!"

From which it may be gathered that Cuthbert had overheard more of the conversation in the bar than he had chosen to admit.

CHAPTER X

It was ten o'clock that night, and lights were out at St. Mildred's. Gentle sleep was kissing some of the urchin eyelids. Esme, however, was very wide awake. His light was out, but he stood, fully dressed, by the window, holding in his hand one end of a length of string which dangled down into the darkness beneath.

Had he been fishing with a line, as his attitude suggested, he would have been aware of a distinct nibble. The string was taut and being violently agitated from the other end. At last a husky whisper from Cuthbert was wafted up from below.

"Haul away, miss. It's all there. A bottle of Bass, twenty Gold Flake, and a letter from a gentleman."

"A letter from a gentleman! " repeated Esme to the unheeding dusk.

He pulled up the string hand over hand, and it was not until the parcel had toppled clumsily on to the window-sill that he thought of Cedric Bingham.

"My hat!" he murmured to himself. "I wonder if he's got hold of Cuthbert. Rather bright for him if he has!"

Esme was so anxious to read the note that he broke a rule and risked lighting a candle. He found the envelope which contained it folded.

"My first love-letter!" he whispered to himself, squinting abominably. "Be still, my girlish heart!"

He slit open the envelope and read as follows:

"Dearest Claribel :

"If I may so address you. I have found a means of communicating with you through the boy who works at your school. I think Fate intended us to meet to-night. We spoke together for only a few minutes, and yet I felt that I had known you long before. I am deeply grieved about your brother and will never mention him to you again, but at the same time I cannot believe that he is guilty of anything really wicked. How could he be, with such a sister? Perhaps some day I shall do something to deserve your friendship by bringing you good news of him. Meanwhile, I want you to realise one thing, Claribel, that you have a friend. Whatever happens you have a friend. Will you please write to me sometimes and give your letters to the boy, who will deliver them safely?

"With all friendship and respectful devotion—dare I risk your displeasure by adding love?

"Yours very, *very* sincerely,

"Cedric Bingham."

For the space of about a minute and a half Esme writhed on the floor, stuffing a bunched-up handkerchief against his mouth. He had always known Cedric for an ass, but Cedric had far exceeded his expectations, had out-assed himself. Choking and gurgling, he read the letter through twice more, and was holding it out to the candle flame, when he stayed his hand. To keep it would be risky, but the temptation was too strong for him. If the Fates were kind he would be back at Wryvern next term. The temptation to preserve this and any further correspondence from the same source for the delectation of his friends was too much for Esme.

He knew his weakness even as he prised up the board beneath which were hidden certain of his private possessions which would have astonished Mrs. Toy had she known of their existence. He was courting disaster for the sake of what he called a "rag." He had had a narrow escape, and instead of being grateful to the chance which prompted Cedric to jump to a wrong conclusion, he was determined to walk back into danger. Sheltered behind the walls of St. Mildred's, he could easily be rid of Cedric, easily avoid seeing him again. He could easily stop Cedric from sending him notes; he could even tell Mrs. Toy that a man was annoying him and leave her to deal adequately with the situation. Cedric would never suspect the truth unless he gave that impressionable young man further opportunities of seeing him.

But the temptation to make a fool of Cedric altogether exceeded his powers of resistance. He was already determined to lead him on, to behave like a genuine schoolgirl—as far as he knew how—flattered by the attentions of her first immature admirer. In doing so he not only ran the risk of detection—and Cedric, in his righteous wrath, would not be likely to show much mercy—but it was also possible that the lynx-eyed Mrs. Toy might discover what was going on and expel him at a very critical time. But he could not help it. It was too joyous an opportunity to be lost. Even Uncle Dick would hardly expect him to miss it.

Next morning, during the half hour's break at eleven o'clock, Esme sought and found an opportunity to slip into the boot-room, where he found Cuthbert at leisure, studying the early racing edition of an evening paper and a slip of pink cardboard headed "Joe the Jockey's Daily Wire."

"Didn't know you were a racing man, Cuthbert," he observed.

"I does a bit, miss. And I does a lot with football coupons."

"Yes," said Esme, "you would! But how do you manage to get your money on? Credit account with Welsh and Hoppit?"

"No, miss. There's a man as comes into the pub round the corner and takes slips. He's quite safe. All the police bets with 'im."

"So you can get a bit on for me if I ever want it?"

Cuthbert rolled round eyes upon him.

"I've never knowed anybody like you, miss," he said. "I swear I 'aven't." His expression suddenly changed, a sly grin curving his mouth. One of his eyes almost winked. "Did you get your letter orl right last night, miss?"

"Yes, thank you, good Cuthbert."

"A nice 'andsome gentleman, miss."

"Far too good for me, I fear," said Esme, with a maidenly sigh.

"Don't you believe it, miss. Nobody ain't too good for you. Fair struck on you he is, miss, too! I could tell that by the soft look on 'is fyce."

"It's a permanent expression, Cuthbert. Tell me, fair youth, have you ever felt as if you had beetles walking up and down your spine? Have you ever wakened in the morning with a glad cry, singing, ' Tra-la-la, the same sun is shining upon my loved one '? Or, to cut it short, have you ever been in love?"

"Not lately, miss," said Cuthbert. "If you was a feller who 'ad to spend the best part of 'is life cleanin' young ladies' boots you wouldn't see much in the opposite sect. Same as these 'ere fellers in the drapery. I expect they get 'ardened to it, like."

"Ah, then," said Esme dreamily, "you wouldn't understand."

Cuthbert regarded him craftily over the top of the paper.

"Always willing to do anything to 'elp you, miss," he murmured insinuatingly. "'Ave you got a note for me to give 'im?"

Esme shook his head, and Cuthbert looked disappointed.

"Ah, that's a pity, miss. 'E won't 'arf feel 'urt." Esme regarded him with sudden enlightenment.

"Nice oif you to take such an interest in us, Cuthbert," he said. "What are you making out of it?"

"Well, miss, I'd better tell you the troof, in case you finds out later. The gen'leman's givin' me two bob for every note I brings you from 'im, and a bob for every one I brings back from you."

Esme stared at him and whistled.

"That shows you 'ow struck 'e is, miss," the boot boy added.

"A shilling for every note I write! Cuthbert, I've a good mind to write one every day and stand in with you."

"Well, miss," said Cuthbert briskly, " I don't say as I should mind cornin' to an arrangement with you."

Esme smiled and shook his head.

"No, no," he said, " my dignity as a gentle—as a gentlewoman forbids it. Still, Cuthbert, I wish you well. You've done me a lot of good turns, although I've paid you well for them. With very little trouble I can earn you an extra bob a day, so you can count on me. What are you going to do with all that money? Marry and settle down? Oh, I forgot! You're not a marrying man!"

Inside the house a bell rang, and Esme turned towards the door.

"I'll go up to my room immediately after tea," he said, "and write a note. Come out of the boot-room when it's all clear and start singing ' I love lime-juice ' or some other popular ditty. That'll be a signal and I'll drop the note out of the window to you."

While Christine was walking with Esme in the dingy garden after the mid-day meal, the former made a reference to the thrilling happening on the previous evening.

"You told me once," she said, " that you had a secret. Was that the one?"

Esme shook his head.

"No," he said, " my other secret's a better one than that. I'll tell you some day, and then you'll die laughing."

"Oh, it's a funny secret," said Christine, disappointed.

"Partly."

"Mine isn't. I'm going to tell you one day, Esme, dear; only I think I ought to ask Aunt Edith first."

Esme, who could not guess the nature of Christine's secret, was not unduly excited. His own affairs seemed a great deal more interesting.

"I had a note from *him* last night," he said. "Cuthbert brought it."

Christine gave vent to a little squeal of rapture.

"Oh," she cried, "how lovely! And how clever of him to think of giving it to Cuthbert. Did he—Was he?"

"He did!" said Esme. "He was! My girlish heart was touched."

Christine began to giggle.

"You do say such funny things, Esme. Fancy talking about your girlish heart. It's a good job none of the other girls can hear you, or they'd rag you terribly. But of course you haven't been brought up amongst girls, have you."

"No, thank no, of course I haven't."

"Still, you're awfully sweet," said Christine, "aren't you? I'm so glad he wrote to you, because I really believe you do love him, in spite of that ginger girl."

"*Cave,*" Esme muttered in a low voice, "here's the Spotted Wonder."

Caroline Bax was approaching them, swinging a hockey stick. Her blemishes were more than usually inflamed this afternoon and shone like little beacons against the natural pallor of her face. Her expression was far from kindly: an arch-duchess, whose nostrils were being offended by a tannery, might have worn the same sort of look. Not only was she Esme's avowed enemy, but just then she was on bad terms with Christine for championing the pariah.

"Isn't she a little darling!" Esme murmured. "Looks more like a piece of Stilton every day. I wonder whether anybody'll ever marry that? They say there's a mug bom every day." Christine tried hard but unsuccessfully to hide a smile, and Caroline became instantly aware that Esme had been talking about her. She ignored Esme and addressed Christine in a tone which was cold and haughty.

"The others want to know whether you're going to have a game of hockey," she said.

Christine shook her head.

"I don't think so, thanks. Esme can't play, and somebody ought to talk to her."

"Oh, bother Esme! We must practise up for the High School match."

"It doesn't matter how much we practise, my dear. They beat us ten-one last year, and they've got a better team than ever, and we're not so strong."

"Oh, well," said Caroline, frowning, "of course we shan't have any chance if people aren't going to trouble."

"It's a pity you're such an invalid, and can't play," Christine remarked, turning to Esme.

"Yes," agreed Caroline, cuttingly, "Esme 'ud have a good chance of getting into the third eleven—if we had one."

Once more sheer vanity tempted Esme into danger. They play hockey at Wryvern in the spring term, and Esme was more than hopeful of getting his second eleven colours after Christmas. Moreover, Wryvern has always been famous for its hockey. There are seldom less than half a dozen Old Boys playing for the two Universities. First-class London sides have been to Wryvern before now and met more than their match.

Between a good boy player and a good girl player there is a great gulf fixed. If he played at St. Mildred's, Esme knew that he must stand out as a giant among pigmies. He knew that any triumph of his in that respect would be a poor and hollow one, and he knew also that his safest plan was to be as little conspicuous as possible. But, on the other hand, he had a vulgar hankering after causing sensations. And Caroline had spoken slightingly of him. The temptation to "show Caroline" at the same time as being thought the most wonderful thing on earth found a large chink in his moral armour.

"I don't know how to play hockey, of course," he said, " but I wouldn't mind trying this afternoon." Christine stared at him. "You!" she exclaimed.

"Of course," Esme almost purred, "I shan't be any good."

"But I thought you weren't allowed to play games."

"My nervous anaemia is a little better this afternoon."

"Well, you can't play," Caroline said abruptly. "You're not in the Big game."

This was quite enough for Christine.

"Well, Margaret's captain," she said, "suppose we ask her? I don't suppose we can raise twenty-two this afternoon. Come along, Esme, I've got a spare stick I can lend you." Caroline sniffed.

"She'll only make a fool of herself," she remarked, "especially if she's never played before."

"Well, even you had to learn," Esme remarked meekly. "Of course, my people aren't hot stuff at games like all yours. I never had a second cousin who got her half-Blue for honey-pots at Girton. But I can have a shot at the game, I suppose?"

It has been mentioned before that St. Mildred's consisted of two old houses knocked into one. In one of the gardens a hockey pitch had been laid out. It was not a good hockey pitch by any means, nor was it full size, but it "did for practice." On half-holidays the girls marched in pairs to a lumpy field about a quarter of a mile away.

Margaret good-naturedly allowed Esme to play, as, counting him, there would only be ten aside. When Caroline argued with her, she clinched the matter by saying that she supposed Esme was charged on the bill for games, like everybody else. Christine ran inside and returned with two sticks. In the minute which elapsed between her return and the beginning of the game she hastily explained the more important rules to the neophyte.

"The game is to see which side can hit the most goals. . . . Only you can't hit goals until you're inside the circle. . . . And you mustn't swing your stick as if you're playing golf. ... Not allowed to lift it above the height of your elbow. . . . You're playing centre- half-back, so you won't have to score goals. . . . You'll have to help the backs—the two girls behind you—and pass to the forwards when you get the chance."

Esme listened silently and politely to these instructions. Christine was playing centre-forward for his side. On the other side Caroline, who played centre-half for the school, was occupying that position opposed to him. His intention was not to trouble too much about the opposing centre-forward, but to concentrate on Caroline.

From the first bully the forwards opposed to Esme obtained the ball and made a scrambling rush. They surged past Esme, and left him unaccountably with the ball on his stick. Christine shrieked with delight at what she believed to be a glorious fluke. "Well played, Esme! Come on! Pass! Pass! "

But Esme was bent upon showing off. He ran with the ball, tricking two opponents with consummate ease. Caroline tackled him, and grunted with surprise and discomfiture as Esme slipped past her and out towards the right wing. He showed a sudden turn of speed which produced a gasp of admiration. Caroline, gasping for another reason, panted along behind him. Esme waited for her politely, feinted to the left, and slipped by her again on the right. He then set off at what was to him a jog-trot in the direction of goal. The defence closed in upon him. Esme dazzled them with a little stick-work. His own forwards surged past him shouting. He, however, continued his triumphant progress into the circle and, with the goal at his mercy, passed the ball back to Christine to smack it into an empty net.

Most of the girls could scarcely credit the evidence of their senses. They had never seen a girl run as Esme ran. Apart from that, she was either a super-girl or had brought off a series of the most astonishing flukes.

Esme obtained the ball exactly one second after the subsequent bully-off, and, with an air of polite boredom, took it through the opposing team by himself, and banged it contemptuously into the net at the other end. He amused himself in a like manner for most of the remainder of the game, varying the proceedings by arranging little one-sided duels with Caroline, who fancied herself as a hockey player. He would deliberately wait for Caroline to tackle him, run past her, and wait for her to tackle him again. Sobbing with rage, fatigue, and wounded vanity, Caroline invariably charged like an infuriated bull, while the rest of the girls looked on, as mediaeval warriors sometimes paused in the midst of battle to watch a contest between two champions.

Esme's conscience pricked him about it later, but at the time his sense of chivalry was dulled. He had suffered a great deal at her hands. She had set herself openly and secretly to make him look ridiculous. Now their positions were reversed. He knew that he was taking an unfair advantage, but he could not help himself, and the cries and gasps of admiration and astonishment were as music to him.

Esme's side lost count of its score. Esme himself got thirteen or fourteen goals, and Christine nearly as many, thanks to Esme.

At the end of the game Esme's unpopularity was all forgotten, and the girls came crowding around him— all save Caroline, who leaned on her stick, puffing and scowling.

"Esme, you're simply wonderful!"

"I've never seen anybody *run* like you!"

"Esme, you'll have to play against the High School!"

"We can beat them if you'll play, Esme!"

"Esme, is it really true you've never played before?"

Esme shook them off him good-humouredly.

"Of course," he said, "I daresay I should improve a bit with practice. But I don't think my Uncle Dick would like me to play in any matches, even if I was good enough. You see, I'm delicate!"

He left them gasping. Caroline, catching up with a group of girls on their way back to the house, aired her views gaspingly.

"Says she hasn't played before! I bet! She isn't a girl at all; she's a freak. She's one of those things in Darwin—a missing link. Of course, I was rather out of form to-day, otherwise I'd have shown her something!" The others took no notice of her.

"She *must* play for us against the High School!" Margaret exclaimed.

"I don't think she will," said Christine, enjoying this turn of the tide in Esme's favour. "And I don't blame her either. You've all gone about saying that she isn't a real lady, and being perfectly horrible to her. The Moths passed a vote against her, and they expelled me for sticking to her. You've all given her the cold shoulder. I shouldn't play if I was her."

"Wouldn't it be better if you said, 'If I were she?' "suggested a purist mildly.

"Oh, bother that! But you'll find she won't play, and I don't blame her."

"She would if you asked her," Margaret said insinuatingly.

"Why should I? Why don't you ask her yourself? I haven't been beastly to her, and you have. If anybody asks her, I think the one who's been horridest ought. Why don't you make Caroline?"

"Me!" exclaimed Caroline. "Thanks!"

"We'd better have a committee meeting immediately after tea, and talk it over," Margaret said.

CHAPTER XI

It has been the present writer's painful duty to describe Cedric Bingham as a bonehead. Any brain- fever germs which had ever attacked him must have retired nonplussed and chagrined. His head was pure solid ivory throughout. But the lad had qualities. He was a youth of action. No grass seed pushed up tender green blades under the soles of his feet. He obtained permission to leave the bank a little earlier than usual that afternoon, and came to pay a call on Miss Budging, in the hope of catching a glimpse of Esme.

In this he was unsuccessful, for he was invited to tea in the stuffy little drawing-room with Mrs. Toy, Miss Budging and Miss Chadpole, while the girls took theirs in the long bare dining-room which always smelt of yellow soap and recent scrubbing. But if he did not see Esme he certainly heard him mentioned, for his phenomenal success as a hockey-player had reached the ears of the mistresses and provided them with a topic of conversation over their tea.

"Everything about that girl is extraordinary," Miss Chadpole remarked, while Cedric listened, all ears.

"Particularly her vulgarity and insolence," Mrs. Toy commented grimly. "What is the matter, Mr. Bingham? Is your tea too strong for you?"

The headmistress had caught Cedric in the act of frowning heavily upon her. His brow cleared as he realised that he could not openly champion Esme.

"No, it's all right, thank you, Mrs. Toy," he said with a rather rasping laugh. "A little indigestion."

"At your time of life, Mr. Bingham!" exclaimed Miss Budging.

"You forget I'm a man now, Miss Budging," said Cedric, with dignity. "And a man's *entitled* to have indigestion."

Miss Chadpole once more steered the conversation in the direction of Esme and hockey.

"All the girls are quite mad about her," she remarked. "They say she's simply marvellous—easily good enough to play for the women's county eleven. They think they can beat the High School this year, if only she'll play."

"But Esme has no right to play games at all," said Mrs. Toy tartly. "You see," she explained for Cedric's benefit, "she's supposed to be an invalid. What really is the matter with her I don't know. But she's been brought up by an eccentric old uncle who doesn't believe in doctors, and she's not allowed to have one near her."

Cedric's mouth fell open. The Esme Geering he had I known at school—and whom he supposed to be the brother of this female Esme—had been vaccinated like everybody else during a small-pox scare.

"Her brother—" he began, and broke off suddenly in cold horror. What was he saying? Into what dreadful trap had he been led? How was he to account for knowing the girl of whom they were speaking?

He coughed and shuffled his feet. The three women stared at him in silence. Mrs. Toy's beady eyes seemed to eat into him like acid.

"You were saying, Mr. Bingham?" she said in a bleak voice.

"From what I can see," Cedric muttered, "the Government will simply *have* to do something about the unemployed."

"We were not discussing politics just then. We were talking about a girl named Esme Geering, and you began to say something about her brother."

"Oh! Ah! Ha, ha! Yes! Quite! I was only going to say that he ought to be a pretty stout fellow at footer if she's as good at hockey as all that. What?"

Mrs. Toy's features relaxed.

"As it happens," she said, "she hasn't got a brother."

"And perhaps it's just as well," Miss Chadpole laughed. . "Heaven knows what *he'd* be like!"

Cedric stared from one to the other in bewilderment. Then light dawned upon him. As the brother was in disgrace, and never mentioned by his family, it would account for their not having heard of his existence.

"I must see Esme about this hockey-playing," Mrs. Toy declared. "If she is really an invalid, and knocks herself up, I shall be responsible. And as I am pledged not to call in a doctor to her, I might easily find myself in a difficult position."

Cedric left soon after tea, and the three mistresses fell to discussing him.

"What an awfully nice boy," Miss Chadpole remarked. "Such a thorough little gentleman."

"Yes," agreed Miss Budging, "I think it's awfully sweet of him to come and see me sometimes. It's nice to think that people remember one."

Miss Budging was a small, spare, skimpy woman, almost entirely without personality. Middle age was rapidly overtaking her, and she made no effort to delay her own capture. She had been born a schoolmistress and an old maid.

Mrs. Toy glanced at her appraisingly. It *was* rather remarkable that this young man should come to see her, simply because she had once been governess to his sister. So far as she could tell there was nothing very attractive about Miss Budging, but she had to admit to herself that she could not see any member of her own sex with the eyes of a young man. And very young men, she knew, often fell in love with women much older than themselves.

The headmistress's thoughts ranged a long way in a few moments. She devoutly hoped that this Cedric Bingham was not consumed with a precocious passion for Miss Budging. Dear me, so unsuitable! So very unsuitable! But, if so, could Miss Budging be trusted to be kind but firm in her discouragement? There was a vulgar saying to the effect that there was no fool like an old fool . . .

She pulled herself together suddenly, stopping the long train of thought with a jerk.

"Miss Chadpole," she said, "would you mind running up to Esme's room and telling her that I want to see her?"

The girls' tea had then been over some little while, and there was an interval for play before the start of evening preparation. Esme had gone straight up to his room to answer Cedric's note and drop it out of the window as soon as he received Cuthbert's signal, and the bigger girls had put their heads together to decide who was to ask Esme to play in the hockey eleven.
The choice fell upon Caroline. She had been Esme's worst enemy, and if she bore the olive branch it would be a tacit way of informing Esme that everybody wanted to make friends. Caroline protested volubly. The very thought of the mission was gall and wormwood to her. But she was out-voted and threatened with expulsion, both from the Moths and the hockey eleven, if she declined to comply with the general request. So, with a very bad grace, she climbed the stairs.

She could not have chosen a happier time to ask anything of Esme. The boy was in a mood of dejection and repentance, both angry with and ashamed of himself for the way he had behaved at the practice match.

"Even if you were found under a whelk-stall," he told himself savagely, "you needn't have behaved like it! You utter little bounder! You low, crawling cad from Margate beach!"

From which it will be observed that Esme, with all his faults, had his moments of grace. He had deliberately used the strength and speed of his sex to make a girl look foolish, and now that he had time to reflect on the matter he could not forgive himself. He disliked Caroline as strongly as ever. She deserved little kindness at his hands. She had done everything in her power to make life unpleasant for him—not that he really cared about that. But she was a girl after all, and as much entitled to his chivalry as Christine.

It was in this chastened and self-accusing spirit that Esme sat down to write to Cedric, and he set about the task with almost a savage zeal. Anyhow, Cedric wasn't a girl. Cedric was not entitled to his chivalry. Cedric was a man—or nearly—older and bigger than Esme himself. Since he had to rag somebody, he would rag Cedric for all the game was worth.

He had written a few lines, such as he imagined a young girl might write in such circumstances, when he heard footsteps outside and a tap at the door. Esme took fright at once. Close by him on the little table was a book which somebody had lent him. It was a school story for girls, entitled "For the Honour of St. Brazil's." He had not read it, nor did he intend to, for one glance at the first page had been sufficient. But the book remained, and it provided Esme with a hiding place for this particular piece of correspondence.

"Come in!" he shouted, jumping up, and at the same time pushing the unfinished note between the pages. "Who is it?" he added as somebody strained in vain against the door.

"It's Caroline," said a voice from outside.

Esme was surprised, wondering what on earth she could want with him. But his conscience had been troubling him about her to such an extent that he was prepared to be civil, even gracious, to her.

"Half a sec," he said. "The door hangs a bit on the bottom. I'll come and open it for you."

When he had wrenched it open, Caroline made no sign of wishing to come in.

"They've sent me up to ask if you'll play for the first eleven," she said briefly.

"Won't you come in?" said Esme, with a politeness which would have staggered any of his friends.

Caroline entered unwillingly and only because she was anxious, for her own sake, for her mission to succeed. Unless she were successful in getting Esme to play, she was well aware that the other girls would say that she hadn't tried.

"Sit down, won't you?" said Esme. "You'll find that chair quite comfortable. Have a chocolate?"

He pushed an open box towards her. Caroline took one, wondering. Esme had suddenly changed out of all knowledge.

"Have the box," said Esme; "I've got plenty more."

"It's very good of you," said Caroline, choking.

"Not at all. I say, Caroline, I'm frightfully sorry about this afternoon. I didn't mean to show you up. At least, I suppose I did mean to, but, anyhow—well, dash it all, I'm beastly sorry."

"I was off form," said Caroline coldly, "otherwise— "

"Otherwise," Esme interrupted gladly, "I shouldn't have had an earthly with you. I know that! Now, look here, I'd like to play for St. Mildred's, but I don't think I shall be allowed to. You see, I'm very delicate and sickly—"

Caroline sniffed loudly.

"—very delicate and sickly," Esme continued unwaveringly, "and I'm not supposed to play any games.

But if I feel all right, and can get leave to play—"

He was interrupted by a sudden commotion at the door. Somebody outside was trying to thrust it open.

"That's one of the mistresses," he remarked, ostensibly to Caroline, but in a very loud voice. "Anybody else would have the decency to knock before trying to butt in."

"*How* many times," demanded the voice of Miss Chadpole from without, "must I tell you not to speak like that?"

"I'll buy it," said Esme cheerfully. "*How* many times?"

"Open this door at once!"

"It only needs a little shoving," said Esme, and wrenched it open.

Miss Chadpole, her face flaming, stood on the other side of the threshold.

"You are a very naughty girl, Esme!" she cried. "I shall report you to Mrs. Toy. Once more, I shall *not* knock when I come to your room."

"All right, Miss Chadpole," said Esme equably. "Don't let's argue about it. I can't *make* you. And as you don't seem to have the strength to shove the door open at once, it doesn't much matter."

"Insufferable!" breathed Miss Chadpole.

Esme chose to assume that she was speaking of the door.

"Yes," he agreed, glancing down, "it does want seeing to."

Miss Chadpole bit her lip.

"You are to go straight down to the drawing-room," she said, in the tone of a wardress addressing a confirmed female criminal. "The headmistress wishes to speak to you at once."

"Right-oh!" said Esme, wondering what now could be the matter. Turning to Caroline, he added "Don't run away. I shan't detain the headmistress very long." Were there a Greek chorus to this narrative, it would hereabouts break in very much as follows: "Alas! luckless youth, you have forgotten the unfinished note to Cedric between the pages of yonder volume. You are now full of a kindly intent to Caroline, but she is still an enemy. While you are gone she has but to open those pages in an idle moment. Woe, woe to you, Esme! Woe, woe!"

So Caroline remained, while Esme trotted downstairs. Miss Chadpole followed him, fuming. But she was tired of reporting Esme, and did not precede him into the presence of the headmistress.

Meanwhile Caroline sat on in Esme's chair, sucking chocolates and drumming her fingers on the table. Some long minutes passed. The window was open, and presently she heard the door of the boot-room slam far down below. A few moments later the voice of Cuthbert was lifted far down below in the dusk.

"Yer called me Byeby Doll a year agow,
Yer sed as I was very noice ter know-ow . . .

It will be remembered that this bursting into song on Cuthbert's part was a signal by which Esme might know that the coast was clear and drop his note for Cedric out of the window. Receiving no response from the casement above, Cuthbert burst into even louder song.

"An niff yer gow awye Yer'll be saw-ry some dye
Yer leff me loike a brow-ken dor-holl."

Caroline listened, wondering. She was aware that Cuthbert over his work often made a noise which he was pleased to call singing. But Cuthbert was not at work, nor was he moving about. Strange that he should be standing still outside the boot-room, howling like a stray dog.
Cuthbert tried again. The gathering dusk grew hideous with his voice.

"Mah, 'e wants ter mah-ry muh.
Be my 'unny bee-hee ..."

Still mystified Caroline heard him out. The music ceased. Then the whispered voice of Cuthbert, hoarse with his recent vocal efforts, floated in at the window on the wings of the breeze.

"Are yer there, miss? 'Ave yer got that note? Yer can drop it now. It's all clear!"

Caroline's heart gave a great jump. That note! It was all clear! Esme could drop it now! What did it mean?

She had the good sense not to answer and to keep away from the window. So Esme was writing notes to somebody, and Cuthbert was acting as messenger. A grin of triumph rounded her flat, pasty cheeks.

Cuthbert, having by now assured himself that the attic room was empty for the time being, loitered in silence below, kicking at the dingy brickwork of the wall. Caroline put on her thinking cap. Had Esme written that note? If so, where was it?

She was still Esme's enemy. Whatever kindlier feelings she may have entertained for him after the pleasant way he had received her, and his gift of chocolates, were dissipated by his conduct towards Miss Chadpole. Rudeness to darling Miss Chadpole was the unforgivable sin. Very intensely did Caroline desire to see that note.

In many respects the girl was no fool. She was able to reason. She was very good at those sums in which x equals the number of plumbers it would take to repair a four-inch leak in a cistern containing y cubic feet of water. She had now a problem in real life with which to wrestle, and only a limited amount of time, since Esme might be back again at any moment.

Perhaps Esme was writing the note at the very time when she came to the door. If so, Esme naturally hid it somewhere, and with haste. She tried to put herself in Esme's place, and her gaze alighted upon "For the Honour of St. Brazil's." She opened the book at once, and at the right place. The folded sheet of notepaper acted as a marker. The front half of it was covered by Esme's small and rather untidy scrawl. Caroline scrupled not to read.

"Dearest Cedric,

"Thank you for your sweet, sweet note. I have read it through a hundred times, and, ever since, I have been looking into my girlish heart, and murmuring to myself, 'Can this be love?' Well, I'm blest if I know. I don't think I've ever liked anybody before quite in the same way as I like you. But I am so young and inexperienced, Cedric, a gentle flower, which, as Shakespeare says, has only blushed unseen. Suppose my girlish heart was to change—"

Here the note ended in a smudge, where the ink had run on Esme's hastily thrusting it into its place of concealment. Caroline stared at it full of righteous horror. No nice girl, she was sure, could ever have concocted such an epistle. And who was the boy—this Cedric? Somebody vulgar and horrible, she was sure.

There was almost enough already to procure Esme's expulsion. Almost enough, but perhaps not quite. Esme—loathsome girl!—might yet sob repentantly on Mrs. Toy's bony chest and wring forgiveness out of a heart which would be very loath to lose £70 per annum. Besides, even at St. Mildred's "sneaking" was anathema. Caroline knew that she could only procure Esme's downfall at the price of her own ostracism.

No, she must not denounce Esme openly, and the time was not yet ripe. She must watch and wait and bide her time, and contrive in some way to bring Esme's "affair" before the notice of Mrs. Toy without even that good lady being aware that she had a hand in the matter. To that end she must cautiously sound Cuthbert. She was certain that if she kept her eyes open ways and means would be revealed to her.

Caroline's thoughts had carried her thus far, when the sound of Esme's hurried footfalls on the stairs brought her to a sense of the immediate present. She slipped the note back into the book, and, when Esme burst into the room, she was apparently absorbed in the study of Nesfield's English Grammar.

Esme arrived in a state of profuse perspiration. While he was talking to Mrs. Toy he remembered that he had left his unfinished note ready to Caroline's hand if she chanced to open the book on the table. The thought had caused him to fidget a great deal, but Mrs. Toy, who was in a comparatively good-humoured mood, had declined to be brief. He stared first at Caroline, then at the book, and back again at Caroline as he crossed the threshold.

The book was exactly where he had left it, and Caroline's face, as she gazed mildly up at him, was almost devoid of expression. He blew a great breath of relief.

"The headmistress wanted to see me about playing hockey," he said. "I'm not allowed to play unless my Uncle Dick gives me leave. You see, I'm not supposed to play any games at all. But I feel much better than I did. St. Mildred's is so bracing! So I'll write and ask him."

Mrs. Toy took no interest in games, but she wanted her girls to beat the High School for much the same reason as she liked them to score more successes in the Oxford Locals. Esme himself was not averse from playing. In one sense it wasn't fair, but looking at it in another way, who cared tuppence about a girls' hockey match. It would be rather a rag to win the game for St. Mildred's off his own stick.

"Do you think your uncle will let you play?" Caroline asked.

"I should think so. He does most things I ask him. And of course if he lets me, I'll play."

Caroline, having accomplished her mission, rose and talked herself slowly out of the room. Esme, although he was still polite to her, made no effort to detain her. He wanted to investigate the hiding place of his note and finish writing it as soon as possible. As soon as he was alone, with the door closed, he made a dive for the book, opened it and found his unfinished composition just as he had left it.

"Now, has she seen it, or hasn't she?" he reflected. "She didn't look as if she had. Anyway, she can't get me into much of a row, even if she wanted to. I've still got the note, and she can't prove anything. Besides, p'raps she mightn't want to get me into a row, although she owes me one. Daresay she's quite a decent sort really, in spite of her spots."

No sooner had he settled down to write than the voice of Cuthbert was once more upraised in song. Esme crossed to the window and leaned out.

"Shur-rup, Cuthbert!" he said in a growling whisper. "You're giving me goose-flesh."

"That you, miss?" said a husky whisper far down below. "Lumme, I been singing my inside out for the last quarter of an hour."

"Sorry, fair Cuthbert. I was out of the room while you were carolling your little lay. I hope nobody else came to the window? "

"Oh no, miss."

"One moment, then, and I'll chuck the note down to you."

Esme gave vent to a long and luxurious sigh as he went back to the table.

"Everything's all right, then," he reflected in his innocence.

CHAPTER XII

It is necessary to remark once more that Cedric was a lad of action. On the following morning Vince, head prefect of Esme's house at Wryvern, received a letter from him which filled that youthful dignitary with mirth and amazement. During the eleven o'clock break that morning he buttonholed two other members of the Sixth Form and sauntered with them around the quadrangle.

"You remember Bingham, don't you?" he asked.

"What, that silly little wet?" drawled Culmer, a tall, lean dark boy, who wore the first delicate flowering of an early moustache.

"Came a floater at Sandhurst, didn't he?" said Uffington-Page, the third of the trio. "Dam' good job! If they'd let him into the Army, I swear I'd have made my pater ask a question about it in the House. I wonder where he is?"

"I can tell you," said Vince. "He's living in some God-forsaken suburb. I heard from him this morning, and, ye gods, what a letter! He was awfully sorry to hear that young Geering had been bunked and was now in prison—"

"*What!*" shouted the other two in chorus.

"Wait a minute, you haven't heard the best. He wants to know what young Geering's been up to. Says he's sure there's no vice in the kid, and he's sure he must be innocent of whatever he's supposed to have done. Wants me to tell him all about it so as he can investigate the matter."

There was a moment's silence.

"Didn't you tell me," Culmer asked, "that young Geering was away for a term because his pater, whom he's never seen, was coming home from Africa?"

"Something of the sort," said Vince hazily.

"Then how on earth did Bingham get hold of that yarn?"

"Can't you see, my dear old lightning thinker, that somebody's been pulling the idiot's leg?"

"It's not fair," said Uffington-Page, shaking his head. "It's a rotten shame of people to pull Bingy's leg. It's too easy. Well, what are you going to tell him, Vince?"

Vince smiled. "Who am I to spoil the gaiety of nations?" he said. "I shall carry on the good work, I suppose. I think I'll write and tell him that young Geering was found in unlawful possession of the head's wife's *jools*. You've seen her *jools,* haven't you, Uffy? But I'll also say that I think there must have been some mistake, and that if young Geering's people had only troubled to employ a decent counsel for the defence he might have got off."

The other two chuckled. Culmer, however, said: "Steady on, Vince. You don't want to start a rumour that young Geering's in prison. Besides, they wouldn't send him there at his age. He'd be in Borstal."

"Right!" said Vince. "I shall be careful to refer to Borstal in my reply. Of course, I shan't be starting a rumour. Everybody here knows where young Geering is. He's coming back next term. And everybody knows what an unholy idiot Bingham is. Only he gave me the impression that he was going to start some amateur detective work on young Geering's behalf. Perhaps my letter will help him a bit."

So in the fulness of time Cedric heard from Vince, and was confirmed in his belief that Esme was now languishing in a penitentiary in expiation of an offence which he had never committed. But it were best not to run too far ahead, and to return to that messenger of Cupid, known to the world as Cuthbert, entering the " King and Keys" with Esme's first note to Cedric in his pocket. He handed it over and was duly paid.

"So you delivered my letter safely?" Cedric said, with a devastating grin.

"Oh yes, sir!"

"Good! You're an intelligent sort of fellow. I wonder whether you'll be able to arrange for us to meet occasionally—what? I know the old lady keeps a pretty sharp eye on 'em, but I think you and I might be able to hoodwink her, eh?"

Cuthbert shook his head. Carrying notes was all very well, as profitable and comparatively safe. But there was very little of a romantic strain in Cuthbert. He was not going to risk his job for the sake of love's young dream.

"Don't see 'ow it could be done, sir. And if the young lady did 'appen to get copped talking to you, Mrs. Toy 'ud give 'er the push as soon as look at 'er."

Cedric was sufficiently sensitive to want to avoid such a calamity for his own sake. He was rather in awe of Mrs. Toy, and it was not pleasant to speculate on what she might say to him. And a man can't run after a schoolgirl and retain his dignity if there is any fuss about it. That sort of thing was called cradle- snatching.

"Oh, ah, quite!" he said hastily. "For her sake we must be very careful. Always consider a lady first, my lad, that's a gentleman's first instinct."

Cuthbert concealed a scowl. He did not like gentlemen. They battened and fattened on the downtrodden workers, and, not content with that, they couldn't even mind their own business, and had been known to come between man and wife. His uncle, while in the act of correcting his aunt with an empty beer bottle, had once been most brutally assaulted by the son of a lord. These things rankle.

"I'll tell yer wot I *can* do, sir," he said, after a moment's silence. "I can manage for yer to see 'er at a distance sometimes."

Cedric visibly brightened. "Splendid!" he exclaimed. "Go on. How?"

"Yer know St. Mildred's is on a comer of Sumphill Road, don't yer, sir? Well, the young lady 'as a room to 'erself at the top of the 'ouse at the back. From 'er window she can see 'arf way down Arran Road, which leads into Sumphill Road. Well, if you likes to come along o' me, I'll show you 'er window. Then p'raps you could arrange by notes when she'd be at 'er window and you'd be standin' in the road. Like Romeike and Curtis, sir."

"Romeo and Juliet," corrected Cedric. "By Jove, that's a good idea. I'll walk along with you now." They had not far to go. Cuthbert duly pointed out the window.

"And you see, sir," he said, "even if they sees you they can't see Miss Geering, so they won't know nothing. Be careful of that window there, sir. That's Mrs. Toy's study. But if you stands closer to the fence she won't be able to see you. But Miss Geering will, 'er window being 'igher up."

"You're a genius, Cuthbert," Cedric exclaimed with real enthusiasm. "Now just come back with me to the 'King and Keys' while I write a few lines."

Half an hour later, when Cuthbert, suitably rewarded and bearing with him another note for Esme, returned to St. Mildred's to tackle the day's crop of more or less dainty footwear, he found Caroline Bax awaiting him.

The girls were then at evening preparation, but Caroline had obtained leave to withdraw awhile bn the pretext of feeling faint. This gave her the opportunity of a talk with Cuthbert at a time when they would be least likely to be interrupted. The youth lifted his eyebrows at the sight of her. Caroline was one of the stiff and haughty sort who rarely spoke to him. Even when she had complaints to make about the way he cleaned her boots she was in the habit of going straight to one of the mistresses.

" 'Evenin', miss," said Cuthbert suspiciously.

Caroline did not respond to this civility. She was there to take Cuthbert by surprise, to force a confession from him before he knew where he was. The heroine of "That Dare-Devil Girl, Babs," one of her favourite works of fiction, was particularly good in that sort of situation. She did not speak for a full minute, thus allowing Cuthbert time to feel vaguely uncomfortable.

The youth peeled off his coat, picked up a brush and a pair of mud-stained boots, and was about to resume his work when Caroline opened her batteries on him.

"Well," she said, "did you take that note for Miss Geering?"

Cuthbert had been rolling some saliva in his mouth, preparatory to moistening the blacking in his accustomed way. The words had a disastrous effect on him, for he missed the tin by nearly a foot.

"Wot, miss?" he exclaimed, looking round with a start.

"Did you take that note for Miss Geering?" Caroline repeated.

"Wot note?"

"Yes, you're very innocent, aren't you?" Caroline sneered. "How's Cedric?"

Cuthbert stared at her woodenly, and wasted a gem of sarcasm.

"Never 'eard of 'im, miss. 'Oo does 'e play for? The Spurs?"

"If you're going to tell lies," said Caroline, frowning, "I shall go straight to Mrs. Toy and tell her all I know."

"If I was you I should go now, miss—in case you forgets."

Caroline became uncomfortably aware that things do not always run so smoothly for the heroines of real life as for their sisters in fiction. By this time "Babs" would have had the delinquent at her feet, confessing all and begging for mercy. But Cuthbert was rather more than her match. He had sharpened his wits, so to say, against the street-comers of life, and learned to use them against predatory relatives, bookmaker's touts, roughs, and occasionally policemen.

"Very well, Cuthbert," said Caroline, pretending to turn away. "You will be sorry for this."

"The same to you, miss," retorted Cuthbert politely, "with the usual knobs."
Caroline swung round upon him, simmering with weak wrath.

"How dare you talk to me like that!" she squeaked. Cuthbert, in replying, was able to give quite a tolerable imitation of the squeak.

"And how dare you come 'ere, bringin' accusations against an honest feller wot's tryin' to do 'is work?" He ended up on a note of triumphant virtue which fairly floored Caroline. When she spoke next it was in a tone of reasoning, which was almost plaintive.

"Cuthbert," she said, "I don't think you understand what a serious thing it is. There's the—the good name of the school to be considered. And—and suppose Esme—I mean, Miss Geering—was to elope or something?"

Cuthbert spat nonchalantly into the blacking—an excellent long-range shot—and answered her wearily.

"I don't know wot you're torkin' about, miss— straight, I don't. I should go and see a doctor if I was you. Molly Flummery was took the same way at first. *She* began with deloosions. Thought as 'ow Mrs. Toy was the rightful Queen o' Italy, and used to begin 'er compositions with 'May it please yer R'yal Majesty.'" Caroline snatched at what remained of her dignity. "Very well," she said, coldly and haughtily, "I shall go straight to Mrs. Toy."

"Right-oh, miss. Got yer evidence?"

Caroline turned again.

"Evidence!" she repeated.

"That's wot I said, miss. Yes, we 'ave *no* bananas. You goes to Mrs. Toy with your tale about a note to a bloke named Cedric. Why don't you call 'im 'Arry, miss? I don't believe there ever *was* a bloke named Cedric outside of a book, and no more will Mrs. Toy. Mrs. Toy'll ask to see the note. You 'aven't got it. She'll ask Miss Geering about it, and Miss Geering won't know nothing. Then she'll ask me, and *I* won't know nothing. Then you'll look a bit of orl right, won't you, miss?"

"Cuthbert, you don't mean to say you'd lie!" cried Caroline, deeply pained.

"Not 'arf," he retorted, promptly and cynically. "Now, look 'ere, miss. You've got one up against Miss Geering, and you wants to put 'er through the 'oop. I don't blame you for that, I'm sure. Only you've come to the wrong shop. Our little Esme 'as always been a perfect lady to me. Wotever I does for 'er I don't do for nothing. I gets well paid. So now you know."

Caroline grasped the situation at once. Bitterly did she regret not having seized upon that unfinished note. She had never intended to go straight to Mrs. Toy and brand herself as a tale-bearer, save as a last resort, and even if she did, what chance had she, if Esme and Cuthbert conspired to tell wicked lies? She had formulated a hazy plan of so frightening

Cuthbert as to obtain his entire confidence, and making him, in the fulness' of time, cause all to be "accidentally" discovered. That plan, however, had already expired in its own mists.

"Suppose," she said hesitatingly, "I were to pay you too?"

Cuthbert brightened visibly.

"That, miss," he said, "is wot might be called fair and 'ealthy competition. And now, as Labour is a-sayin' of to Capital, 'ow much 'ave you got?"

Caroline had eightpence ha'penny to see her over the next five days. She mentioned this sum tentatively to Cuthbert, who laughed derisively.

"But I'm going to have a birthday soon," she added. "My father always sends me a sovereign then, and I've a lot of uncles and aunts I can write to."

"Well," said Cuthbert, getting busy with a boot, "I 'ope it'll keep fine for yer. You come and see me when you've 'ad yer birthday, miss."

Cuthbert did some hard thinking when his visitor had left him. He was not in the least afraid of Caroline. Evidently she knew a great deal, but she could prove nothing. He was quite willing to sell Esme—at a price; but he doubted if Caroline would ever be able to pay that price. A girl who could mention such a ridiculous sum as eightpence halfpenny evidently knew nothing of the vertiginous heights of real finance. But meanwhile, pending the possibilities of her birthday, there was no harm in her remaining in the market, as it were. He was not pro-Esme or pro-Caroline, he was entirely pro-Cuthbert.

So busy was he with his thoughts that he put a most unwonted polish on one of Cissie Marriott's boots, and had to smudge it all over to save himself the trouble of making its fellow equally magnificent. During his labours he decided that it were best to say nothing to Esme or Cedric about Caroline's visit. He knew that everything at present was quite safe, and it was not his desire to make them cautious. Caution on their part would mean fewer notes, and fewer notes meant less money for himself. Altogether Cuthbert was a nice, bright, clear-thinking boy.

CHAPTER XIII

Meanwhile a little ship was on the sea, and Tom Geering was aboard her. Father was coming to his babe in the nest. Every day brought him some hundreds of miles nearer.

Uncle Dick, snug in his Bloomsbury lodging, took no count of time. He never had the least intention of meeting the boat. He never even glanced at the shipping news in the papers. At the back of his mind he was aware that Tom Geering would soon be home again, but he did not morbidly encourage himself to dwell on the fact. Uncle Dick had his own way of dealing with unpleasant thoughts. He shut the door of his mind upon them, and left them like so many shabby unruly children condemned to play outside in the streets. He called this "not meeting trouble halfway." Tom Geering knew where to find him. He would hear from Tom as soon as he arrived. Until then, for goodness' sake let him forget as much as possible the horrible muddle he was in.

Yet, although he knew that he must be prepared to meet Tom Geering almost any day, it was a profound shock when he received a telegram, handed in at a London post office not much more than a mile away, which made him realise that the hour he had been dreading was now at hand.

"Can you call for me seven thirty bunneys hotel covent garden dine with me if possible bring esme greetings —geering."

Thus said the telegram, baldly, uncompromisingly, with neither punctuation nor capital letters, a passionless summons to the lists. A prepaid form arrived with the telegram, and almost before he had had time to think, Uncle Dick scribbled on it and handed it back to the boy : "With you seven-thirty, impossible bring Esme."

Thank goodness, it was impossible to bring Esme! Quite bad enough to be going to meet Tom Geering and have his own p's and q's to attend to. The ordeal of introducing Esme was at least deferred for a little while. No need to think of that now.

Uncle Dick slid down into his favourite chair, pressed his hands to his brow, and tried to concentrate his mind on what was immediately before him. He was going to meet a stranger. They had been comparatively young men when they parted, and instinct told Uncle Dick that time had wrought greater changes in Geering than in himself. What would he be like—this stranger whom he had wronged?

He found himself staring at the telegram, where it lay on the edge of the table. At first it told him little more than it had told the post office clerk who took it down; then his deductive faculties, sharpened by the urgency of the situation, began to work for him.

Why on earth had the man asked for Esme? He had never written to the child all these years, never even asked for news of the little unwanted girl who had killed her mother. And now, no sooner was he in London than he must needs wire for her.

Bunney's Hotel? Why, in the name of heaven, Bunney's? There was the Savoy or the Cecil, if Tom Geering were well-to-do. If he had returned poor, there were some tolerable caravanserais in the neighbourhood of King's Cross. But Bunney's!

Then Uncle Dick remembered that Geering had lost touch altogether with London. Bunney's, now a place of frowsy bedrooms and homicidal cuisine, its bars hideous with the din of the market men, had seen better days. Some of the Great Ones in the land used to sleep there on the mornings after Covent Garden balls. Uncle Dick remembered it in the old Cambridge days. Surely Tom Geering was a member of that party! And back it all came to the air of a waltz of Strauss, and Tom Geering, as Charles II., playing with Mephisto—name now forgotten—a game of skittles with champagne bottles and an orange while the sun was waking over London. Dear heaven, how young everybody used to be!

He peered through the mists down the long roads of memory for glimpses of the boy who was Tom Geering, and the young man who was Tom Geering, in the hope of recognising them in the stranger from Africa whom he was soon to meet. In an instant he was back at Wryvern, walking under the plane trees in the close beside a small, dark, sensitive-looking new boy, who was saying: "Am I *really* to call the house matron Mrs. Buggy? Is that really her name? Or are they trying to be funny?" Alas the matron's name was not Mrs. Buggy.

That small sensitive face was with him all through his school life, watching him with eyes which worshipped his strength and prowess at games. Tom Geering had been a queer, passionate, dreamy boy, a great enthusiast and a poor performer. Uncle Dick had given him his friendship because it was sought, that being the way of him. He was kind to him as he was kind to dogs and children, but without conscious patronage. He often expressed a belief that "there was something in young Geering."

Whatever there may have been remarkable in Tom Geering did not obtrude itself at school or university. At Cambridge he was lost in the crowds of Trinity, while Uncle Dick's light shone brightly in a smaller college. Geering became a rowing man because Uncle Dick was one, but he never obtained a place in one of his college boats, whereas Uncle Dick rowed three times through cheering Cockneys from Putney to Mortlake.

At Cambridge and afterwards Geering scribbled a great deal of unintelligible verse, and passed from one desperate love affair to another. A declining business in the Midlands awaited him when he came down. He had no taste for sordid manufactured wares, and it was the wrong man who came to stem the tide of disaster. He spent too much time in Town worshipping at the shrine of Uncle Dick. Then came his marriage. Widowhood and financial disaster followed within a year. The man had no backbone, and the two blows crumpled him up. But the "something in him" had shown itself at last, and during sixteen years of exile he had managed to struggle back upon his legs and was home again at last.

This was the man whom Uncle Dick had known. The stranger he had become he was yet to meet. Of one thing he could be fairly sure—that Tom Geering was still a sentimentalist. Only a sentimentalist would have gone to Bunney's in memory of a night or two of youth.

Uncle Dick roused himself to look at his watch. Half-past six already. In one more hour ... He fell to wondering if he should dress. Certainly not, if they were going to dine at Bunney's; but they were not going to dine at Bunney's if he could help it.

Reflecting that one may sometimes be right in wearing morning dress of an evening, but one can never be wrong in wearing evening dress, he went into his bedroom and donned a twelve-years-old dinner jacket suit, slipped his arms into a rusty thin black overcoat, crammed a disreputable old soft felt hat on to the back of his head, and was soon striding across New Oxford Street, a Micawber of twentieth-century London.

He decided to walk to Bunney's. It was not far, and the cool evening air helped him to think. The shop windows were ablaze, and in one of them he saw himself reflected from head to foot in a mirror, and smiled as if in greeting. Really, he was most ridiculously young for fifty. He *was* young, too. He could outdistance most youngsters on the river now, and run ten miles with a little training. Tom Geering would know him at once. He doubted if poor old Tom had worn half so well . . .

It was twenty past seven when he reached Bunney's, and, seeing that he had ten minutes to spare, he did not go straight to the office to inquire for Geering, but went instead into one of the ill-lit bars to fortify himself for the meeting with a whisky and soda.

The bar was empty save for a sour-visaged female attendant behind the counter, who grudgingly laid down some knitting to attend to him, and a tall, spare, elderly shabby man who brooded in a dark corner over an empty glass. It was the wrong time of day for Bunney's to be busy.

"Well, here's luck to Esme and me," said Uncle Dick to himself as he raised his glass. "May we come out of this most infernal mess with colours flying. May—"

"Dick!"

Uncle Dick swung around. The sound of the voice had touched a chord of memory. The tall, spare, elderly man had risen from his dark comer and was advancing towards him, smiling. Uncle Dick stared at him, while the glass in his fingers began to shake. This lean, sallow, bloodless old man was never Tom Geering! But it was, and he knew it, although it was by inference that he knew, and not from recognition.

"Dick! Don't you know me?"

Uncle Dick's voice shook when he answered. "It's never Tom Geering!" he exclaimed. "It's all that's left of him, Dick. You're looking well. You haven't altered a day. I should have known you anywhere."

They shook hands in silence, while the sour-visaged barmaid, still occupied with her knitting, looked on with a face as expressionless as a cow's. A chill struck Uncle Dick. The atmosphere of the place was all wrong for such a meeting; and then to find Tom so changed, so old, so bloodless!

He stared at him frankly, searchingly. If he were prosperous he did not look it, for his open greatcoat and the lounge suit under it were both of an appalling cut. But Uncle Dick did not know at the time that the world's worst tailors all go to South Africa. The man himself had grown spare and leathery, with a lined face that was sallow beneath its bronze. The cheeks sagged in folds, giving him something of the look, of a mastiff, something of the look of an ancient Anglo-Indian colonel. He did not look ill; only very old and j very tired.

"I was waiting in here until you came," Tom Geering remarked. "The public rooms, apart from the bars, aren't up to much. This place has gone down a lot since the old days. Don't you remember that early morning in 'ninety-six, when I played Reggie Heritage a game of skittles with champagne bottles in this very bar?"

He ended with a smile, but there was not much mirth in the smile.

"I was only thinking of that just now," said Uncle Dick. "Was it Reggie Heritage? I was wondering who it was. Well, Tom, how are you? "

"All right. Better than I look, I daresay. You look in the pink, as you always did. How you do carry your years!"

"This fellow's going to make me feel old," said Uncle Dick to himself, and fell to wondering whether he would have been glad to see Tom Geering again without the present complexities of the situation. In his heart he knew that he might not have been. The friendship on his side had existed only because it was forced upon him, and he had been too lazy and too good-natured to uproot it. And what had he in common with Tom Geering now? he asked himself. The man belonged to the dead past of which he did not care to be too poignantly reminded.

"What are you going to drink?" Geering asked, "Champagne?"

"What? Before dinner?" said Uncle Dick dubiously. "Besides, I've just had a whisky."

"I thought on an occasion like this . . . Besides, we're always drinking champagne in Jo'burg. I've been mixing with a lot of Jo'burg Jews. I'm afraid my manners aren't what they were. It'll take me a bit of time to be civilised again."

"I'll have a whisky if I have anything," said Uncle Dick; and they drank gloomily together. No, it was a joyless meeting. Something was depressing both of them—as if there were a death in the house.

"How's the world been using you?" Uncle Dick asked, breaking a spell of silence.

"Pretty fairly, thanks. It's funny how the luck comes to people who don't want it. You know the mood I went away in? I didn't want to make money, and really I didn't care tuppence whether I lived or I died. And I couldn't do anything wrong. I got a job which brought me in more than I needed to live on, and saved a little money automatically. Then the father of a young Jew whom I'd done a good turn gave me the tip about some shares in a new diamond mine. They do repay a good turn, those people. And I just drifted into wealth as easily as most poor devils drift into penury. Pm not a millionaire now, but I'm better off than I ever dreamed of being. What are you doing?" Uncle Dick told him, and the thin sun-dried face smiled.

"Drifting as usual," said Geering. " Well, old man, where are we going to dine? You know London better than I do. Is Romano's still going?"

"Yes," said Uncle Dick. "We'll go down there if you like. They've opened up an American bar there now."

A youth outside in a shabby uniform got them a taxi which had only to take them a few yards. Inside, Tom Geering turned to Uncle Dick and said awkwardly: "Well, how's Esme?" Uncle Dick was thankful for the partial darkness.

"She's—she's all right, you know. Grown into a fine big girl."

"Why couldn't you bring her along to-night."

"She's away at school."

"Ah, of course, I hadn't thought of that. Far?"

"No, only in one of the outer suburbs. But there was no time to send for her when I got your wire."

"No, of course . . . Tell me, Dick, what she's like."

"I've got a photograph of her in my pocket. I'll show you when we get into the light. She's quite pretty, but—but she's at rather an awkward age, you know. Rather large—er—hands and feet. Ought to have been a boy. We had her photograph taken as a boy. I'll show you that one too."

Uncle Dick was rather pleased with his own daring. Anybody seeing that particular photograph of Esme might have believed he was a girl in boy's clothes. Geering nodded thoughtfully.

"I wish to God she *had* been a boy" he said.

So did Uncle Dick. If Geering's lost child had been a boy he would have been without a care in the world.

"Then I'd have had her sent to Wryvern," Geering pursued with a flash of sentiment. "Good old school! You never go down there now, I s'pose? No? But coming back to Esme, I must have a settlement with you, Dick."

Uncle Dick started and stared at him.

"You know what I mean," Geering continued. "You've been out of pocket over that girl of mine. Sixty pounds a year was all right at first, but, as soon as she was old enough to go to school, what with clothes and fees and pocket money—we'll go into figures presently, Dick." Uncle Dick reddened and began to fidget. The difficulties were beginning already. How could he possibly take any more money from Tom Geering?

"You don't owe me anything," he growled.

"But I must do, Dick. I meant to write. I was always meaning to write to you, but perhaps I was a little hurt because you never wrote to me. Every quarter I was expecting to hear from those lawyer fellows that you wanted more money. I thought you were probably better off than you seem to be, and I knew we'd have a reckoning one day, so I let matters slide." Uncle Dick nodded sympathetically. He knew how easy it was to "let things slide" and could appreciate this trait in another.

"You don't owe me anything," he said solemnly, "and I may as well tell you here and now that I'm not going to touch an extra penny of your money. Ah, here's Romano's, you see."

He got out first, paid for the taxi, and stood waiting for Geering with one foot on the first of the flight of steps leading up to the vestibule. But his companion lingered behind him.

"I'm not very hungry yet, are you?" he said. "Didn't you say something about an American bar?"

"All right," said Uncle Dick doubtfully, "if you like. Down those steps."

"We'll have another glass," said Tom Geering, " for Auld Lang Syne."

Uncle Dick acquiesced a little unwillingly. He was fond of his glass, but he hated to drink gloomily, and there was little that could be called hilarious about the occasion. With Tom Geering he felt like an old ghost pathetically trying to recapture something out of the life which had been lost forever.

Downstairs they did not go to the counter, but sat at a small table close to a wall, where a waiter came to them and took their orders. There Uncle Dick rummaged in his pockets and produced two photographs.

"There's Esme," he said, "dressed up as a boy. And here's another one of her as—as she really is." Geering took the photographs with almost a feverish haste and studied each in turn. Uncle Dick watched him covertly, thinking hard and impatiently. Confound the fellow, why on earth should he seem so excited? He had hated the child when it was born. All these years he had never written nor expressed a desire, even through his infernal firm of lawyers, to receive a letter from the child. What was the matter with him now? Uncle Dick suddenly perceived that his eyes were dim. Good Lord!

"Of course," said Geering slowly, "photographs are deceptive."

"Y-yes."

"Don't see much of me in her."

"There is a bit of a likeness," stammered Uncle Dick L" I notice it sometimes."

"Nor of her mother. Dick, I hoped—I hoped she'd be like her mother."

Uncle Dick's conscience gave him a twinge of almost | physical pain. He felt just then the lowest and meanest criminal in or out of any prison.

"It suits her to be dressed as a boy. There's something very boyish about her."

"She's like a boy in most respects."

"I wish she were ... I don't know ... a little softer and more feminine. Of course, one can't tell from photographs. When can I see her?"

"Oh—er—are you in any hurry?"

"Hurry! Good God, man, I'm her father, and I haven't seen her for sixteen years—not since she was about a month old. And you ask me if there's any hurry!"

"Uncle Dick finished his cocktail, lifting the glass with an unsteady hand. The wind was blowing from a dangerous quarter.

"Old man," he said, "as I can't conceive of any human being in this world understanding me properly, I can hardly expect to understand you. You left that kid on my hands, hating the sight of it. You've been away sixteen years without making one direct inquiry about it, without writing her a single letter or requesting one from her. I'm not upbraiding you; I'm just stating plain facts. And now you've arrived here at last, you seem to have worked yourself up into a state of excitement about her. Now I'd like to know exactly what it means."

"It means," said Tom Geering huskily, "that I want my daughter. I want my little girl. That's why I'm here."

Uncle Dick wiped the sweat from his brow.

"You don't mean," he gasped, "— you weren't thinking—of taking her back with you?"

"I had thought . . . Why, what's the matter?"

"Nothing," muttered Uncle Dick, rapping his knuckles on the table. Desperately he called a waiter. He required something to sustain him in this his hour of need.

"Listen here, Dick," said Geering, bending earnestly towards him. "It isn't given to human beings to make themselves perfectly intelligible to one another, but I'll do my best to make you understand me. I hated the child at first—I know that. I loved her mother. I knocked about a bit as you know, but she was the one real love of my life. She remains so still; I have never been able to look at another woman. But time, which has left that love unchanged, smoothed away that unreasonable antipathy to the child. It happened gradually. But for five or six years I've been thinking about her. I know I didn't write. It's a funny thing, but I felt shy about it. Somehow I thought the ice was too thick, had been standing too long, to break with a letter. The only thing to do was to come home. I'd been meaning to for years, but something always cropped up to make me defer it. Do you understand me, Dick?"

His companion nodded evasively. Geering suddenly clutched him by the arm.

"Don't you see? I'm a lonely man, Dick, and not so young as I was. There isn't a single person in this world who cares a tuppenny damn about poor old Tom Geering. *You* don't! You wish to God I hadn't come home; I can see it in your eyes. I'm only Geering, who was never any good at anything, and used to hang on to your coat-tails when you were one of the bloods. I'm loveless and lonely and I'm getting old. And I want my little girl—I want my little girl, Dick."

Uncle Dick contained his emotion with difficulty. He was genuinely touched. A man of ready tears, he would certainly have shed some then, but his sense of ' the ridiculous whispered to him of the sort of figure he would cut weeping copiously over a dry Martini in a public place. "Look here," he said jerkily, "you may think it's my fault, but—but Esme's a bit sick with you for never having taken any notice of him—her—or writing, or wanting her to write. You mustn't think I've brought hi—*her*—up to dislike you. It's just how she looks at the way you've behaved."

Tom Geering nodded. His face was expressionless for the moment.

"I must try and win her over to me," he said.

Uncle Dick cleared his throat. The time had come for him to fight.

"You want to take her away from me?" he demanded. "You leave me to bring up a child for sixteen years, and then suddenly you want to swoop down and snatch her away. The law's on your side, Tom, but I wonder if you think it's playing the game. You say you're lonely. So am I. I knock about a bit, and pass as a good fellow, and people suffer me gladly, but I'm bitterly lonely sometimes. Esme's the only person in the world who really understands me, really cares for me. I've brought her up as my own child. We've always been like father and daughter. I couldn't bear to part from her, nor she from me. Don't you understand, Tom? It would be cruel of you, damnably cruel."

Uncle Dick was spared the ignominy of acting. Save for the gender of the pronouns applied to Esme he meant every word he said. His voice rang true, and Geering flinched.

"I shan't," he said heavily, "take Esme away from you unless she wants to come."

A sigh of relief fluttered from the lips of Uncle Dick.

"Oh, she'll stick to me," he said confidently. "I'm sorry, Tom, but I doubt if you'd get her to go to you now, even if you got the law to help you. I'm sorry, old man. Heaven help us, we have made a mess of things, haven't we?"

"When can I see her?" Geering growled.

"Oh, any time. We can run down any afternoon."

"Can't we take her away from that school for a bit?" Uncle Dick shook his head vehemently.

"The headmistress would object most strongly. Besides, I—I've entered her for an exam. She must have a chance on form if her training isn't interfered with. Bound to catch the judge's eye, I should think." Quite unconsciously he had plunged into racing vernacular. Geering merely inclined his head. Uncle Dick held the reins, and just at present his companion saw little chance of snatching them from him.

A lot of Tom Geering's dreams were vanishing in the dawn-light of reality, a lot of dream castles were toppling down into a rubble of mist. Uncle Dick saw the look in his eyes and felt something rise in his own throat. An impulse seized him. Better to end it all now, to be honest, to confess, to throw himself on Tom Geering's mercy.

"Old man," he breathed, "there's something I want to tell you."

Geering stared at him curiously. "Well, what?" he said.

Uncle Dick opened his mouth to speak, but the good moment was already gone, the resolution faded. If Tom couldn't forgive him it meant prison. Prison!

"I—I know of something good in the two-thirty race to-morrow," said Uncle Dick.

CHAPTER XIV

Letters posted in London very late at night are delivered in the suburbs before eight o'clock. Thus Esme received the news in a hectic note from Uncle Dick, while he sat at breakfast in the bare dining-room at St. Mildred's in a comfortless atmosphere of recent scrubbing. The girls were gobbling porridge and drinking indifferent tea when Mrs. Toy came round with the letters.

Mrs. Toy had a wonderful memory for handwriting, and could tell at a glance what letters were from parents or from such uncles and aunts as were regular correspondents. These were handed unopened to the girls to whom they were addressed. Letters arriving in a strange writing—even a feminine hand, for young men have been artful enough to get their sisters to address envelopes before now—were all ruthlessly slit open with a paper knife and browsed over by the headmistress.

That morning Mrs. Toy, leaning over Esme's shoulder, dropped a letter on to his plate.

"There's some good news for you, Esme," she said, almost archly.

Esme stared at the letter. It was from Uncle Dick and the flap of the envelope was stuck down. He examined it closely to make sure.

"Must have steamed it!" he remarked audibly.

Mrs. Toy heard and swung round, but she thought better of saying anything and bit her lip. Esme opened his letter, drew out the folded sheet of notepaper, smoothed it out and began to read. Almost immediately his parted lips emitted a volley of weird oaths.

"Crimes of Paris! Ye gods and little fishes!"

There was a general titter and Mrs. Toy, now some yards distant, stamped her foot.

"Esme! Esme! How dare you make use of such horrible expressions?"

"Well, my old blighter of a pater has come home at last!" Esme exclaimed, as genuinely disturbed at the news as Uncle Dick had been. "Wow, wow! *Two* w'ow-wows!"

The whole school paused to listen. Save for a muffled sob of laughter here and there the ensuing silence was complete. Mrs. Toy turned as red as the comb on a turkey cock.

"I don't know what to do with you," she said, from the bottom of her heart. "You get coarser and coarser. You really are not fit to associate with ladies. I know that your father has come home. I had a letter this morning from your Uncle Richard. He seems most anxious—"

"Yes, I bet he is!" said Esme, beneath his breath. "I'd put my shirt on Anxious to win in the Uncle Dick stakes. You don't have to back that one each way. Anxious! Wow!"

"He seems most anxious," Mrs. Toy was saying, "that you should appear in your most favourable light. If you behave in his presence as you have been doing, I really don't know what he will think of us all at St. Mildred's. But you seem to be without feelings and without shame. The father you have never seen, and whom you ought to love with your whole heart, is coming to see you at last, and instead of being delighted and expressing some ladylike sentiment of joy, you refer to him as a—as a blighter!"

The girls near Esme, knowing themselves to be included in the sweep of Mrs. Toy's gaze, regarded him with a pious air of concern.

"Edison Bell record!" murmured Esme, just loud enough for his nearest neighbours to hear.

"What was that?" demanded Mrs. Toy sharply.

"I was only murmuring to myself," said Esme, 'just a little expression of girlish glee at the thought of seeing the dear old Dad again."

Murmuring to herself, "The girl is mad," Mrs. Toy shrugged her shoulders and passed on. She was at her own breakfast twenty minutes later, when Esme tapped at the door and walked in.

"What do you want?" the headmistress demanded sharply, looking up. She was masticating conscientiously, having heard that every mouthful ought to be chewed thirty times, and she had the appearance of a very thin Alderney chewing its cud.

"Mrs. Toy," said Esme, "I'm so excited! Pm all of a dither!"

An invisible east wind seemed to strike Mrs. Toy, for she wilted and shivered.

"I'm afraid I don't know what that means," she said icily.

"Goosey all over," Esme explained blithely, "and can you wonder? If you heard *your* father was coming to see you—"

"My father," said Mrs. Toy in a hollow voice, "has been dead for more than twenty years."

"Then I expect you would be even more excited than I am."

Mrs. Toy heaved a long sigh, highly flavoured with Danish bacon.

"What do you want, child?" she asked in a quiet voice of martyrdom.

"I've come to ask leave not to go into class this morning, Mrs. Toy. It wouldn't be a bit of good if I did. My thoughts would be elsewhere. I wonder what my father's like. Wouldn't it be awful if he was a beaver? Should you think he was a beaver, Mrs. Toy?"

"What do you *want?*" demanded the goaded headmistress.

"Well, Mrs. Toy, as it won't be much use my going into class this morning, I've come to ask if you'll let me go out and do some shopping. I want my dear Papa to be proud of his little girl, and all my stockings are in ladders. Look!"

He turned, caught one foot by the instep, and, standing balanced on one leg, presented the calf of the other for Mrs. Toy's inspection.

"Properly speaking, of course," said Esme, "that isn't a ladder, it's a fire escape."

"Haven't you any clean stockings upstairs?" demanded Mrs. Toy.

"Yes, but they're all like that," said Esme. "Aren't I a naughty girl? And there's a new pair of boots ordered for me. I have to have them specially made, you know. I want to see if they've come yet. I'd like to look as doggy as possible this afternoon."

Mrs. Toy considered. When occasion demanded, she had no objection to allowing one of her senior girls to go out by herself in the mornings.

"Very well, then," she said, "you'd better go, although your conduct would warrant my refusing your request."

"Thank you, Mrs. Toy," said Esme. He produced a cheque and laid it on the table. "My Uncle Dick has sent me some pocket money. It's a cheque drawn on his bank in London. Would you mind changing it for me, please?"

Mrs. Toy stared at the cheque with a blank expression. It was for two pounds. Pocket money at St. Mildred's averaged about sixpence a week.

"It's a lot of money," said Mrs. Toy sententiously.

"I expect he came by it honestly," Esme returned blandly. "Unless, of course, he got it off a bookmaker." The headmistress made no comment on this. She was tired of checking Esme.

"Bless the child," she said wearily, "I'm afraid I haven't two pounds. I never keep money in the house, but if you'll give me this, and I give you one of my cheques for the same amount, you can take it to the bank and cash it."

And so it happened that Esme went out that morning as free as the air, and Fate took him straight to the bank where Cedric wore the nap off his trousers on a high polished stool. It will have been apparent that Esme was in a "silly " mood that morning, and less inclined than ever to put a guard upon his tongue. At the bank Cedric saw him as he entered, and while the cashier was handing him two one-pound notes, Cedric slipped off his desk at the back, and having murmured something in the cashier's ear to the effect that he "knew this young lady," ducked under the counter, and intercepted Esme close to the door.

"Hullo!" he bleated rapturously.

"Hullo, my old and noble," Esme returned, shaking the proffered hand.

"What are you doing out this morning?"

"Shopping. My father's home from Africa, and he's coming down to see me this afternoon. Bon, eh?" He would have been wiser to have said nothing. He knew that Cedric was an ass, but it did not occur to him then that he might be ass enough to try to see his father.

"Yes, rather!" said Cedric with a giggle. "I expect he will take you out and give you a good time."

"He'll be marched straight to the Oriental Cafd," Esme announced.

Cedric sunk his voice. "I've got some news of another member of your family," he whispered.

For the moment Esme forgot all he had told Cedric. "Another member of my family!" he repeated blankly.

"You know—the one we mustn't mention. I've heard something about him. And I'm more than ever convinced of his innocence."

"O-oh!" Esme was completely bewildered. Cedric, all unconsciously, was paying him back in his own coin. What could Cedric have heard about his non-existent brother? Was he only yarning? Or had the idiot been making inquiries, and somebody, seeing that his leg was being pulled already, had given it another gentle twist? Everybody pulled Cedric's leg.

"Ah, never mention him to me!" he murmured dramatically.

"All right, I won't, then. I say, I loved having your notes. I've kept all of them. Have you kept mine?"

Esme nodded.

"I sleep with them underneath my pillow. I read them over every time I look into my girlish heart. You're a stout old sportsman. Ta-ta!"

So saying, he waved his hand, and vanished through the swing doors.

It was just after half-past two when Uncle Dick and Geering arrived at St. Mildred's. Many pairs of eyes watched them from the windows, as it was considered in St. Mildred's that Esme's father would probably be a curiosity well worth seeing. The critics were, however, somewhat baffled by the appearance of two men instead of one. Nobody knew for certain which was which, and many penny bets were made on the subject. But neither of the two men who mounted the steps passed the standard for fathers which St. Mildred's had set up. Uncle Dick was a fine figure of a man, as all admitted, but he was a great deal too Bohemian in his attire to please young ladies, whose fathers for the most part went daily to their respective offices as if to weddings or funerals. Moreover, Uncle Dick was suffering agonies of apprehension, and, although the day was cold, his face was a deep scarlet, and damp with perspiration. Tom Geering, in a lounge suit made in Johannesburg, looked like a tram inspector in his Sunday best.

"Rather plebby, both of them,'' Margaret remarked, turning away from the classroom window.

"I told you," said Caroline triumphantly, "that Esme wasn't a lady."

"Of course," remarked Christine in a tone which did not always endear her to her friends, "her father may not be a commercial traveller like yours—or a home ambassador of commerce, as you prefer to call him—but he may be something just as important all the same. You can't always tell by clothes."

Esme was duly sent for, and told to go to the drawing room. Mrs. Toy, with a delicacy hitherto unsuspected, was not present during the affecting encounter. Pushing open the door, Esme found himself in the presence of Uncle Dick and a stranger.

"This is Esme," said Uncle Dick, slightly choking, and turning away.

Esme stared at the stranger. He had always hated him in the days when he believed he had a claim upon him. That feeling still rankled. Such a man had no right to own a daughter.

In a moment Esme saw that he had the advantage. Truly he was nervous, for the moment dreaded both by him and Uncle Dick had come. But Tom Geering was both nervous and shy, and blinked at him almost guiltily.

"Why, Esme!" Geering exclaimed, and stooping a little, thrust out a yellow cheek.

Esme stood at arm's length, ignoring the cheek, and holding out his hand instead. Geering, too shy to insist upon a filial caress, grasped the hand.

"Why, what a big girl you are!" he exclaimed.

"About size nine," said Esme flippantly.

"When I last saw you," stammered Tom Geering, holding his hands apart as an angler describing the length of a fish, "you were only about *so* big."

"That," retorted Esme, "was because I was only a few days old. You expected me to grow, didn't you?"

Tom Geering stared at his supposed daughter almost incredulously. Uncle Dick coughed and blew his nose. Secretly Uncle Dick was pleased. Geering would have deserved no better if Esme had been his daughter, and Esme in behaving thus was showing him pretty plainly that Tom Geering might whistle in vain for the love of this neglected child. An excellent thing in more ways than one. It might send Geering back to Africa all the quicker, and it would discourage him from paying too many visits to St. Mildred's on his own. Bad luck on Geering, but there it was.

Geering coughed and fidgeted. He had no idea what to say to this cold and extraordinary child. The speeches he had prepared were a mere scattering of words at the back of his memory. Vainly he wondered what a man placed as he was ought to say to his daughter. If only Esme would meet him half-way!

"Well," he said at last, with a little mirthless chuckle, "what have you been doing all these years?"

"Growing up a bit," Esme replied, "and living on your money and Uncle Dick's. Mostly on Uncle Dick's."

"Esme! Esme!" cried Uncle Dick sharply. For his own private reasons this was one of the last things he had wanted Esme to say. A faint flush crept into Tom Geering's sallow cheeks.

"I suppose," he said quietly, " I deserve that."

"I don't know what you deserve," Esme retorted. "I don't know anything about you. You're a stranger to me. If I'm your daughter, why have you kept away all these years, without troubling to send me even a penny postcard? Why have you butted in now? I don't know you, and I'm damned if I want to."

Geering stared at him aghast. Strangely enough, it was the profane verb which startled him most. Like so many men who have lived their lives, he was a puritan where his womenfolk were concerned. A girl of sixteen in a nice old-fashioned school ought never to have heard such a word, except perhaps in church, much less use it. He turned a reproachful gaze on Uncle Dick, whom instantly and rightly he held responsible.

"Esme," he said, with a sort of pathetic dignity, "I suppose in these days it is no uncommon thing for fathers to justify themselves to their children, and ask their forgiveness. If I can't justify my neglect of you, I shall ask you to forgive it."

'Oh, all right," said Esme, a little touched in spite of himself. "Only it's a bit too late to expect me to bound into your arms with a glad cry. I shall never be a—a daughter to you. I'm sorry and all that, but it's just as well to say so at once, and save both of us a lot of trouble. Uncle Dick's the only father I've ever had, and the only father Pm going to have!"

Uncle Dick moved restlessly. He was sorry for Tom Geering after what had passed between them on the previous night, and it seemed to him that Esme was going a little too far. Geering himself listened with almost as little expression on his face as may be seen on a distempered wall.

"Perhaps," he said quietly, "we shall understand each other better."

Meanwhile he was conscious of something lacking in himself. He had loved the image he had set up in his mind and called his daughter. The dream was gone now, and for the reality which stood facing him he could not find one crumb of fatherly affection. He looked in vain for some trace of the wife he had loved and lost, and found it not. There was nothing in Esme's features or voice or gestures which reminded him of his old self at Esme's age. Esme was right, and they were strangers. He could not feel that she belonged to him, although his sense of fitness begged of his affection in vain.

This hoydenish young person with her bobbed hair was utterly different from the daughter he had imagined. He hated bobbed hair. He had hoped to find a girl who was soft and feminine and clinging, and there were none of these qualities in this strapping young wench with her enormous hands and feet. She was masculine in every line of her. Those muscular young limbs were built for strength and speed, never for grace and beauty. Some whim of nature had given him for a daughter one of those aggressively mannish young women, a type only less objectionable in his eyes than an effiminate man. So his thoughts ran on, summing up Esme.

"Perhaps," said Geering, with a smothered cough, "you'd like to go out somewhere. Your headmistress says I may take you."

Esme brightened a little.

"Thanks," he said, " I'm always glad to get out of this hole."

"Aren't you happy here?" Geering demanded quickly. He was not very favourably impressed with the little he had seen of St. Mildred's. Uncle Dick interposed with a cough and a warning glance at Esme.

"Of course she is," he said quickly. "It's a very good school of its kind."

"I expect all girls' schools are much of a muchness," Esme remarked, to Uncle Dick's relief. "I shan't be sorry when I'm old enough to leave, that's all."

"Well, we may as well go out somewhere," said Geering, who was tired of standing in the cheerless little drawing-room.

Uncle Dick, who was beginning to breathe freely again, felt constrained to make a suggestion against his better judgment. He trembled at the thought of leaving Esme and Geering alone together, but common decency demanded that he should at least offer to do so.

"I'll clear off somewhere," he said tentatively. "I expect you two have plenty to say to one another." To his relief Esme edged close up to him.

"You needn't go," he said anxiously. "My—er— my father and I won't be wanting to say anything private that you mustn't hear."

Geering nodded rather grimly.

"I think you'd better come along with us, Dick, and keep the peace," he said. "It's quite obvious that we shan't embarrass you with too much sickly sentiment." To himself he was thinking: "The chit doesn't lose any opportunity of showing me where her affections lie. I believe she thinks I'd kidnap her if Dick were out of the way."

So they went for a walk together, surely the strangest trio abroad that autumn afternoon. They had tea at the Oriental Cafe, and conducted Esme back to the school at half past six. From the point of view of Esme and Uncle Dick the afternoon had been a highly satisfactory one. Neither made one of those slips of the tongue which both had been dreading, and Geering was plainly disappointed in his "daughter." The returned exile was not likely to be tempted to prolong his stay in England on Esme's account, or put too much pressure on Esme to accompany him when he left.

He wanted to buy Esme a present and asked him what he would like. Esme declined to make a suggestion, and stoutly maintained that he did not want a present. He did all this with an air of "I'm afraid I don't know you well enough to accept anything."

Only one incident marred the occasion from Esme's point of view. On their way back Esme pointedly refrained from looking at a young man who passed them in the High Street. The young man, however, lifted his hat.

"Who's that?" demanded Geering sharply.

"I didn't see," Esme replied.

"A young man who hatted you."

"O-oh! I expect that was a man named Bingham, a friend of Miss Budging, one of the mistresses."

The explanation served for the time being. Neither Geering nor Uncle Dick would have thought more of the incident had it not been for Cedric's anxiety to make a good impression on Esme's father. Cedric, it must be remembered, was acting the part of hero in **a** novel of his own creation.

CHAPTER XV

Having left Esme at St. Mildred's the two men turned away in silence. A hundred questions trembled on Uncle Dick's lips, but he left them unasked, and waited for Geering to make his comments unprompted. So far, he was well aware, the deception had been a complete success, and, moreover, Tom Geering was so little pleased with his supposed daughter that he was less likely than ever to insist on exercising the full control of a parent.

Geering wore a slight frown, and trudged along with the sullen air of a convict at exercise. Uncle Dick waited in vain for him to pronounce his judgment on the very remarkable young person whom they had just left. At last the congenial conspirator could stand it no longer. "Well?" he said.

That "Well?" was five score questions condensed into one word. Geering understood and made a savage slash with his stick at the empty air.

"Damn her!" he exclaimed. "I suppose it is all my fault, but damn her all the same! She's as hard as nails. There isn't even a touch of kindness about her, let alone daughterly love. Wouldn't even kiss me. Gave me her fist like a man, the little vixen. She seems to have appraised my neglect well enough. One thing I'll say—there's no pretence about her."

"I haven't brought her up to be a hypocrite," said Uncle Dick simply.

"The less you say about the way you've brought her up the better!" Geering retorted.

"According to my lights. You knew the kind of man you were leaving her with. You didn't mention at the time any particular wishes with regard to the child, and had you—er—communicated any to me since, I should, of course, have tried to comply with them." Geering winced. 'Yes, you have a right to say that. You've as much right to taunt me as she has. Are you turning on me too, Dick?"

"Don't be a fool. But, naturally, knowing the child as I do, I understand her better than you do."

"Great lumbering hoyden!" Geering growled, "Look at her hands and feet."

"Damn it all, you're not going to blame me for *them!*" said the other, with a long-suffering air.

"Oh, man, man, you don't understand. Of course you can't help it, but I am hideously disappointed. I was fool enough to think that she might overlook the way I have treated her; that Nature would step in and make her care for me, and make me feel like a father to her. But I don't. The fault isn't all on one side. She's a stranger to me, and I shouldn't care tuppence I if I never saw her again. I don't see a trace of her mother in her, and there's nothing in her that reminds me of myself. I've left it too late, I suppose. All my fault!"

Uncle Dick would have given a great deal just then to show his very genuine sympathy. He refrained however, as a matter of policy.

"Well," he said bluntly, "it's no use crying over, spilt milk, is it? There she is, and she can't be altered. If you're dissatisfied with her, I suppose I'm largely to blame, but I never set her against you, Tom."

Geering felt that his gratitude was being delicately impeached.

"My dear fellow, I didn't mean that. Not one man in a thousand would have done what you have."

"Oh, rot! But never mind that. What are your plans for her?"

Geering shrugged his shoulders. "I haven't any. She's yours. You let me see that, both of you. I, Thomas Geering, do give my daughter Esme to you, and renounce all future claims in her. As a matter of duty, I shall run down and see her occasionally, but I don't think you need be jealous, Dick."

"And you've—you've abandoned all idea of taking her back to Africa with you?" Uncle Dick asked with a faint gasp.

"Oh, quite. It doesn't amuse me to spend my life with people who dislike me. And a nice fool I should look, trailing about with me a daughter, all hands and feet, who hated the very ground I walked on."

Uncle Dick nodded comprehendingly, trying to conceal a joy which he felt would have been hardly decent to flaunt. For a moment his heart was as light and buoyant as a toy balloon. But for a moment only. Then Cedric appeared in the limelight, or rather in the light of a street lamp—Cedric determined to play the *role* of hero to the bitter end, and ingratiate himself with the father of his beloved by displaying a blind, heroic faith in the son who was in disgrace.

He knew that Esme's father was coming down that day, and having seen him in the company of the two men, he assumed that one was Geering and the other Uncle Dick. He therefore lingered until they had left Esme at St. Mildred's, and waylaid them on their way to the station. He approached with an ingratiating smile and half lifted his hat.

"Mr. Geering?" he asked, looking from one to the other.

"That's my name," said Tom Geering, surprised. He had expected few people in England to remember him and none to recognise him. As he gazed at Cedric his amazement grew. This callow youngster was much too young to have known him in the old days.

"That's my name," he repeated, "but I'm dashed if I know how you got hold of it. Oh, wait a moment! Wasn't it you who hatted my daughter about twenty minutes ago?"

"That's quite right, sir," said Cedric, beaming.

"You'll wonder why I've—ah—ventured to address you."

"I should be glad to know how you came to know my daughter," said Geering, with a slight frown.

Cedric, fairly sure of his ground, conjured what he thought was an engaging smile.

"You see, sir," he said respectfully, "I was a great friend of her brother's."

Geering's lips curled in a cynical smile, which faded; as he turned sharply to stare at Uncle Dick. Uncle Dick had uttered a sort of choking cough, and now, with a handkerchief to his nose, trumpeted at the imminent peril of blood-vessels. Wondering a little at Uncle Dick's behaviour, Geering turned once more to Cedric.

"That's very interesting," he said with a sneer. "Her brother, eh? Well, young man, she doesn't happen to have one."

Cedric ceased smiling, his eyes grew round and his brows went up. Uncle Dick plucked at Geering's sleeve.

"Come along," he said. "Don't let's waste time talking to a young lunatic."

"But," Cedric protested, "I know your son—"

"I have this much to say to you," interrupted Geering. "I don't know how you scraped acquaintance with my daughter when she is at school and supposed to be protected from the molestations of young adventurers. Nor can I see what you expect to gain by your effrontery now, in approaching me with a tissue of lies. Once more, I have no son."

Uncle Dick was not quite in the dark as to Cedric's identity, Esme having mentioned him in a letter, and, fearing what that youth might disclose he was suffering agonies of apprehension and tugged once more at Geering's sleeve. Cedric looked from one to the other in nervous amazement. He was pleased at having been called an adventurer, but at the same time he was at a loss to think what he could have done to deserve such treatment. Geering, who had old-fashioned ideas as to the bringing up of girls, was furious at the thought of his daughter having become unconventionally acquainted with this rather unpromising specimen of budding manhood. Confound the girl! Was there no limit to the disappointments she was to give him?

"I know," said Cedric, suddenly recollecting something that Esme had told him, "—I know your son is dead to you".

"Damn it, man, I keep telling you".

"But he is innocent!" cried Cedric, in the manner of Lyceum drama. "I swear he is innocent. When I was with him at Wryvern—"

Uncle Dick made a curious noise like steam escaping from a boiler under heavy pressure. "He's mad!" he muttered. "Come on, Tom."

"So you were at Wryvern, were you?" Geering said witheringly. "So, strangely enough, were we!" Cedric's smile, which had waned considerably, lit up again. Old Wryvernians are traditionally glad to meet, the world over.

"Splendid!" he murmured.

"And you knew my son there?" Geering demanded, with a heavy irony which was lost on the youth.

"He was," said Cedric sentimentally, "one of the best fellows that ever—"

"Yes, I had a son there!" said Geering, with an even deeper note of sarcasm. "He was about as much there as you were. There are too many little cads like you, who go about pretending they were at public schools. Don't tell anybody else that you were at Wryvern, because you won't be believed. They don't breed 'em like you there. Now go away, and if you come hanging around my daughter again I'll make you regret it."

To the great relief of Uncle Dick, who was half-way to an apoplectic fit, Cedric turned on his heel. That youth was a swashbuckler only in theory. Geering was becoming so heated that any retort might have been requited with a punch on the nose; and Cedric did not want to have his nose punched—he hated the sensation. He walked away with, he fondly hoped, a certain dignity, and a bitter sense of injustice. "Of course," he told himself valiantly, "if he hadn't been her father I should have knocked him down."

Geering and Uncle Dick resumed their interrupted journey to the station, one of them growling and muttering under his breath, and the other blowing and gasping as if he had just escaped after having been chased across a ten acre field by a bull.

"I'm going to take Esme away from that school immediately!" Geering announced suddenly.

"I thought you'd surrendered her entirely to me," Uncle Dick retorted sharply.

"But she can't remain at a place where she's allowed to make undesirable friends in the town."

"Didn't Esme say that she had met that—ah— young fellow through one of the mistresses?"

"Yes, she *said* something of the sort."

"Esme does not lie," said Uncle Dick, a dangerous inflection in his voice.

"Well, then, what did that young liar mean by saying he knew my son at Wryvern?"

"I don't know." Uncle Dick reflected desperately for a moment and then lit upon an inspiration. "I'll tell you what happened. That young fellow's an awful fool, of course, but he may be a decent enough chap in other ways. He was introduced to Esme by this Miss Budget, or whatever her name was. Very likely he *is* an old Wryvernian, and there may have been a Geering there with him. And he asked Esme if that Geering was her brother, and, to pull his leg, she said it was. See?"

"I do not care for Esme to pull the legs of young men. And, besides, what did he mean by all that rot about my son being innocent?"

Uncle Dick shrugged his shoulders.

"How should I know. Esme probably stuffed him up with a lot of nonsense. He—she's a champion kidder."

"The little baggage!"

"Well, don't start writing letters to the headmistress. You may only get Esme into a row. And—and you don't want'to increase the estrangement between you."

"It's a nice position for a father to be in, isn't it? Not daring to offend his own daughter!"

"You put yourself into that position," Uncle Dick reminded him mercilessly.

Tom Geering accepted the rebuke by lapsing into silence for a moment.

"But, good heavens!" he exclaimed suddenly. "If your theory is correct I've been unwarrantably rude to that youngster. I ought to seek him out and apologise." Uncle Dick squirmed visibly at the other's perverseness. It would never do for Cedric and Geering to meet again.

"Don't do anything so ridiculous!" he said quickly. "If you do that, the young ass will think he can hang around after Esme as much as he likes."

Geering gave him a sidelong glance. He was beginning to think that Uncle Dick was a difficult fellow. Whatever he wanted to do, Uncle Dick seemed to have some good reason to urge against it.

"Yes, perhaps you're right," he said weakly.

But he noticed a few minutes later, when they were sitting in the train, that disposition to head him off on the part of Uncle Dick.

"Wonder if there *was* a Geering at Wryvern lately," he remarked thoughtfully.

"Probably. That's how that young idiot thought he knew Esme's brother. Don't suppose it's any relation of yours."

"I don't know. I've got some cousins of about an age to have sons at school. I'd rather like to meet them. I've half a mind to write down to the school and make inquiries."

Once more Uncle Dick squirmed.

"I shouldn't!" he said promptly.

"Why on earth not? I'd like to find some relatives. Blood's thicker than water, and I'm a lonely man.

Esme letting me down has made me lonelier than ever."

"Relations are a mistake," said Uncle Dick oracularly. "They won't care tuppence about you. They'll cold-shoulder you if they're well off, and sponge on you | if they're not. If you take my advice you'll leave them alone."

Geering leaned forward with an air of mystification.

"What's the matter with you, Dick?" he demanded. "Why do you sit on everything I want to do?"

"My dear fellow, I don't."

"Very likely you don't notice it, but I do. And it may be my imagination, but sometimes there seems to be something queer about you. It gives me a feeling that I'm living in the midst of a conspiracy."

Uncle Dick roared out a laugh. It was loud enough, but a sensitive ear might have detected a false note in it.

"What utter nonsense!" he exclaimed.

Geering laughed too, but the sound was accompanied by a searching glance at his friend. It was a chilly evening, and yet Uncle Dick's red face was redder than usual and a gentle dew was apparent on his brow.

CHAPTER XVI

Having been left at his prison, Esme went upstairs to his room under the stars with a share of that virtuous peace which the Village Blacksmith took to bed with him every night. Something had been attempted, something had been done. Moreover it had been done well; it had "come off." Tom Geering had evidently been completely fooled; he suspected nothing, and, according to plan, Esme had succeeded in getting himself disliked by the man who had come to claim him for a daughter. Geering wouldn't be likely to worry him much more, wouldn't want to create an impossible situation by dragging him out to Africa. Soon, very likely, he would take himself off again, and Esme would be able to leave this atrocious girls' school, and get into trousers once more, and be natural, and breathe freely.

The prospect so enchanted Esme that, on his way upstairs he burst into song, carolling a merry ditty about "Dan, Dan, the undertaker's man." His voice was more noticeable for strength than beauty, the song was not an example of a perfect lyric wedded to perfect music, and, as he passed Miss Chadpole's room she ran out to revile him.

"*Ssh! Ssh! Ssh!*" said Miss Chadpole.

Esme went on singing.

Miss Chadpole executed a peculiar caper, as if she were marking time at the double. "Ssh! Ssh! Ssh!" she repeated. "Esme! Don't you hear me?"

"Naturally," Esme replied in a tired voice.

"Then why didn't you stop that noise at once?"

"Didn't know you wanted me to, Miss Chadpole. I thought you were playing trains."

Miss Chadpole bit her lip and glared at him.

"Esme," she said coldly, "are you quite sane?"

"I was all right when I came here," Esme retorted, "but I doubt it now. Let's go on playing trains, shall we? You go *Ssh, ssh, ssh* again, and I'll say, 'Right away, Guard! '"

Miss Chadpole stared at him, white with temper.

"Esme," she cried, " is there no limit to your impertinence?"

"I give it up," said Esme, " then I'll ask you one."

"I shall go straight and report you to Mrs. Toy."

"Then I hope you'll do the square thing and tell her that you began it."

"Began it!" repeated the quivering assistant mistress.

"You said my singing was a noise, and then said I was mad. I—I've half a mind to burst into tears." Miss Chadpole made a clicking noise with her tongue and felt constrained to use reason.

"Don't you understand, Esme, that your conduct is, and always has been, most unseemly? However—er— nice your voice may be, you are not allowed to sing about the house. And that song is hardly what one would expect to hear from a nice girl."

"What's the matter with it?" Esme demanded. "Why, it was in one of the Sunday papers!"

Once more was the futility of arguing with Esme brought home to Miss Chadpole. She hesitated in the act of replying, and gave Esme a further chance of stating his case.

"If *you'd* just seen *your* father for the first time in your natural, perhaps *you'd* want to sing going upstairs."

"Of course," said Miss Chadpole, in a more conciliatory tone, "I—I'd forgotten that. How was your father, Esme?"

"Pretty dull, thanks. He didn't come up to expectations. But then I suppose strange fathers never do. Still, it was an interesting experience to meet him. I'm all of a shimmy-shake. My girlish heart is going *flip-flop*. No wonder I am inclined to burst into song."

This speech reduced Miss Chadpole to stony silence. Without another word she withdrew backwards into her room and closed the door. What, she asked her immortal soul, could one possibly say to such a girl as that? Of one thing she was now certain, namely that Esme was mad. She was determined to tell Mrs. Toy so, without delay.

Meanwhile Esme, having sought the privacy of his attic room, turned on the light, removed from one of his secret hiding places a packet of Gold Flake, proceeded to smoke out of the open window and reflect on a life which was full of ups and downs. Just now things were going very well. Not such a bad old world if only you knew how to live in it. Even St. Mildred's had its compensations. In his little room he could smoke almost as much as he desired, whereas at Wryvern the opportunities were less frequent, and fraught with the most terrible dangers. After all, Mrs. Toy didn't do any "swishing", probably didn't know what it was.

Ignorance is happiness. Esme did not know that Cedric had blundered into Tom Geering, nor that Miss Chadpole was even then on her way to Mrs. Toy to urge his removal from St. Mildred's.

Cedric's encounter with Tom Geering had left him sore in spirit. It had not panned out according to plan. In fiction, Tom Geering would have thought him rather a fine young fellow, whereas in fact he obviously had not, and he had also been distinctly rude. What was worse, Esme would doubtless hear of the encounter, and he had enough sense to know that Esme would be angry. Perhaps that fiery and mysterious beauty would decline to have anything more to do with him. His heart grew heavy at the thought. Of course he would write and explain his motive in having approached Tom Geering. But letters were so unsatisfactory.

When you've written them they never seem to express your meaning properly. The recipient misses the look on the writer's face, the inflection of his voice. More than ever did Cedric feel the need of a personal interview with Esme.

Then he bethought himself of the road alongside the school, upon which Esme's window looked out. If Esme could only see him, and he could signal some message, such as "Forgive! I did it for the best!" He understood the deaf and dumb alphabet, if Esme understood it too, all would be well. And surely if he stood there, looking so forlorn, Esme's girlish heart would be touched. Possibly, too, Esme w'ould be alive to the romantic side of the situation. It would be distinctly reminiscent of the balcony scene in Romeo and Juliet.

Fortune favoured the young swain. There was a light in Esme's window, and Esme himself stood there, puffing invisible smoke-clouds into the darkness. Cedric planted himself well in the light of a street lamp and began to wave furiously. At the sight of him Esme leered horribly, crushed out his cigarette, and waved back.

"Now what," he reflected, "does the silly ass want?"

Unconscious of possible danger he leaned out of the window, kissed the tips of his fingers with a sound like the drawing of an obstinate cork, and flourished his hand towards the young man in the road. Cedric returned the kiss and then stood motionless while somebody passed.

When once more he had the street to himself, Cedric, holding his hands high up in the light, began to tap his fingers and make those gestures by which deaf mutes converse. Esme watched him from the window with a broad grin, and nodded at the end as if to say that he had understood the message—which he had not. He knew that Cedric was trying to tell him something, and as that youth was amusing him considerably, he let him go on. Having spelt out "Forgive. I did it for the best," Cedric waited for a reply, and Esme, thus called upon, twiddled his hands and thumbs in imitation of the other. Cedric watching carefully, spelt out, *Chllj*. This did not seem to make sense, and as he did not understand Esme, he assumed quite reasonably that Esme had not understood him. Possibly, he reflected, Esme knew some other deaf and dumb code. Finding himself thus prevented from sending his particular message, Cedric contented himself by making those signs which were intelligible before mankind learnt to speak.

He shrugged his shoulders and hung his head to show that he was dejected about something. He made a magnificent Gallic gesture, and pressed his hand to the region of his heart. He kissed both hands and flung them wide in the air. Esme watched him with the cynical amusement of one regarding the antics of a drunkard or a lunatic.

Cedric had forgotten something which Cuthbert had already pointed out to him, namely, that if he stood back a certain distance from the garden wall he would be visible not only from Esme's window, but also from the window of Mrs. Toy's drawing-room. He was now standing far back from the wall, so as to be right under the street lamp, and chancing to lower his gaze, he suddenly beheld three faces pressed against the drawing room window, all watching him curiously.

Instinct prompted Cedric to turn and run, even although he was sure he had been recognised. But thought is swift even to the most sluggish brain. He could not see who was watching him from the drawing room, but he could make a good guess. How long they had been watching him he did not know, but he realised that he must now make the best of a bad job by pretending that he had been waving to them. As a man and a lover his duty was to protect Esme. Accordingly he looked straight into the drawing-room window, and began to dance and gesticulate like a dervish. How to explain his conduct later he did not know; he could only trust that some likely story would be put into his mouth when he was questioned.

Esme was quick to observe the new move in the game. He saw that Cedric was looking at one of the windows below him and waving frantically in that direction. He knew that window, and realised the import of Cedric's behaviour.

"Help!" he gasped. "The fool's got himself caught."

He closed the window, drew the blind, and prepared the room for an immediate visitation. Cedric could get out of the mess as best he could. If anybody had been seen waving in the street, Esme was determined to be quite unconscious of it. As he got out his school books he began to invent speeches strongly flavoured with injured innocence which would serve him in the hour of accusation. After all, how could he fairly be blamed if an utter stranger made a fool of himself in the road?

Meanwhile Miss Chadpole had already gone down to Mrs. Toy's drawing-room, where she found not only that good lady herself, but Miss Budging cosily ensconced in the second-best chair. Mrs. Toy exposed her long teeth in a smile of welcome.

"We were just discussing," said the headmistress, "the advisability of sending Milly Bell up for the Senior Cambridge. She wants to go in, of course, but it would be inadvisable from the point of view of the school to send her up unless she has a good chance. Losing an uncle and five of her teeth has retarded the poor child's studies. Miss Budging is rather against our sending her on the grounds of her weakness in mathematics. What do you think?"

Miss Budging and Miss Chadpole were supposed to be friendly rivals, but there was more rivalry than friendship between them. If Miss Budging wanted something done, Miss Chadpole did not, and *vice versa.*

"I think she might go," Miss Chadpole said. "She'll pass in *my* subjects."

"But arithmetic is compulsory," Miss Budging urged.

"I said *my* subjects," Miss Chadpole retorted, leaving the delicate innuendo to the headmistress. "After all, the child's studies have not been so greatly interrupted, and she has her false teeth now."

"You don't understand that child," said Miss Budging gently. "She has been moping herself to death. Certainly she has her artificial teeth, but nobody can provide her with an artificial uncle."

Mrs. Toy gave her casting vote. She liked to boast at the end of every scholastic year of the percentage of her pupils' successes in public examinations.

"Well, perhaps on the whole," she said, "we'd better not send her."

Miss Budging and Miss Chadpole exchanged glances. Miss Budging's glance said, "One up to me!" Miss Chadpole's glance retorted, "Cat! "

"We ought to do very well this year," Mrs. Toy continued brightly. "If Esme Geering would only work, she might take honours."

Miss Chadpole made a grimace as if at a twinge of pain.

"Oh, please," she said in half-humorous supplication, "don't mention Esme to me! I was just going to say something about her."

"What's the matter now?" Mrs. Toy demanded.

"Oh, her usual insufferable insolence. I've just encountered her on the stairs. She came stamping up with her great feet, singing some abominable comic song, and when I ventured to remonstrate with her, if you please, she—she was as cheeky as an errand boy."

"What did she say to you?" Miss Budging asked in a tone of treacherous sympathy.

"Oh, I forget exactly what she said. It was the way she said it."

"That reminds me of another comic song," said Miss Budging with a giggle.

"I daresay it does, but as I don't frequent music halls you have the advantage of me. I've only one thing to say, Mrs. Toy, and unless I said it, I shouldn't be doing my duty to you. We've all suffered a great deal at Esme's hands, and I for one blamed the child unjustly at first. It isn't her fault. It's my considered opinion that the child is mad."

Mrs. Toy looked grave.

"Do you really think that? She isn't a bit like that poor little Molly Flummery we had here."

"There's more than one kind of madness," urged Miss Chadpole. "I had a poor little girl cousin who— who went just like it."

"Not having had any lunatics in our respective families," said Miss Budging sweetly, "there you have the advantage of us."

"Of course," said Miss Chadpole warmly, "I could if I chose comment on the bad taste of that remark. Being a lady and the daughter of a solicitor, I refrain, but it is only right that I should say what I think, Mrs. Toy. I'm quite certain that Esme is mad, and Pm just as certain that she is doing the school no good."

"A very difficult child," murmured Mrs. Toy, pursing her lips.

"I find her quite insufferable."

Then it was that Esme found a friend. Miss Budging, who hated Miss Chadpole, came promptly to the rescue. Miss Budging envied Miss Chadpole her influence over the girls, and the esteem and affection in which the good-looking assistant mistress was held. None of the girls wanted Miss Budging to die a picturesque and lingering death, so that they might sit at the bedside and hold her hand, or risk infection for her dear sake. None of them ever gave Miss Budging cheap editions of the " out of copyright" poets with dried pansies pressed between the leaves. None of them ever cherished secret ambitions to forsake home and kin and live all their lives with Miss Budging in a dear little country cottage. She was not a cult as was Miss Chadpole, and being human she was jealous, and seized upon her chances of scoring.

"I can't understand that," she said gently. "Esme and I get on very well together."

Miss Chadpole snorted, and Mrs. Toy stared.

"Really! exclaimed the headmistress. "But you used to complain so bitterly about her."

"Yes!" said Miss Chadpole, looking daggers.

"Ah, I admit that at first I found her difficult, but since I have learnt to understand her, I haven't a word of complaint. Esme's true worth lies beneath the surface. It is the work of the schoolmistress to discover the true gold beneath the superficialities. Of course, Miss Chadpole has not had as much experience as a teacher as I have had—"

"I suppose you had about twenty years' start of me," interpolated Miss Chadpole.

"Experience is not wholly a matter of years, and if you'll allow me to say so, I think you've made a mistake with Esme. If you'll allow me to say so, I think you have too many—I shouldn't like to call them favourites—"

"No, please don't," said Miss Chadpole icily. "but girls whom you—er—favour more than others. And Esme not being one of them is inclined to resent it. Now my system of teaching—"is to set a few sums and go to sleep over a novel."

"Really!" exclaimed Miss Budging, appealing to the headmistress.

"Yes, really," said Miss Chadpole with a forced laugh.

Mrs. Toy interposed.

"Please don't let us quarrel," she said. "The whole art of teaching is a vexed question, which we all—Oh, good gracious me! I ought to have drawn the blinds ages ago. Anybody can see in. I—"

She made a movement as if to rise and draw them. Miss Chadpole intercepted her.

"Let me," she said.

It was just then that Cedric was busily engaged in signalling to Esme. Miss Chadpole went to the window, but she did not draw the blinds.

CHAPTER XVII

"What *is* the matter?" Mrs. Toy demanded as Miss Chadpole instead of drawing the blinds lingered by the window, gazing out into the darkness.

"Most extraordinary," said Miss Chadpole, without turning. "There's a man outside signalling to somebody."

"Signalling where?" asked Mrs. Toy, looking up sharply.

"Here! No, he isn't. He's looking above this window. Why, it's Miss Budging's friend, Mr. Bingham."

"Cedric Bingham!" exclaimed Miss Budging, genuinely mystified. "What in the name of goodness can he want"

"You," said Miss Chadpole, still without turning, " should best be able to answer that. Yes, he's certainly trying to attract somebody's attention."

"Perhaps he wants to see you about something," the headmistress suggested, a faint note of displeasure in her tone.

"I can't think why, then. And why doesn't he ring the bell and ask for me?"

Mrs. Toy left the question unanswered. All her previous suspicions that Cedric had become victimised by Miss Budging's mature—and doubtful—charms came crowding back upon her. There was no accounting for these things.

"Let me see!" she said, and went to the window. Miss Budging followed her.

"It looks," said Miss Budging, "as if he's waving to somebody at one of the upper windows."

"That," retorted Miss Chadpole with a sniff, "is hardly probable."

It was then that Cedric saw them and altered his tactics.

"There's no doubt about whom he's waving to now," said the headmistress ominously. "It must be you he wants to see, Miss Budging."
"Then why doesn't he ring at the door and ask for me?" demanded that lady blankly for the second time.

"Ah!" murmured Miss Chadpole.

"I think," suggested Mrs. Toy, kindly but coldly, "I think you had better ask him in. It doesn't look very well, you know. If anybody were to see him—"

"Quite!" said Miss Chadpole.

Miss Budging understood the innuendo. She was partly annoyed by it and partly flattered. For the first time for many years she felt quite girlish and naughty.

"What a silly boy!" she exclaimed, with a little twitter which was by no means lost on her audience. She pointed twice towards the front door, and Cedric nodded to show that he had seen and understood, and moved slowly in that direction.

The wretched Cedric was in an awkward predicament. Flight would have afforded him only a temporary haven and perhaps awakened a suspicion that he was waving at Esme. He must see Miss Budging and say that he had been waving to attract her attention, but he could think of no reason to offer for his unusual conduct. He was a youth who blushed easily, and, by the time he was admitted to the drawing-room, it would have been almost possible to toast a crumpet against either of his cheeks. He greeted Mrs. Toy, Miss Budging and Miss Chadpole in turn, and blushed deeper in the ensuing silence while all three waited for him to explain himself.

"Did you want to see Miss Budging, Mr. Binghapi?" Mrs. Toy asked at last.

"Yes," stammered the unfortunate youth, "I—er— I was just passing, so—er—I—well, as I was just passing, you see, I—well, there, I was passing."

His embarrassment was so painful that even Mrs. Toy felt compassionate.

"We're always very pleased to see you, Mr. Bingham," she said gently, "but another time when you want to see Miss Budging, I should be so much obliged if you would come to the front door in the ordinary way. This being a school you will understand that it doesn't look at all well for a gentleman to be seen standing outside making signals."

"Oh, quite!" Cedric agreed hastily.

"Do you wish to speak to Miss Budging privately?" Mrs. Toy inquired.

"Oh—er—no. No, not at all. I—er—I was just passing, that's all."

"But surely—"

"I saw a light in the window," rambled the unfortunate Cedric. "I saw a light in the window, and I just waved."

The chilly demeanour of the other two women was an implied compliment to Miss Budging. She felt and looked almost coquettish.

"But surely," she said, " you had something to say to me? Some—some message to give me?"
Cedric seized upon the word Message and took it thankfully to his heart. It seemed to him then nothing less than providential that Miss Budging should once have been governess to his sister.

"Yes," he said, glowing all over, "I had a letter from Viola to-day. She—she sent you a message."

"Yes?" said Miss Budging, sharing with the others an expectation that the mystery was about to be solved.

"She—she asked to be remembered to you," continued Cedric, his powers of imagination suddenly failing him.

The announcement was coldly received.

"Is that all?" Miss Budging demanded in a still small voice.

"No. She sent her love. She said I was to be sure and give you her love. And as I was passing, and saw a light in the window, I—You see, I didn't want to knock at the door and just tell you that. I—I thought if I could see you without troubling anybody— And now I think I had better be getting on."

He was wretchedly aware that his words carried no conviction, but he was unaware of how they were being interpreted. Miss Chadpole was regarding him with cold, contemptuous pity—the sort of pity she was able to feel for a mere boy who had become entangled with a woman old enough to be his mother. There was more anxiety in Mrs. Toy's attitude. She felt that a difficult and delicate situation was being forced on her, and uttered a laugh intended to be light, but which sounded uneasy.

"So the mystery is cleared up," she said. "I declare, Mr. Bingham, we thought we were going to hear something quite thrilling."

"Something about the weather, at least," said Miss Chadpole caustically.

"No," muttered Cedric lamely, "I was just passing, so I—Oh, good-bye!"

Mrs. Toy accompanied him to the hall door, leaving the two assistant mistresses alone together. Miss Chadpole shot an accusing glance at Miss Budging.

"He was standing still," she said, "gesticulating wildly as if he were trying to stop a train. And then he said he was just passing. His message didn't sound very important to me, and never have I seen a young man so painfully embarrassed."

"He certainly seemed to behave very mysteriously," Miss Budging agreed calmly.

"Did he? Really? I thought perhaps you held the key to the situation. But if *you're* mystified, then I fear it is quite inexplicable. I couldn't understand why he came to tea a few days ago. I should have thought there was nothing here to attract a very young man."

At this point Mrs. Toy re-entered the room and Miss Chadpole rose. By her very manner of leaving the room she conveyed the suggestion that Mrs. Toy must have something to say to Miss Budging in private.

Mrs. Toy had. She prefaced it with a little dry cough suggestive of embarrassment and decision.

"Er—Miss Budging," she said, "I have always made it a rule never to interfere with the private affairs of my staff."

Miss Budging looked up, and, flustered, lowered her gaze again.

"But of course," continued Mrs. Toy firmly, "there is the name of the school to be considered, and I hope I can rely on you to see that that unfortunate young man does not repeat his—er—singular performance of to-night. Of course I shall always be pleased for you to entertain your friends here if they come to the door and call in the ordinary way. But I suppose that seems too commonplace and unromantic to a youth in his— er—condition."

"I am quite at a loss to account for his conduct," said Miss Budging with a slight simper. "You surely don't think, Mrs. Toy, that—that he has come to regard me as more than a friend. There is such a disparity in our ages. I—I am in the thirties, you know."

Mrs. Toy, staring straight at her, feared the worst, and had to suppress a vulgar desire to add, " And the rest! "

"There is no understanding a boy of that age," said Mrs. Toy, who had never known one intimately. "You have my sympathy, Miss Budging, in a difficult and delicate situation. It will be no easy matter to be kind to him without encouraging him, to discourage him without hurting his feelings. If I were you I should promise to be a moth—I mean a sister to him."

"I can hardly credit that he—he cares for me," said Miss Budging, with quite a girlish simper. "It does seem almost impossible," agreed Mrs. Toy, with no intention of being unkind, " but there it is. I am sure I can rely on you to be tactful and see that we don't have another such ridiculous scene as we had to-night."

Miss Budging accepted the charge in silence. It was strange how her heart was fluttering. It had not fluttered like that for years, indeed, not since her dashing and wicked cousin Robert had kissed her as a preliminary to borrowing her savings. She would scarcely have believed that Cedric was infatuated with her, it was the other two women who had infected her with that belief.

No wonder she began to dream dreams. Cedric seemed to her a nice enough boy, and he had a rich father. Of course she was much older; old enough to be his moth—no, his elder sister. But she felt young, indeed, just now she was feeling ridiculously young. And perhaps she didn't look her age. And it was nice to think that she attracted somebody. Anyhow, no young man had made himself ridiculous because of Miss Chadpole!

So, when she went to her room a few minutes later, I am afraid it was to think out a new way of doing her hair. Her head was in the clouds and full of bright dreams. Far away, down in the boot-room, Cuthbert's voice assailed her, uplifted in the bowdlerised version of a song which helped many a khaki legion down many a road lined with poplars.

"Madam-was-ell from Armon-teers, parley-voo! Madam-was-ell from Armon-teers, parley-voo! Madam-was-ell from Armen-teers She 'asn't been kissed for forty years—Inkey-pinkey parley-voo! "

The words struck upon Miss Budging's ears like a message of hope.

CHAPTER XVIII

"Did you have a good time yesterday?" Christine asked.

It was during the eleven o'clock "break" in the morning following Tom Geering's visit, and Christine and Esme were walking on the arid waste which was sometimes called the garden and sometimes the playground, dipping alternately into a bag of biscuits.

"Pretty putrid," Esme returned unemotionally. "I went out and had a tea, which was something. And of course I was glad to see Uncle Dick again. But my father and my father's own little girlie weren't exactly wrapped up in one another."

Christine regarded him curiously. He was often incomprehensible to her.

"It doesn't seem natural," she said, "that you shouldn't like your father."

"It 'ud be pretty wnnatural if I did, seeing the way he's treated me."

"Oh, Esme! Do you mean to say you can't forgive him?"

"Oh, bless his heart, I don't bear him any grudge. I just haven't any use for him. Relations are a mistake. People ought to be allowed to choose theirs. Then I'd have my Uncle Dick for a father, and my father could have something sweet and feminine for a daughter. And I'd have you for a sister."

"We can pretend we're sisters," said Christine, heroically declining the last biscuit.

"I don't want it—the biscuit, I mean. Yes, all right. I don't know anybody I'd sooner have for a sister than you. Since you've chucked that mob who go oiling up to that Chadpole woman you're—well you're as good a pal as a boy. Isn't it funny, though? I've got a father that I don't want, and you'd like a father. I s'pose you don't remember yours."

Christine shook her head.

"I'll tell you one day about my people," she said. "I told you I had a secret, didn't I? But I must see Aunt Edith again and ask her permission before I tell you."

Esme smiled. In spite of his skirts he had little curiosity.

"You don't happen to be a duchess in disguise, do you?" he asked.

"No. Just the opposite."

"What's the opposite to a duchess? You can't very well be a bally duke."

"No, you stupid. I mean I'm—I'm quite common, really."

"Not you. Besides, Miss Cheville's your aunt. And she isn't common, is she?"

"No, but—" Christine broke off the thread of the sentence, looking troubled. "Oh, I can't tell you now."

"Right-oh, old girl. Talking about duchesses, I only met one in my life. She was giving away the prizes, and—"

"The prizes? Where?"

"At s—" Esme checked himself in the nick of time. He had forgotten for the moment that he was supposed never to have been to school before, and found himself about to plunge into an anecdote about himself at Wryvern, and a boys' school to boot.

"At some sports I ran in," he corrected himself.

"Esme! Have you ever run in sports? Public sports? You never told me! But how could you?"

"It was a—a maiden race," said Esme, presuming on Christine's innocence by borrowing an expression from the turf. This seemed to satisfy Christine, who said:

"But how wonderful! Did you win?"

"Yes—a big tantalus. And that reminds me. My Uncle Dick says I may play hockey—just in the one match against the High School. Oh, blazes! There goes that bally bell. More of that Chadpole woman! And I haven't looked at my French author yet."

They began to wend their way back in the direction of a door upon which a number of girls was already converging.

"I've never paid you back yet," said Esme suddenly, " for asking me out when your Aunt Edith came down."

"Oh, don't be silly!"

"But I'd like to. If my respected Papa comes nosing around here again—I hope he won't, but I'm afraid he will—I'll get him to ask for you to come out to tea with us."

"I should be horribly in the way," Christine protested.

"Not a bit of it. Just the abso-bally-opposite. If we were alone we should only stare at each other and think out snappy bits of back-chat to hand across. It won't be half so bad if you're there. But perhaps he won't come down again. He's seen me once, and once ought to be enough."

But Tom Geering did come down again. A week later Esme was sent for early in the afternoon, to find Geering awaiting him in Mrs. Toy's drawing-room.

Geering had no more looked forward to the visit than had Esme. It was only a sense of duty which had prompted him to see Esme again, to give both of them another chance to establish more cordial relations. They shook hands, each wearing a forced smile, and might well have been two polite strangers.

"I'm starting for Capetown on Monday fortnight," Geering said.

Esme heaved a sigh of relief and did his best not to look too indecently pleased.

"I hope it'll keep fine for—I mean, I hope you'll have a decent voyage. And don't you get playing poker with strangers. I've heard there's a lot of sharks travel on those boats. You stick to auction bridge at a bob a hundred."

Geering stared at Esme out of eyes which, for a moment, threatened to burst.

"Extraordinary child!" he breathed, as if to himself.

"I may be only an innocent schoolgirl," said Esme, " but I've read all about the pitfalls in this wicked world. Did you read ' Behind the Scenes in Bayswater ' in the *News of the Globe?* And 'Guilty Splendour at Muswell Hill.' "

"No, I didn't," said Geering, and, in spite of himself, he began to laugh weakly.

"Of course," said Esme, "you've been out of England a long time, and you'd hardly believe some of the goings-on. I don't believe in suppressing facts. There are some things which, for your own sake, you ought to be *told.*"

"That," he reflected, "ought just about to settle him."

He was right. Geering, bereft of words, could only stare, and smile the foolish smile of one left speechless. This was Dick Farman's upbringing, of course. If only he could have known! And then Conscience spoke for him, saying: "If only I had cared!"

Esme, having partly paralysed the man who called him daughter, strolled around the room, commenting on Mrs. Toy's possessions, murmuring between while snatches of song with a refrain which ended: "And now I 'ave to call 'im Father!"

"What do you want to do?" asked Geering at last, feeling himself unable to stand it any longer.

"Which would I rather, or go fishing? Are you going straight back to town, or have you come to take me out?"

"We'll go out somewhere if you like."

"Thanks very much. Then may I bring a friend with me? We don't want to talk privately about anything, do we? And it's quite usual here, if a fellow's —if a girl's people come to see him—her—for—er—her to invite somebody else to come along too. You see, my pal, Christine Richards, took me out with her when her Aunt Edith came to see her. I daresay you've heard of her Aunt Edith. Her name's Miss Cheville, and she's Uncle Dick's old flame. Decent sort, too, although she did let poor old Uncle Dick down with a bump."

"I used to know Miss Cheville slightly in the old days," said Geering. "So she has a niece here, has she?"

"Not a bad sort, either. May I bring her. Mrs. Toy's sure to let her off afternoon class if you ask. She'll wriggle and show all her teeth—Mrs. Toy will— and pretend you're a naughty man for interrupting the work, but she'll let Christine come all the same. Have you ever seen Mrs. Toy being girlish? It's great!"

He gave an imitation of Mrs. Toy being girlish, before which Geering winced. In the same fashion he could imagine himself being imitated by Esme, for Uncle Dick's benefit. She seemed altogether without pity or mercy, this strange unlovable daughter of his.

"Bring her if you like," he said aloofly, "if Mrs. Toy will let her come."

Mrs. Toy, interviewed on the subject, behaved precisely as Esme had foretold, and Geering, although he was in no mood to be amused, had some difficulty in keeping his face, particularly as he was aware that Esme was trying to exchange glances with him.

So Christine came. And as she entered the drawing room Tom Geering saw at once the girl he would have had for a daughter.

She was pretty, this Christine; not gifted with any distinctive beauty made for tragedies and immortal love tales, but sweet and pleasing in the homely commonplace fashion of the Anglo-Saxons. One might have passed her in the street, and for the moment have been glad at the sight of her, and in the next moment forgotten her. She was soft and clinging and fragrant, and wore an air of open-eyed innocence which is not always deceptive, even in these sad times. It was such a girl as this that Tom Geering had once hoped he owned for daughter; to such a daughter had he dreamed of returning home.

Geering took her hand shyly, bashful as a boy, because he had an unaccountable instinct to kiss her. It would have seemed to him quite natural to kiss this charming child, stranger as she was. It would not have seemed at all natural to him to kiss Esme, and he was glad that Esme shrank from such demonstrations.

Christine thanked Geering prettily, while the man fell unconsciously to comparing her with Esme. "So awfully nice of you to ask me out. But I'm sure you don't really want me. Shan't I be horribly in the way?"

And Geering felt that Esme and not Christine would be in the way. For a moment he almost hated Esme for not being like Christine. It seemed incomprehensible to him that these two should be friends; Esme the hard and rough and Christine the soft and sweet.

It was Christine who "made" the afternoon. Clearly she liked Tom Geering. She was nice to everybody, but specially nice to him. She got him talking, loosened his tongue, and egged him on to tell stories of his life overseas, while Esme sat and looked, cynically amused.

Esme did not actually dislike Tom Geering. He was not given much to self-analysis, and would have been hard put to it to say exactly what he felt. He had had a justifiable grudge against Geering in the days when he believed that the man was his father. Some of that grudge may have remained as part of his habit of mind, and he told himself that if he had been the real Esme

Geering, Geering would have deserved no better treatment from him. But part of his callous ungraciousness was put on with the purpose of making Geering dislike him, for if Geering claimed him as a daughter it must lead directly to disastrous consequences. He neither liked the man nor disliked him, certainly he was sorry for him, but his love and loyalty to Uncle Dick overrode all other emotions.

On the whole, the afternoon was a great success. Geering and Esme both enjoyed it in their different ways because Christine was with them. Cedric was not mentioned. Possibly because of Christine's presence Geering refrained from asking for an explanation of what had occurred on the occasion of his previous visit.

They sat long over tea, and afterwards Geering took them out and bought them boxes of sweets—although Esme protested—and afterwards took them back to St. Mildred's.

"I think your father's a dear," said Christine, as soon as they were alone.

"Oh, he's all right," said Esme indifferently.

"There's something about him—I can't explain— I wish he was *my* father."

"Well, I can't give him to you. If I could I would, like a shot. I daresay he'd much sooner have you for a daughter than me." He stared suddenly at Christine and a frown wrinkled his brows.

"For the love of Mike!" he exclaimed, "you're not going to start blubbing about it, are you?"

"I'm not. Only—only it's rotten not having a father."

"Well," said Esme, "if you'd had him for one he'd have deserted you for sixteen years, and then rolled up and expected you to sit on his knee and stroke his head and ask after his rheumatism."

"You don't understand him, Esme, I'm sure," Christine pleaded. "He—he must have had a lot of trouble that you don't know anything about."

"He's got a whole packet now, that I do know something about! Well, I'm glad you like him, Chrissie, old thing. If you like I'll ask him to leave all his money to you. *I* don't want it."

A little later in the evening Tom Geering expressed to Uncle Dick his appreciation of Christine.

"I've just seen the girl I should have liked for a daughter," he said. "She was—well, she's just everything that Esme isn't. Esme got me to invite a friend of hers out with us. I think we were both relieved at not being *tete-d-tete.* That's how I met her. By the way, her name's Christine Richards, and she's a niece of Edith Cheville's."

Uncle Dick nodded.

"Yes," he said, "I've heard of her. She's Esme's great pal."

"Can't think what she sees in Esme."

"That's a truly paternal remark," said Uncle Dick, flushing slightly. "Esme's all right, and a damned sight better daughter than you deserve to have. If you desert a child for sixteen years you can't expect—"

"You've taunted me with that before," Geering interrupted sullenly, "and Esme seems only too well aware of my shortcomings as a parent. It's not a question of my deserts, it's what I want. And I wish to God that other child were mine. I could settle down for the rest of my life quite happily, with a girl like that for a daughter."

"Yes, you'd settle down—for about four years. And then some young puppy 'ud come along and whisk her off to church without so much as 'by your leave.' Come and do a show with me somewhere and make your miserable life happy."

"All right," said Geering indifferently, "I'll go and dress."

On his return he found Uncle Dick staring out of the window, deep in reverie. He had fallen into one of his absent-minded moods.

"I wonder where she comes from," said Uncle Dick. "Who?"

Uncle Dick started slightly, and curved his lips in an apologetic smile.

"This Christine Richards. I wonder what relation she really is to Edith. I don't remember the Chevilles having any relatives named Richards. I must get Esme to find out."

CHAPTER XIX

Meanwhile Esme continued his clandestine correspondence with Cedric, and was amassing in his secret hiding place quite a bulky collection of letters. In this way Esme heard of Cedric's encounter with Tom Geering and of his being caught signalling in the road. Cedric confessed to the former incident, lest Esme should hear of it from his father. Esme was angry and alarmed at first, but finding that nothing happened he soon dismissed the matter from his mind.

Although he had suffered considerably at the time, Cedric made light of the signalling incident, and gave Esme a highly-coloured account of the affair, boasting of the excuse he had made and of his escape. And Esme, once he was convinced that Mrs. Toy really believed he had been signalling to Miss Budging, could afford to laugh.

"Help!" he mused. "I wonder if Old Mother Toy thinks there's something on between Cedric and the Budging woman. I wonder! Daresay Mrs. Toy thinks she's a jolly old cradle-snatcher. Wow, what a pair they'd make! And if the Budging woman herself thinks—Why, dashed if she hasn't been doing her hair a new way and wearing new jumpers. The giddy old crow!"

Once Esme had got an idea into his head it did not take him long to evolve from it some form of devilment. He started a rumour in the school that Miss Budging had a young man of about half her own age, that the young man was an easy victim because of not being quite right in the head, and that his name was Cedric. Nobody really believed the rumour at first, but the girls took it to their hearts as an attractive fable, and uttered the name Cedric, accompanied by slight coughs, in Miss Budging's hearing.

Save for Miss Budging herself the rumour would soon have died a natural death. But she bridled and simpered whenever Cedric's name was mentioned, and even raised an occasional faint imitation of a blush.

It was not bad form to "rag" Miss Budging—only Miss Chadpole was held sacred—so the girls, vastly amused, began something which was intended to be a mild form of persecution, only to discover soon enough that Miss Budging actually enjoyed it. She pretended, of course, to be quite innocent of the meaning of the hints thrown out to her, and giggled and looked coy, and behaved like an ingenuous girl in her teens when being teased about her first admirer.

Esme, one morning, took advantage of a lull in the algebra class to ask Miss Budging if a husband ought to be older than his wife, or *vice versa*. Miss Budging was generally shy of answering questions relative to holy matrimony, having had some startling ones put to her in her time, but the subject being near and dear to her just then, she made reply:

"There is no rule to go on. It is generally understood that a married couple should be of about the same ages, or the husband perhaps a little older. But there have been very successful and happy marriages when the wife was considerably older than the husband."

"Yes, Miss Budging," cried a chorus of voices, "there were the Brownings. There were the Brownings, Miss Budging."

Everybody, it seemed, knew about the Brownings, and although they had nothing to do with quadratic equations, Miss Budging was not averse from talking about them for a little while. In the midst of the talk the name Cedric was heard in a loud whisper, several of the girls coughed, and Miss Budging, trying to look severe, and wearing a gratified smile, called the class to order.

But Esme soon tired of the sport, and scowled at Miss Budging in undisguised contempt. He was of an age which holds too much in derision, and was merciless in his attitude of mind towards the failings and foibles of others.

"It gives me the Willies," he said to Christine, "to see that silly old geyser, with a face like a slab of bread pudding, giggling and doing the little girl business every time that chap's name is mentioned. She's ninety in the shade if she's a day, and any man who looked twice at her ought to be pushed straight into a padded cell. Silly old hag!"

"Who is this Cedric she's supposed to be in love with?" Christine asked. "It isn't *your* Cedric, is it?"

Esme rolled his eyes as if in pain.

"If I thought so," he said, " I think my girlish heart would break."

The allusions to Cedric in Miss Budging's class, and Miss Budging's coy behaviour whenever the name was mentioned, soon reached Miss Chadpole's ears. She had at least half a dozen admirers who would have told her anything. Miss Chadpole only smiled at the time, but she afterwards went snorting to the headmistress.

"It's becoming a positive scandal," she said. "The whole school seems to have got to hear of it. How the girls found out, I don't know."

Mrs. Toy frowned. She knew of the enmity between Miss Chadpole and Miss Budging, and she thought she knew Miss Chadpole.

"Unless," she said dryly, "you happened to mention it."

"Naturally, I did no such thing."

"I mean inadvertently, of course," said Mrs. Toy hastily.

"No, I haven't said anything, but somebody must have done. And Miss Budging, it seems, enjoys being teased. And only the other afternoon she was telling the girls how much older Elizabeth Barrett was than Robert Browning. Of course I know these things have nothing to do with me, but it is my duty to mention them to you."

"Thank you, yes," murmured Mrs. Toy, "but I don't really see what I can do about it. I can hardly stop my assistant mistresses from having men friends, or, if they want to, from becoming engaged to be married."

"But it's all so very unpleasant. There's the disparity in their ages. And Miss Budging is surely old enough to know better."

"It seems she isn't," said Mrs. Toy, "and in that case I don't see what I can do. I can hardly turn round and dictate to my mistresses in such matters. After all, it is Miss Budging's own affair. Candidly, I think she is very foolish, and I shall tell her so if the opportunity arises. But unless she does something to warrant my speaking to her, I can't say anything. If she permits the girls to tease her, that is also her affair. I have always found her an excellent disciplinarian." Miss Chadpole felt herself growing heated.

"When a woman makes herself and the school publicly ridiculous, isn't it time to take notice?" she demanded. "I daresay plenty of people outside saw that great oaf dancing about and waving his arms the other evening."

"I don't think Mr. Bingham will behave in that way again," retorted Mrs. Toy. "He seemed acutely conscious of the foolish exhibition he had been making, and I am sure that when he wishes to see Miss Budging again, he will approach her in the proper manner."

"But—"

"When I require any advice in the management of the school," said Mrs. Toy coldly, and with a sudden edge to her tone, "I shall always ask for it."

Miss Chadpole took herself away, angry and defeated, and her anger was in no wise lessened by the sight of the school notice board, upon which Margaret Buddery had just hung the names and positions of the hockey team which was to play against the High School on the following Saturday. Esme was down to play centre- half, and there was no mention at all of Caroline Bax.

Caroline was a favourite of Miss Chadpole's, so, fuming, she sent for Margaret.

"Why isn't Caroline playing on Saturday?" she demanded abruptly.

"Because the selection committee," said Margaret, with a touch of grandeur, "agreed that Esme ought to take her place."

Miss Chadpole's frown deepened.

"Even supposing," she said, "that Esme is better than Caroline—"

"Oh, Miss Chadpole, she is! Much better."

"But she's never had any practice—except that one game."

"Esme doesn't seem to need any practice. She's easily the best player we've ever had."

"Well, but couldn't you play Caroline at right- or left-half?"

"She's so used to playing in the centre, Miss Chadpole. And the other girls are playing quite well in their positions. It would only disorganise the team if we made any more alterations. All the committee voted for the team as it stands—except Caroline."

"I see!" Miss Chadpole frowned gloomily, seeing that there was nothing to be done. She had influence enough to have her wishes obeyed, but she prized the popularity which gave her that influence. If she had another girl turned out of the team to make room for Caroline, that other girl would immediately have a grievance. Perhaps it might even get to Mrs. Toy's ears, and Mrs. Toy would be certain to tell her not to interfere with the games committee. Besides, if the High School won, as they probably would, it might be said that it was all due to Miss Chadpole's interference. It were better, therefore, to remain quiescent. Then, when St. Mildred's had lost, she could say that it was due to her advice having been disregarded.

"Oh, very well," she said coldly. "Have your own way."

And Margaret departed heavy of heart, because dear Miss Chadpole seemed to be angry with her.

Esme himself was not pleased because Caroline had been stood down. He disliked the Spotted Wonder intensely, but he had tried to be nice to her of late, being contrite for having made her look small in the practice game. He went to her as soon as he had seen the notice on the board."

"I say," he said, "I'm beastly sorry. I swear I didn't think I was going to take your place."

Caroline turned her head away.

"Well," she said, "you knew you were going to take somebody's, I suppose. We can't play twelve a side. It doesn't matter to *me*. *I* don't want to play in the silly match. I hope you'll enjoy it, I'm sure. I daresay you think you're better than I am, because I happened to have an off day, and I never trouble about how I play in practices."

"Have a chocolate," said Esme, persevering.

"No, I don't want your beastly sweets. And I don't want you to speak to me either. I don't want to have anything to do with a girl who—"

She checked herself suddenly, biting her flabby under-lip.

"Who what?" Esme asked encouragingly.

"Never mind. I know something about you, Esme. And you'd better be careful."

Esme grinned.

"Jolly little sport you are," he said. "What with your kind heart and your good looks and your sporting instinct—"

Caroline interrupted violently, raising her voice.

"Shut up!" she cried. "I warn you again to be careful, Esme Geering."

"Failing that," said Esme, "I'll be good."

He turned away whistling, with a glance of amused contempt.

"Now what does that silly little skug think she knows about me?" he mused. "Nothing, I bet. Or something silly that doesn't matter tuppence. All bluff. Wow, though, if she only knew everything!"

Esme did not let his mind dwell overmuch on the subject of Caroline and her threat. He had other things to think of. That morning he had received a letter from Uncle Dick, congratulating him on having still further alienated Geering's sympathies. Like all Uncle Dick's letters of late it enclosed a currency note, and, like many more of his letters it contained an interesting postscript. On this occasion the postscript said : "Am going down to Kempton on Saturday, and if you see in the paper that Drunk as a Lord won the three o'clock race, you'll know that your old Uncle D. hasn't done so badly."

"I suppose," reflected Esme, "it's worth five bob if I can only get it on." And with that object in view he strolled in the direction of the boot-room, where he found Cuthbert, shirt-sleeved and smeared with blacking, hard at work among the boots.

"Good morrow, good Cuthbert," Esme said, lounging with an elbow on the bench. "You are looking, if I may say so, all hot and bothered. It's like a tonic to me to see anybody else working so hard. But rest from your labours for a moment. I have something to shoot into your dainty shell-like listener-in."

"The old 'ag's just been round 'ere, pl'yin' me up. You take it from me, miss, I've got a rod in pickle for 'er w'en Labour 'as its rights and we 'as Belshevism. You'd better not let 'er see you 'ere, miss. She's like a cat with a sore tail wot's just lost a whole nest of mice."

"She will not see me here, good Cuthbert. She has just gone out to interview the laundry. I gather from some fragmentary remarks exchanged between her and one of the female domestic staff, that the laundry people have basely stuck a ha'penny extra on pillow slips.

That has naturally had a detrimental effect on a disposition otherwise sunny, and may well have caused her to speak sharply to you just now."

Cuthbert dropped a boot and a blacking brush, and transferred some of the blacking from the palm of his hand to his damp forehead.

"Oh, if she's gom out!" he said, and breathed stertorously with relief.

"I remember," said Esme, "when we were having a little heart to heart talk some time ago, you said you could get money on a horse."

"That's right, miss." Cuthbert's small shifty eyes regarded him in awed admiration. "You aren't 'arf a nib, miss, I must say, wot with your beer and your fags. Yes, I can get a bit on for yer. There's a ready-money bloke calls in at the pub round the comer every dinner time."

Esme nodded doubtfully.

"Does he pay out when he loses?" he asked.

"Gor' bless yer, miss, he's been takin' bets around 'ere these twenty-five years. Honest Ole John Cooper, 'e calls hisself. Why I've seed 'im pay out a bloke forty-eight quid with me own eyes."

"He ought to be good for five bob, then. Will you put five bob on a horse called Drunk as a Lord for me on Saturday?"

"I like its nyme," said Cuthbert. "Is it going to win?"

"It'll be back again in the paddock before the others know they're off."

"Then I don't say but I won't 'ave a bit on it myself," Cuthbert observed. "You gets some inflammation I can see, miss."

"It's going to be good enough for my uncle to back, so it's going to be good enough for me. Here's five bob. And if it wins there'll be something for you, Cuthbert."

Cuthbert seized the two half-crowns which Esme offered him, and thrust them into his trouser pocket.

"Thank'ee, miss. Just write the name of the 'orse and your own name on a bit of paper, and write five shillings on the top of that."

Esme hesitated.

"I suppose," he said, " there's no chance of this bit of paper getting copped."

Cuthbert shook his head.

"Not the least bit of chance in the world, miss," he said.

But he was wrong, as in due time Esme was to discover to his sorrow.

CHAPTER XX

Although Esme could not have guessed it, events were now marching rapidly to a crisis, and the sudden indisposition of Cuthbert may be reckoned as one of the beginnings of the end.

On the Friday night, just as he was about to start work in the boot-room, Cuthbert was aware of certain inward qualms combined with a tendency to shiver, and a feeling of being acutely sorry for himself. At his best he was no great lover of work, and to-night the idea of handling boots was utterly repulsive to him, so he went to see Mrs. Toy and laid the case before her.

Mrs. Toy was not unduly sympathetic, but her dread of epidemics compelled her to take Cuthbert's temperature. The thermometer registered a hundred and one.

"Um, yes," said Mrs. Toy thoughtfully. "Um, yes, you *are* a little above normal."

"I 'xpec' it's a chill on the stummick," said Cuthbert, with a sickly and patient smile. Mrs. Toy winced.

"Possibly," she said, "it may only be a chill on the —er—what you said. But you must go straight home to bed, and you mustn't come back to work until the doctor has been to see you. I will send him to you to-morrow. Er—have you had the usual childish ailments? Measles, mumps, whooping cough?"

"None of 'em, mum," said Cuthbert, who knew how to play his cards.

"None of them?" exclaimed Mrs. Toy in horror.

"None of 'em," Cuthbert repeated, "except thrush."

"Then go home at once! At once, do you hear? Go straight out of the front door and try not to breathe while you're going through the hall. I shall have the boot-room disinfected immediately."

Mrs. Toy duly sent her doctor to see him on the following morning, and was relieved to hear that his temperature had returned to normal, that there was no symptom of any infectious ailment, and that he would probably be able to return in time to deal with the crop of boots on Monday evening.

Now while Mrs. Toy was taking Cuthbert's temperature and sending him home, Christine and Esme were sitting together in a comer of the senior playroom close to the moribund fire of coke and slack which was one of the "home comforts" provided by St. Mildred's. Between them was a draught-board and some scattered pieces. To the accompaniment of many apologies Christine had just beaten Esme for the third successive time. Esme disliked draughts and freely owned that he was no good at the game.

"Never mind," Christine said, genuinely sorry that Esme had not won at least once. "I can't touch you at anything else. I only wish I could play hockey like you."

"Oh, bosh!" said Esme, and his voice, beginning in one key, went suddenly off into another. Christine stared at him curiously.

"What a funny way you speak sometimes," she said. Esme nodded and frowned. For the past two or three days his voice had been playing him queer tricks, and he knew that it was breaking.

"Something wrong with my nose or throat, I s'pose," he said. "Mrs. Toy's been at me to see a doctor, but of course I mustn't. She thinks I've got adenoids."

"Poor old Esme. Does it hurt? "

Esme shook his head violently and switched the conversation on to another line.

"I say, what on earth can we do? Draughts is a perfectly putrid game."

"There's nothing else to do in this prison," said Christine—"except talk. Esme, dear— Oh, I forgot.

You don't like being called dear. I want to tell you something."

Esme nodded and glanced around the room. Some other girls were present, but none was sitting very near them.

"Anything private?" he asked.

"Yes, but nobody'll hear if we whisper. You know I told you I had a secret. I felt awfully mean when you told me yours about Cedric and I couldn't tell you mine. You see I had to ask Aunt Edith's permission first, and she's written back to say I may tell you if I like. Promise you won't tell anybody? Not a soul?"

Esme nodded.

"I know I can trust you," Christine proceeded in a muffled whisper, "or I wouldn't tell even you. The other girls would be so horrid about it if they knew, but you're different somehow."

"Just a bit!" Esme agreed, grinning.

"You know I told you the other day that I was really quite common?"

"Yes," said Esme, "you're not so bad as the others, but you—do talk a lot of bilge sometimes."

"No, but it's true. I'm really no relation to Aunt Edith. She—she adopted me."

Esme nodded. His face was quite expressionless.

"Then who were your people?" he asked.

"I don't know. Nobody knows. But they couldn't have been anything very special, could they?
Nice people don't desert their children like that."

"It doesn't follow," said Esme, acutely conscious of having been found under a whelk-stall. "And, anyhow, what does it matter?"

"There's just a chance that I was kidnapped or stolen, because the old woman who brought me up until I was about three was quite mad. That's what Aunt Edith says, for I don't remember her, of course. The old woman was a seaside landlady, and she died while Aunt Edith was staying in the house. So Aunt Edith adopted me. Before she died the landlady told Aunt Edith that I was no relation of hers and she didn't know who I was. And Aunt Edith thinks that the old landlady, who was very queer in her ways, and mad about children although she had none of her own— Aunt Edith thinks she may have stolen me. . . . Why, Esme, how funny you're looking! "

Esme certainly felt funny. He gulped twice, and his eyes grew round and stared fixedly at the face of the girl before him. In a flash he was back on the Cornish cliffs, and hearing the story of Uncle Dick's muddle from Uncle Dick's own lips. It was in a seaside apartments house that Uncle D ck had left the real Esme, never to set eyes on her again. And in such a house had Edith Cheville found Christine. And Christine was about his own age. The natural conclusion leaped at him, and his mind staggered under the impact. The affairs of himself and Uncle Dick were already sufficiently tangled, but if Christine Richards should prove to be the real Esme Geering it introduced a complication sufficient to drive most normal people into the nearest asylum. But he had only jumped at an idea. It remained to be proved. He could not, would not believe it.

"When Miss Cheville found you at Margate—" he began, stammering.

Christine jumped violently in her chair.

"I didn't say she found me at Margate!" she exclaimed.

Esme bit his lip and went slightly red.

"Yes, you did," he growled defiantly.

"I didn't know I did. It must have slipped out. Anyhow, it's true. It was in Margate that Aunt Edith found me. Of course I don't remember it, but—Oh, Esme, what *is* the matter?"

Esme rested his head between his hands. It was beginning to ache and his forehead felt very hot.

"What's the matter?" he repeated. "The *matter!* Oh, holy smoke! Wow, wow! *Two* wow wow's! Crimes of Paris! Suffering cats! What *isn't* the matter?"

Christine was staring at him in blank amazement, unable to think of anything in her short narrative which could normally have produced such an effect.

"Aren't you well?" she asked softly.

"Well? You wouldn't be well, if—"

"If what, Esme?" Christine asked, as the wretched boy came suddenly to a pause.

"If you had adenoids," he added desperately.

"Oh, poor Esme! Do they hurt?"

"Like Hell mean, yes, they do!"

Christine rose up at once.

"Esme," she said firmly, "it's all dreadful nonsense about not going to a doctor! You ought to have one.

I'm going straight to Mrs. Toy to tell her—"

Esme too got up and faced her, panting.

"If you do go to Mrs. Toy," he said, "I'll never speak to you again."

"But, Esme—"

"And then I shouldn't be able to play hockey tomorrow, and we should lose."

"But you can't play if you're ill."

"But I shall be all right to-morrow, you idiot. I shall be all right to-night."

"Oh, well," Christine murmured doubtfully, "if you're sure about that—"

"I've only got to say over to myself a few times:

"Every day and in every way I'm getting better and better.' You say it for me, and that'll help. Every day and in every way—"

He began to mumble to himself, and Christine joined in, murmuring, "Every day and in every way Esme is getting better and better."

"Twice more," said Esme, "and then once for luck, and I shall begin to feel a new m—a new girl."

The ritual was proceeded with. Then Esme smiled, filled his lungs and exhaled with a long sigh.

"All right now," he said.

Christine stared at him incredulously.

"Do you really mean you're better?" she demanded.

"Heaps, thanks. Just saying those few beautiful words is better than all the doctors. It cures everything except softening of the brain and clergyman's throat. But I think I'll hop up to my room now and take things a bit easy."

"I should," said Christine. "Good night, Esme. You—you don't think any the less of me because of what I've told you?"

"Don't be a freak!" Esme implored wearily. "Besides, why should I?"

"Oh, it's all right. Only you looked so funny while I was telling you."

"That was only the adenoids," said Esme. "Goodnight, Chrissie, old lady."

The fact was that Esme wanted to be by himself in order to do some hard thinking. He had stumbled across a coincidence so wild and improbable that even now he could scarcely credit it. But the more he thought, the less doubt remained that Christine Richards was the real Esme Geering. Added to the evidence of Christine's own story, overwhelmingly strong in itself, was the mutual liking between Christine and his supposed father, which he had seen with his own eyes. They had taken naturally to each other; and in that word "naturally" he found that proof to which all the circumstantial evidence pointed. Christine, all un-knowing that she was Tom Geering's daughter, had seen in him the kind of father she would have liked to have. Geering had seen in her the ideal daughter.

Esme, sitting on his bed in the dark, tried to collect his thoughts, to marshal them against one problem at a time. In spite of a manner which might justly have been called unfortunate he had a conscience; his instincts were good; he was a boy with a heart. If he had been otherwise this momentous discovery would have done no more than jerk from him a few exclamations of astonishment, and it would in no way have added to the complications of the affair.

But he saw clearly that Christine had a right to her father, and Tom Geering had a right to his own daughter. Besides, when Geering died there would be money left. What then? The easiest way would be for him to go to Tom Geering, tell him the whole truth and throw himself on his mercy. Esme did not mind very much what happened to himself.

But there was Uncle Dick. The way to doing the honest and right thing was barred by the shadowy bulk of Uncle Dick. Suppose Tom Geering would not forgive him, and chose to prosecute? Esme knew that if this happened he would never afterwards forgive himself. His loyalty to Uncle Dick bound and gagged him on the instant. It was to Uncle Dick that he owed everything, and for whose sake he had embarked on this mad escapade. His first duty was to protect that good- natured shiftless child who masqueraded as a giant.

His first instinct was to shift the responsibility from himself and write to tell Uncle Dick of his discovery. But he knew in his bones that his guardian's nerve would fail him; that Uncle Dick would either invent some other wild-cat scheme for getting out of the mess, or beg for silence with the promise of righting everything in the indefinite future. Esme knew his Uncle Dick too well to trust his judgment in anything but racing.

So Esme, after much cogitation, ended by deciding to do exactly nothing for the present. Like Uncle Dick, he was a born compromiser, and able to take comfort in the thought that possibly to-morrow, or the day after, or next week, would reveal to him some brilliant and safe solution to the present difficulty.

So Esme went to bed and slept; but that night he did not sleep as well as usual.

CHAPTER XXI

Next day, Saturday, was the day of the great hockey match against the High School. Work during the morning was a mere pretence, and Esme's preoccupation in class passed without much notice. All the while he was revolving in his head a problem which defied all efforts at solution. It was impossible to inform Tom Geering of the identity of his real daughter without compromising Uncle Dick, and rendering Uncle Dick liable to two years in prison. Perhaps Geering would let him off, but one couldn't be sure before actually putting it to the test, and Esme shrank further and further from the thought. Already in imagination he could see the headlines in the newspapers, and read the humorous remarks of the judge. Not only would Uncle Dick be sent to prison, but he would be made to look ridiculous; and ridicule would hurt Uncle Dick even more than imprisonment.

Although Cuthbert had been absent only for a few hours, Esme was already beginning to miss him. He had expected a packet of cigarettes on the preceding evening, which had not been forthcoming owing to the boot-boy having gone home with a temperature. His supply was getting low, and he was thankful that the hockey match was on the High School ground, since in going or returning he might get a chance of slipping into a shop. Daring spirits had previously been known to do a little surreptitious shopping on such occasions, but the mistresses on duty stopped this to a large extent by making the girls walk in couples, in a formation known as the crocodile. Thus one could look down the ranks and quickly notice any gaps. Esme, however, was not unhopeful of being able to elude vigilance on the way back. As a matter of course Christine and he elected to walk together.

St. Mildred's was deserted that afternoon. Those mistresses who took an interest in hockey went willingly to watch the match, and those who did not felt morally compelled. Even Mrs. Toy decided to go, and brought up the rear of the procession in a dark tailor-made coat and skirt which, she knew for a fact, cost two guineas more than a somewhat similar creation just bought by the headmistress of the High School. All the girls who were not playing accompanied the eleven with instructions to cheer. The procession formed up outside the school and moved off at two o'clock.

On these occasions the smallest girls walked in front, and between them and the rearguard of mistresses the scale was nicely graduated. Thus Esme and Christine found themselves comprising the last file but two, a circumstance which Esme found annoying for reasons which he presently explained to Christine.

"Will you do a guy with me on the way back?" he asked, as they tramped stolidly along.

"A what?" Christine demanded.

"A guy. A bolt. If I go by myself one of these eagle-eyed wardresses will spot half a file missing. But if we both go they won't notice. We can dodge into a shop going round a comer, before they've had time to get round it themselves. I only wish we were up in front. Then it 'ud be easy. But I think we can manage as it is."

"But how are we going to get into the school again?" Christine whispered.

"Easy. We'll catch 'em up. There's always a crowd round the gate, and we can just nip up from behind them and mix in it. I don't want to stop out, you see. I only just want to nip into a shop and get sweets and a few gaspers."

"Oh, Esme, you are awful!" Christine laughed.

"Well, will you? I don't want to gct you into a row, of course, but I don't think we shall get caught. And now Cuthbert's on the sick list Pm being horribly let down for the necessities of life."

After a little persuasion Christine agreed to slip away with Esme if a good opportunity arose, and with that Esme was content for the time being.

The match of itself would make a story, but as it was a mere incident in Esme's life at St. Mildred's and led to nothing very important, it need not be described with much detail. The

High School, remembering its easy successes in previous seasons, regarded the victory as already won, St. Mildred's, putting all its hopes in Esme, went with the quiet intention of giving its rivals a surprise. And to the accompaniment of bird-like twitterings and soprano screams—which was the nearest to "cheering" that the girls on either side could accomplish—St. Mildred's won by five goals to three.

This was almost entirely due to Esme. In the position of centre-half he was the mainstay of both attack and defence. Two of the goals came from his own stick, and the other three were scored by Christine from deft passes which he gave her when she was well placed to score. Esme became the hero of the hour, and received the congratulations of both teams. Even Mrs. Toy was pleased with him, and afterwards made at him a horrible grimace which she intended for a smile. She cared nothing about games, but was delighted to see her girls beat the High School, even in something quite unimportant.

As for Esme, he bore his honours with unaffected modesty. It was a hollow triumph for him, since, after all, he was only playing with girls. Had he chosen, he could straightway have been the most popular "girl" in the school, since now only Caroline regarded him sourly. Christine, who had carried off second honours with her three goals, was nearly wild with delight, and when on the return journey Esme again asked her to break ranks with him she was ready for anything.

"Round the next comer, then," Esme whispered, "Hop into the first shop—doesn't matter what it is— and let the mistresses get by. Get the two girls walking behind us to close up in the ranks."

The next comer was a very sharp one, and Esme calculated that there would be just time for them to conceal themselves before Mrs. Toy and Miss Budging, who were walking together, could regain a full view of the entire length of the crocodile. No sooner was the comer turned than Esme and Christine sprang out of the ranks and into the nearest shop, which happened to be a poulterer's. It was an open shop, but two or three customers were standing about, and Esme, pulling Christine by the arm, used them as cover, lest Mrs. Toy or one of her lieutenants should happen to glance in that direction.

They heard the uneven footfalls and loud chattering of the crocodile die away, and were preparing to depart when a fat bald-headed man in the white smock of his calling confronted Christine with a smile and a gentle rubbing together of the palms of his hands. This was Mr. Dickey, poulterer and purveyor of game, a prominent member of the Purlingdon District Council, secretary of the local branch of the Toast and Water Temperance League, and vice-president of a society for the Prevention of Being Happy on Sundays.

"And what can I do for you, little missy?" asked Mr. Dickey, rubbing his fat hands together as if he were wringing out a sponge.

Christine had not a word to say. It was impossible to tell Mr. Dickey that she was not a prospective customer, but had merely jumped into his shop to hide while the mistresses passed. She was not always quick witted, and just then she could not for her life have invented an excuse.

But Mr. Dickey did not notice her silence and her imploring glance at Esme. He liked talking to young people. He considered that he had a wonderful way with him in dealing with the young; and he invariably attended the local school treats and made long speeches.

"And how is our dear sister, Mrs. Toy?" he inquired, recognising the hat ribbon of St. Mildred's. "Such a sweet lady. Whenever I meet worldly and wicked people who don't believe in angels I always say to them: 'Why, we've angels walking about our very streets. Look at Mrs. Toy!' And when at last we see her in Heaven—"

"They'll have to give the old geyser a harp," Esme interrupted. "What with having false teeth and no wind, she'd never manage a trumpet."

Mr. Dickey caught his breath, fell back a step, and stared hard at Esme whom he had not previously seen.

"I—I hope I did not hear you aright," he said quaveringly.

"Well, then, I hope you will. Not much use in leaving an order if you don't."

Now Mrs. Toy often gave messages to the tradesmen through girls who had leave to go out. Mr. Dickey had previously received orders in this way, and was less surprised at Esme's last remark than at the tone in which it was uttered. Mrs. Toy occasionally had poultry and game for her own use.

"What may I have the pleasure of sending?" Mr. Dickey asked in a more business-like tone.

"Fifty brace of pheasants," said Esme. "They're wanted on Monday."

"Fifty—*what?*"

"Perhaps," said Esme, "you wouldn't mind sending one of your assistants over. One that isn't deaf."

"Ha, ha! Yes, miss, I understood what you said. But it's a very large order for Mrs. Toy, and I was— ah!—naturally surprised."

"May be her birthday, for all I know," Esme remarked. "Well, thank you, miss, I'm sure. Will you tell Mrs. Toy with my compliments and best respects that her esteemed order shall meet with my immediate attention. I'll ring up the man who buys for me at the market."

"Right-oh." Esme turned to Christine. "Come on," he said.

Outside Christine turned upon Esme a face half laughing and half troubled.

"Why did you tell him that?" she gasped.

"Well, we had to give some reason for butting into his shop, hadn't we?"

"But there'll be a most awful row, and we may be caught."

"Not an earthly. Mrs. Toy'll say there was some mistake and send the pheasants back. Couldn't stand the way that chap was talking. He was putting grey whiskers on me, and giving me a dire attack of the Willies."

"But suppose he *makes* Mrs. Toy keep the pheasants?"

"In that case," said Esme brightly, "we shall have a decent meal by way of a change. Now let's get some chocolates and gaspers. There's a little shop across the road where they seem to keep everything. Newspapers as well. And, coming to think of it, I want an evening paper."
Esme included an evening paper among his other purchases, and turned at once to the sports page.

"Wow I" he cried joyously. "Drunk as a Lord roiled home at ten to one."

"How disgusting I" Christine exclaimed.

"Dis—what?"

"To come home at that time in the morning, and in such a state. Who was it?"

"My dear old priceless one," Esme exclaimed, "Drunk as a Lord is the name of a horse, and it won at ten to one this afternoon. I bet Uncle Dick made a packet. I had a bit on myself. Cuthbert put it on for me".

"Really, Esme, you *are* dreadful!" Christine gurgled. "I think it's too wicked of you. Er—how much did you win? "

"Oh, a pound or two," said Esme airily. "But I shan't see it until Cuthbert comes back to work. Now we'd better run like steam and catch the others up."

They reached the school just as the crocodile was breaking up and crowding through one narrow gate. Mrs. Toy, Miss Budging and Miss Chadpole stood on the fringe of the crowd barking commands like so many sheep-dogs. Esme and Christine came up behind them unobserved, and lingered as if they were waiting for the gateway to be clear before going through. Presently Mrs. Toy turned round and saw them, and said with a toothy grin :
"That's right. There is no hurry at all, and no occasion for all this pushing. I am glad to see two of my girls at least behaving with a proper dignity." This, thought Esme, might be useful as an *alibi* later, in the event of Mr. Dickey making trouble. So, on the way in, he trod on Mrs. Toy's toes to impress the occasion more vividly on her mind.

CHAPTER XXII

During the absence of Cuthbert Mrs. Toy employed a substitute, an old man who sometimes did odd jobs for the vicar. Mrs. Toy engaged him because he was cheap, but at the same time she had been warned that he was very slow and inclined to scamp his work unless he was watched. Accordingly she went stealthily to the door of the boot-room on the Sunday night, but she was unfortunate in choosing her time, for, peeping in, she found the ancient working quite conscientiously. She returned to her study where Miss Budging was seated, the assistant mistress having been invited to a cup of cocoa and a chat.

She had been back in the room less than a minute when Miss Budging began to sniff like a terrier in the presence of game.

"Can't you smell something?" she asked.

Mrs. Toy concentrated all her thought on the matter and her nostrils twitched.

"Something burning?" she asked.

"It certainly smells like that. Where can it come from?"

Mrs. Toy looked around at all the most unlikely parts of the room.

"We must find it," she said. " I can't bear the idea of anything smouldering. If it's allowed to go on we may have the whole house on fire. Dear me, it's getting stronger and stronger. Can't you locate it?"

Miss Budging continued to sniff, and, as Mrs. Toy approached her, exclaimed: "It's getting stronger now."

"It's very strong indeed," Mrs. Toy agreed. "Such a horrible odour too. As if something most unpleasant were being burnt."

She wandered towards the window and had only taken three or four steps when Miss Budging said: "It seems to be going away now."

Mrs. Toy halted and turned.

"How very remarkable!" she said. "To me it is stronger than ever. It's just as if old boots or india rubber were smouldering."

Miss Budging stared hard at her.

"I suppose *you* can't be on fire, Mrs. Toy?" she said anxiously.

Coming immediately after the headmistress's remark, this was perhaps scarcely tactful, but neither noticed it. Mrs. Toy started, frowned and glared at her assistant.

"Ridiculous! How could I catch fire? As if I shouldn't feel it!"

It was then that Miss Budging uttered a little squeal and hastened towards her chief.

"But you *are* on fire. I can see it now. Stand quite still. It's your hair. It's all smouldering."

"My hair!" cried Mrs. Toy, appalled. "But how—"

"Stand quite still!" Miss Budging cried. "There! Look at this."

Having burrowed with her fingers in Mrs. Toy's scanty locks she produced the smouldering end of a cigarette. Mrs. Toy stared at it stupidly.

"But where could that have come from?" she demanded.

"How should I know? But it was *there!*"

The two women regarded each other incredulously, and Mrs. Toy's hand went up and caressed her singed locks.

"Perhaps it dropped on to your head from somewhere?" Miss Budging suggested.

"I didn't suppose that it grew there or jumped up at me off the ground," the headmistress retorted dryly.

"Somebody might have thrown it out of a window. But then you haven't been out, have you?"

"Yes, I have. I've just been down to the boot-room to see how Biggs was getting on."

"Then it must have been thrown out of a window in St. Mildred's."

"Precisely."

"And yet," said Miss Budging, " there isn't a man in the house."

They stared at one another again.

"Perhaps," said Miss Budging, "I scarcely ought to mention it to you, but I know Miss Chadpole smokes during the holidays. She was seen by one of our girls with a fast-looking crowd in the Popular Cafe—or some other haunt of the idle rich—smoking Egyptian cigarettes and drinking black coffee. In the circumstances I feel that you ought to know about that."

Mrs. Toy pursed her lips.

"Of course," she said, " I should very strongly object to Miss Chadpole smoking here, but what she does during the holidays—within certain limits—has nothing to do with me. But it could not have been Miss Chadpole who smoked this cigarette, because she happens to have gone out for the evening. Now who could have been smoking this cigarette, and who could have thrown it out of a window? Don't let us be precipitate. Let us try to think how Sherlock Holmes would have dealt with such a case."

"First of all," said Miss Budging sapiently, "we eliminate the impossibilities, and that which remains".

"The trouble is," interrupted Mrs. Toy, "that when we've eliminated the impossibilities there's a large number of girls and not a few servants to be accounted for. I passed under several windows on my way to the boot-room."

"Yes, but you probably stood outside the boot-room for a little while. So the chances are more in favour of the cigarette coming from one of those windows overlooking the boot-room door. Why—"

The same thought leaped simultaneously upon both women.

"Esme!" they both exclaimed simultaneously.

"I hate to judge a fellow creature rashly," said Mrs. Toy deliberately, "but I must admit that if I were asked which of the girls would be most likely to commit the unseemly and unladylike offence of smoking cigarettes, I should have to say Esme Geering. And when we come to consider that the window of her room is immediately over where I was standing."

"Why, it proves it!" cried Miss Budging.

"To our satisfaction, perhaps. But hardly sufficiently for me to take immediate steps."

"I'll go up to Esme's room," volunteered Miss Budging, "and bring her down at once."

"That would not be the least use. She'd only hear you coming, and hide her supply. I've come to the conclusion that that wretched child is as cunning as she is obnoxious. If we taxed her with her offence she would contrive somehow to wriggle out of it. She would be all injured innocence and put us in the wrong. No, we must wait our time."

Miss Budging tried to conceal her impatience by biting her lip.

"May I ask what you propose to do, then?" she asked.

The headmistress spent a long minute in consideration.

"I will tell you," she said at last. "We will choose some time when Esme will be absent from her room, and give that room a thorough search. If she is a regular smoker, which I fear may be so, she has probably a store of the vicious contraband concealed somewhere. Once we have found it I will confront her with it, and of course I shall get rid of the girl immediately. We will visit the room while the girls are doing their preparation to-morrow evening."

That was Sunday. The morrow was Black Monday for poor dear Esme.

Preparation that Monday evening had been in progress for only a few minutes when Esme, who had contracted a slight cold and had been sniffing all the time, put up his hand.

"May I go and get a handkerchief?" he inquired of Miss Chadpole, who was in charge.

Miss Chadpole frowned and then nodded, and Esme, having sidled out between the desks, made his way up to his attic room, where he found a ridiculously small handkerchief and slipped it into his ridiculously small pocket.

Once there he was in no great hurry to come away. When he returned Miss Chadpole would inquire sarcastically how long it took him to get a pocket handkerchief, and he would reply that it depended upon the difficulty he had in finding one. That was very well. He was standing irresolute, wondering whether he dared find time to smoke half a cigarette when he heard footfalls and voices on the stairs. They were the voices of Mrs. Toy and Miss Budging.

It occurred to Esme immediately that they were coming up to his room, and, naturally enough, they would not expect to find him there. Now what, he asked himself, were they after? Curiosity bit into him like acid. If they saw him there they would merely send him away, and he might never know the object of this strange visit. Esme was a creature of impulse, and, without counting the consequences which would follow on his discovery, he blew out the candle, dropped on his hands and knees, and wriggled under the bed. He lay there, still as a stone, pressing his body against the wall at the back.

The footfalls came to his threshold and he heard the two ladies struggling with the door, which he had long since made to stick. Presently it opened almost explosively, and a dance of lights and shadows informed him that one at least of his visitors was carrying a candle. It was Miss Budging who carried the light, and she set it down on the mantelpiece beside Esme's own candle.

"Where do you think we should begin searching? Mrs. Toy?" she asked.

A spasm of horror took hold of Esme. "*Wow!*" he whispered to his immortal soul.

"I suggest her box, and the mattress, and the chimney," said Mrs. Toy.

Blessed relief surged over the youth beneath the bed.

"All wrong, you silly old geyser!" he chuckled to himself.

The headmistress and her assistant wasted no time. Standing with their feet so close to Esme that he could have tweaked their ankles—and would have loved doing it—they began to strip the bed. They felt the pillow, the bolster and the mattress all over, and then set to work to replace everything as they had found it.

"Nothing here," Miss Budging remarked.

"No," agreed Mrs. Toy, shortly and grimly.

"Have you sent those pheasants back?" Miss Budging asked.

"Yes—with a pretty sharp note to Dickey. I never heard of such a ridiculous mistake. All right, Miss Budging—I'll finish making the bed. Would you oblige me by pushing the poker up the chimney and seeing if it brings anything down."

"Good luck, old dear!" thought Esme, grinning all over his face.

Miss Budging did bring something down. She brought down a quantity of soot, and sneezed as if it were so much red pepper.

"There—*tchar!*—really isn't anything there," she said, "but—*arashoo!*—soot."

"Well, we must try her trunk, then," said Mrs. Toy.

Together they went carefully through Esme's clothes while Esme himself lay chuckling silently.
"Well," said Mrs. Toy gloomily at last, "there's nothing here either. I hardly know where else to look."

"I've just been thinking," said Miss Budging reflectively, "that one of the boards seems to be loose. I've noticed it creaking. I wonder—"

Cold horror crept over Esme once more. The two ladies, picking their steps across the room, at last found the board. It chirruped like a cricket under their feet. Mrs. Toy bent down and held the candle low to examine it.

"It *is* loose," she announced triumphantly. "And you can see where somebody's been prising it up."

The huddled Esme felt himself turning slightly green. So may Catherine Douglas have felt when the men who were to murder James of Scotland discovered the loose boards in the floor under which the king lay hidden. He lay in an agony of apprehension while he heard the laboured breathing of the two women as they strained at the board. Underneath they would assuredly find all Cedric's letters, a supply of cigarettes, and several empty beer bottles. It was what he afterwards described as a Kruschen moment.

"I'm afraid I'm not strong enough in the fingers," said Miss Budging at last, rather plaintively.

"Nor am I," said Mrs. Toy, "and my nails are short. Would you mind going down into the kitchen and asking for some tool which would pull up a loose board?"

"Very well," said Miss Budging, and went.

Left alone, as she thought, Mrs. Toy paced up and down the room like a sentry, occasionally muttering under her breath. Esme lay groaning in spirit, watching her feet and ankles moving, and the hem of her skirt. It was all up now; he was as good as lost. It only remained for him to think what he had best say when confronted with his hidden treasures. Or should he refrain from waiting to say anything, but make a bolt for it instead? It was an awkward fix, but his real secret had yet to be discovered, and his supposed father would now be hardly surprised at anything he did. As the footfalls of the hangman might sound to the ears of a man awaiting execution, so did the returning footfalls of Miss Budging, ringing on the landing below, sound to the wretched boy under the bed.

Mrs. Toy went to the door.

"Have you got something?" she called down.

"No," replied the voice of the assistant mistress. "They say in the kitchen that they haven't anything that will do."

Mrs. Toy snorted impatiently.

"Oh, nonsense!" she exclaimed. "All we want is a big screw-driver. Oh, I'll go and see!"

A moment later Esme, hardly able to appreciate his good fortune, realised that he was alone. He came out from under the bed like an eager dog emerging from a kennel. In a moment or two his strong young fingers had pulled up the board.

He had to find a fresh hiding place, and without very much time. They had already searched the bed, and it was inconceivable that they would search it again. So he placed Cedric's notes and his supply of cigarettes between the sheets. He had yet to deal with the empty beer bottles when he heard footfalls on the stairs. Miss Budging, tired of waiting for the headmistress on the landing below, was coming up.

There was not nearly time enough for him to grope for and remove those empty bottles, but in the midst of his trepidation it occurred to him that empty bottles are not necessarily incriminating. So he replaced the board and slipped once more under the bed.

Miss Budging re-entered the room and waited, but she had not to wait for long. Mrs. Toy joined her after a minute, flourishing a large screw-driver. The board groaned and shifted sufficiently for eager fingers to be slipped around its edges. The candle was lowered over the cavity. In another moment a startled exclamation from both women informed Esme that the two amateur detectives had lighted upon the empty bottles.

"*Bottles!*" cried Miss Budging, in an awful voice.

"*Beer* bottles!" echoed Mrs. Toy in horror, and dropped one of them as if it had turned into a live snake.

"They're—they're all empty," Miss Budging spluttered.

"This is awful!" groaned Mrs. Toy. "I would never have believed it of the girl. Never, never, never!

I had expected to find cigarettes. But beer, beer—Oh, the abomination! Oh, the wickedness! Oh, my poor school! That this should have come to pass! Oh, St. Mildred's!"

Miss Budging was so moved by this display of emotion as to pat the hard stiff back of her principal.

"Calm yourself, dear Mrs. Toy," she said. "It may yet not be as bad as we think. Remember they're *empty* bottles!"

"That only makes it all the worse," wailed Mrs. Toy.

"It simply means that the wretched girl—"

"Not necessarily," cried Miss Budging, upon whose mind had been suddenly shed a gleam of real if misplaced intelligence. "We don't know how long those bottles have been there. Isn't this the room that that wicked cook had last year?"

"Yes, but—"

"And didn't you dismiss her because—?"

"She certainly used to get into bed on one side and fall out on the other," said Mrs. Toy with a sudden change of voice. "She said it was through having vertigo. That's why I had the bed placed against the wall. But the evening she came home from the christening and scandalised the other servants by taking off her boots and dancing on the kitchen table she was certainly   Oh, if I could only believe that these bottles are what that wretched woman left behind!" Esme, prone under the bed, was now hugging himself gleefully.

"You'll believe it all right by the time I've done with you!" he chuckled to himself; for had not the enemy prepared a defence for him within his own hearing '

"We'll hear what Esme has to say this evening," Mrs. Toy concluded.

"You will, old dear!" thought Esme. "You will!"

CHAPTER XXIII

That same evening Cuthbert, now perfectly recovered from his indisposition, returned to work, having first called in at the "King and Keys" to receive from Cedric the usual half-crown and the usual note for Esme. The envelope was as usual sealed but not addressed, since Cedric was in the habit of taking this precaution in case Cuthbert should lose the note on the way back to St. Mildred's. It would never do to have some interfering and benevolent person find it and hand it in at the front door.

As the girls were filing out of the dining-room after their frugal supper, Mrs. Toy appeared in front of Esme like a figure of doom.

"Come straight to the drawing-room, Esme," she said ominously. "I have something to say to you." Caroline overheard the words with some satisfaction. It was clear to her that Esme was in some kind of trouble. In the last two or three days her hatred of Esme had increased a hundredfold, due mostly to his success as her substitute in the hockey team. And because she could bear it no longer she was determined that now was the time to strike. Cuthbert was back. Cuthbert would have a note for Esme from this Cedric. She would get hold of that note and take it straight to Mrs. Toy. If it were to become known throughout the school that she had done this thing she was willing to endure all the consequent unpopularity; but it might yet be possible to convey the note to Mrs. Toy in such a way as to make it appear that her intentions towards Esme were entirely innocent.

She waited a little while and then went round to the boot-room, where Cuthbert was busily at work.

"Good evening, Cuthbert," she said, smirking. "Glad to see you're back."

"Thank you, miss," Cuthbert retorted dourly. "And I shall be glad to see your back, too, miss. I've got plenty to do, I 'ave."

On the edge of the bench in which Cuthbert was working, so placed as to keep it removed from splashes of blacking, was a plain stuck-down envelope which obviously enclosed something.

"Who's that for?" Caroline demanded, pointing.

"Never you mind, miss," Cuthbert growled.

Suddenly suspicious he made a grab at the note, but Caroline was quicker. She pounced on it and seized it, and Cuthbert, uttering imprecations which should never have been heard in a girls' school, dropped the boot he was polishing, and sprang at her with the, intention of wresting it away.

But once more Caroline was too quick for him. She made a dash for the door, hurled herself through it, and slammed it in his face. By the time Cuthbert had opened it, she had too long a start for him to overtake her, and he realised the futility of chasing her into the playroom. He would never be able to recover the note, and he would assuredly be dismissed for conduct unseemly in one of his lowly position. He could only stand staring at nothing and passing a dirty hand across his brow.

"Blimey!" he muttered. "That 'asn't 'arf torn it now!"

But let us take a peep at Mrs. Toy's drawing-room, on the threshold of which the headmistress and Esme found Miss Budging waiting.

"Come in, Esme," said Mrs. Toy in a voice of doom, "and stand over here in the light where I can see you. Now look me in the face."

Esme looked her in the face. On ordinary occasions it seemed a funny enough face to him, but just then he found it irresistible. A grin slowly spread over his countenance; and Mrs. Toy, who guessed the cause of the grin, coloured to the roots of her skimpy hair.

"Now look at the sideboard—where I am pointing!" commanded Mrs. Toy.

Esme looked, and beheld eight empty beer bottles which had once contained the brew which has made Messrs. Bass & Co. so justly famous.

"What do you say to those?" the headmistress demanded, croaking like a raven.

"Nothing," said Esme. "I never talk to bottles. I'm not dotty."

"Wretched girl!" shouted the headmistress stormily. "I can overlook that impertinence for the time being. You are charged with something much more serious. Look at those bottles once more. What do you see? Eight empty beer bottles! Have you no comment to make on them?"

"Looks as if you've been making a night of it," said Esme lightly.

"How dare you! How dare you! Girl, they were found in your room."

"In my room!" Esme repeated blankly.

"Under the floor."

"Then you must mean in the room underneath mine," Esme retorted.

"P'phar! You are only paltering with words. Miss Budging and I discovered them in your room this evening under the floor-boards. Have you been guilty —a girl of your age!—of the disgusting and revolting act of drinking beer? Have you? *Have* you?"

Esme turned away with a slight gesture of weariness.

"Mrs. Toy," he said in a subdued voice, "I am only a poor weak defenceless schoolgirl, but I have my rights. I shall tell my Uncle Dick about this. You have brought a very serious accusation against me, and I decline to answer any questions addressed to me in that tone."

Mrs. Toy and Miss Budging were both considerably taken aback. Never in the whole of their experience had a girl adopted such a manner towards either of them.

"Have you been drinking beer?" Mrs. Toy asked, much more mildly.

"I must decline to answer any questions at all now," said Esme huffily. "You have brought a most serious accusation against me, and you must now prove it. And if you can't prove it, I shall ask my Uncle Dick to bring an action against you for deforming my character."

"Don't talk such ridiculous nonsense!" said Mrs. Toy, reddening; but at the same time Esme saw that he had scored. Anything, Mrs. Toy thought, might be expected of the eccentric uncle of this eccentric girl. "We found the bottles there," she added in a tone which was almost mollifying, "and what else were we to think?"

"I should like to know," said Esme in the subdued tone of one with a just grievance—"I should like to know who had that room before me. Some servant, I suppose?"

Mrs. Toy and Miss Budging exchanged troubled glances.

"Yes," said Mrs Toy unwillingly, "a servant."

"Was she a teetotaler?" Esme demanded, and the two women noticed that he was slowly assuming the air of a counsel conducting a cross-examination. It sat ridiculously enough on this great awkward clumsy "girl," but, ridiculous or not, they found it highly disconcerting.

"No," said the headmistress in a troubled voice, "she wasn't a teetotaler."

"May I ask if you dismissed her?" Esme demanded relentlessly.

Mrs. Toy could only nod.

"Was it for drinking? Please answer me that, Mrs. Toy. My reputation is at stake and I have a right to know."

"I think she—I think she must have been drinking," Mrs. Toy conceded.

Esme was silent a long moment. He was not the only person in that room to be aware of how completely he had turned the tables.

"Thank you, Mrs. Toy!" he said at last, in the cold precise tones of righteous wrath kept well under control. "You find empty beer bottles under the floor of a room which used to belong to a woman who drank. And you accuse a poor, simple, innocent little g-girl!" His voice almost broke on the last word, and for a moment it looked as if he were about to burst into a flood of tears. Mrs. Toy and Miss Budging were alike moved. Knowing who had slept in that room previously to Esme they both wondered how they could have come to accuse her.

"There!" said Mrs. Toy, after a long silence, "we have made a mistake. We will say no more about it."

Esme poked up his head defiantly at that. This was the first and only chance he had had of scoring off these women.

"Excuse me, Mrs. Toy," he said haughtily. "You may have finished with this matter, but *I* haven't. You've made a very serious charge against an innocent schoolgirl and nearly broken my girlish heart. I want an apology. Otherwise I shall write to my father and Uncle Dick, and *they* won't let the matter rest."

Mrs. Toy bit her thin lips. Her pride was in revolt at the thought of apologising to an impudent chit of a girl; but she was not unaffected by Esme's threat.

"Very well, Esme," she said; "I am very sorry indeed that I made the mistake. I apologise."

"Dear Esme," murmured Miss Budging, "I apologise too. I really don't know how we could have come to think it of you."

"Very well," said Esme magnanimously, "let us say no more about it. I am bitterly hurt, of course. But what do my feelings matter? All the time I have been here you have treated me as if—"

He was interrupted in the process of piling coals of fire by a tap at the door and the sudden appearance of a maid.

"Mr. Dickey to see you, mum," said the maid. Esme started visibly, but neither the headmistress nor Miss Budging noticed it.

"Tell him I'll see him in a minute or two," said Mrs. Toy.

"With all respect," said a voice outside, "a minute or two won't do. I'm a busy man, ma'am, same as you are, and I'm not a-going to keep a council meeting waiting if I knows it."

So saying, Mr. Dickey, the poulterer and purveyor of game, pushed his way past the maid into the room and stood bowing to the two ladies.

"Mr. Dickey," said Mrs. Toy haughtily, "I have already told you I am engaged."

"And so am I, ma'am, and a bit late as it is, and this here business won't take two minutes to settle up. I have always looked upon you, ma'am, as a good Christian lady, and what you've done fair beats me. On Saturday you orders fifty brace o' pheasants for to-day. I goes to all manner of trouble to get 'em and send 'em round; and when they come you just sends 'em back and says you don't want 'em!"

"But I never ordered them, my good man," Mrs. Toy exclaimed haughtily.

"You sent one of your young ladies to order 'em though. Two of them came together late in the afternoon, and one gave the order."

"Impossible!" Mrs. Toy exclaimed.

"But they did, ma'am. And much as I should wish to keep friends, in my 'umble way, with a lady like yourself, I must ask you to take them pheasants or pay for 'em, ma'am. How long d'ye think it'll take me to sell fifty brace o' pheasants?"

"I only know," said the headmistress testily, "that I gave no such order, and that I shall not pay for the pheasants. If such an order actually reached you it must have been a hoax, and it could not have been one of my girls who left the order."

From the moment Mr. Dickey had entered the room Esme turned away with a polite air of not being concerned in the present business. Taking great care to keep his back turned towards the indignant purveyor of game, he seemed to be taking great interest in some of the pictures hanging on the walls.

"But it *was* one of your young ladies, Mrs. Toy," Mr. Dickey insisted. "There were two of them, sweet- looking young angels if I may say so, and one gave the order. The one who gave the order was just the build of that young lady over there. Why, I believe—May I look at that young lady, ma'am?"

"Esme," said Mrs. Toy, "turn round."

Esme turned slowly round, holding his breath, and regarded the poulterer and purveyor of game with a certain young-maidenly hauteur.

"Yes, Mrs. Toy?" he said. "What does this person want with me?"

A triumphant light shone in Mr. Dickey's eyes.

"I thought so," he said. "That is the young lady who gave the order, ma'am."

CHAPTER XXIV

Esme was only a little agitated at this new turn of affairs. He was beginning to realise his power. He had just learned the value of bluff, and the learning of it had given him self-confidence. He had also learned by his very recent experience that attack is sometimes the best form of defence.

"What order do you say I gave you?" he asked.

"Fifty brace o' pheasants for Mrs. Toy," said Mr. Dickey; "and you know very well you did, miss. I'd know you anywhere."

"Once seen," said Esme, "never forgotten. But you are sure it wasn't fifty braces—I hate talking about braces in front of one of the opposite sex, but I can't get out of it—are you sure it wasn't fifty braces of fiddlesticks?"

Dickey's face darkened with wrath.

"You can try to get out of it 'ow you will, miss, but it was you right enough."

"Oh, you say so, do you?" Esme regarded him almost pityingly. "And when do you say I gave this idiotic order?"

"Saturday afternoon."

"Saturday afternoon," said Esme, looking at Mrs. Toy and Miss Budging in turn, "I was playing hockey, as—" here he favoured his audience with a somewhat dramatic gesture— "as St. Mildred's will not forget!"

"This was about half-past four," said Mr. Dickey coldly.

"That must have been just after the match," said Esme. "If I'd gone into your shop I couldn't have marched back with the rest of the school. I think you saw me at the gate, Mrs. Toy. You said something nice to Christine and me because we weren't shoving. And afterwards I accidentally trod on your foot."

"Yes," said Mrs. Toy, wincing at the recollection, "I remember." Turning to the indignant poulterer, she added: "I assure you it couldn't possibly have been this young lady."

"But I say it was, ma'am. She must have give you the slip some way or other. There was two of 'em. Don't I know the school colours?"

"It seems to me," said Miss Budging, "that you may have been the victim of a hoax, Mr. Dickey. Unfortunately there is no copyright in the school colours. Anybody can buy them. I have noticed, particularly on bank holidays, young men who could scarcely have been to either of our great universities wearing the ties of the various colleges."

Esme turned, appealing to Mrs. Toy.

"I've had a pretty tough time to-night, one way and another," he said. "I've got the hump and the needle and the Willies—"

"Esme!"

"—and I'm fed up to the back teeth with being accused of things. It seems to me that this man wants to wish his pheasants on to you. He says one of the girls ordered them for you; and, finding me in the room, he pitches on me. I'll buy a bun for anybody who can tell me how I managed to march up from the High School here with the other girls, and at the same time be in his shop. Here, my man, was I carrying a hockey stick?"

"Yes, you was!" replied Mr. Dickey, somewhat heatedly, and not in the least enjoying the manner in which he had just been addressed.

"Yes," said Esme witheringly, "you know that, because I've just told you I'd been playing hockey. But you say there was another young lady with me. Was *she* carrying a hockey stick?"

Mr. Dickey reflected for a moment. Really, he did not remember much about Christine. From Esme' tone he suspected a trap, and replied boldly: "No, she wasn't."

"Well," said Esme to Mrs. Toy, "I can prove that I was walking all the time with Christine. And she'd been playing hockey, same as me, and was carrying her stick."

"And Christine," said Miss Budging, "certainly would not be a party to such a wicked and mischievous joke."

"There you are then!" said Esme, mildly triumphant, and waving a hand towards the indignant tradesman. "I haven't anything more to say, except to quote my Uncle Dick's beautiful words: 'When you start seeing things, take more water with it.' The man wearies me. Let him be removed."

"Esme," rasped Mrs. Toy, "I wish—"

And then, remembering that she had just been compelled to apologise, she checked herself. Although she would not have owned it, she was becoming a little afraid of Esme. Turning to Dickey she said: "That there has been some mistake is only too evident, and I am very sorry for your sake. But the order did not come through me, and could not possibly have reached you through any one of the young ladies here. I was with all of them that afternoon and myself superintended their journey to the High School and back. I certainly shall not pay for the pheasants."

"Very well, ma'am," said Dickey explosively. "I'm not going to stay here arguing. But I 'aven't finished with this yet. You'll pay for them birds or hear from my solicitors. Good night."
He turned on his heel and walked out, leaving behind him a somewhat chilly silence.
After a long moment Mrs. Toy turned to Esme.

"I can hardly rebuke you, Esme," she said, "for the way you addressed that man, especially as this is the second false accusation with which you have been confronted this evening. But I wish you would learn address people in a more ladylike way. Well, I will ay no more about that. Poor child, you look quite overwrought. I think a biscuit and a tiny, tiny glass of claret might do you good."

Esme smiled his thanks.

"But fill me with the old familiar juice,'" he quoted, "' methinks I may recover by and by.'"

"Esme!" gasped Mrs. Toy.

"It's only Omar Khayyam," Esme explained blandly. "My Uncle Dick's always quoting him." "I don't think it's at all nice—Yes!"

There had sounded a knock on the door. The door now opened and Caroline's head appeared.

"Yes, Caroline," said Mrs. Toy.

Caroline looked straight at Esme, concentrated venom in her eyes. She had not expected to see Esme there, but, since it was so, so much the better.

"Excuse me, Mrs. Toy," she said silkily. "I've got a note for Esme. May I give it her? "

"Certainly," said Mrs. Toy, without thinking, and then suddenly checked herself. "A note!" she exclaimed, in a mystified tone. "Who from?" Caroline halted between the two. She saw to her satisfaction that Esme had gone red and then white.

"I don't know, Mrs. Toy. Cuthbert had it, and as he had his work to do I said I'd take it to Esme."

"This is very extraordinary," said the headmistress in a thin dry voice. "Give me that note, please. Are you sure it is for Esme?"

"I *think* Cuthbert said it was for Esme," Caroline said, suppressed triumph in her voice.

Mrs. Toy took the note and broke open the envelope. "Caroline," she said sharply as she did so, "you may go!"

"Thank you, Mrs. Toy," said Caroline.

She shot one look of concentrated triumph and venom at the suffering Esme and went softly out. Esme stood by, shuffling his feet, a sensation of impending doom in his heart. Mrs. Toy's face, as she read the contents of the note, was not reassuring. From her expression, she might have been reading the ghastly details of some particularly appalling murder. Presently she crushed the note in her hand and turned upon Esme a pair of eyes which protruded like door handles.

"Esme," she exclaimed in a voice which cracked with emotion, "are you—are you in the habit of receiving love letters from young men?"

"Love letters from young men?" Esme repeated dazedly.

"You heard what I said!" Mrs. Toy exclaimed, almost with a snarl. "Answer my question. Are you?"

With an effort Esme kept his head.

"I can't help it if people write to me," he muttered. "My face has been my undoing. My fatal beauty has been a positive curse to me."

"How dare you say such things! How dare you! I asked you if you were in the habit of receiving such notes. I am well aware that an isolated instance might be no fault of yours, although it is difficult to conceive of a young man writing to a young lady without any encouragement at all. But evidently in this case there has been some encouragement. It is the most sickly and maudlin rubbish I have ever read. *Dis-gus-ting!*"

"May I see it, please?" Esme asked humbly.

"Certainly you may not!" Mrs. Toy snapped. "I will—I will read it to you. Difficult as I shall find it to force myself to pronounce some of the disgusting terms of endearment, I will read it to you. You will then see to what a horrible—what a humiliating pass—your disgraceful precocity and unladylike conduct have brought you. Listen! And listen too, Miss Budging, to the kind of letter this shameless child has—has sent to her."

Mrs. Toy smoothed out the note again, and, wrinkling her nose as if it smelt offensively, and unconsciously parodying the tones of sickly sentiment, began to read Cedric's effusion. She had already seen his signature at the end, and had alighted upon an explanation to something which had hitherto puzzled and troubled her. Cedric's apparent infatuation for Miss Budging had been in the nature of dust thrown in her eyes. The wretched boy had been making up to the assistant mistress merely in the hope of catching a glimpse of Esme, with the idea of making her a possible ally. This was so exactly true that it was strange that Mrs. Toy should have thought of it.

"My darling Claribel," read Mrs. Toy, and swallowed twice as if the adjective had given her certain physical qualms—"I have not seen you for so long that I am quite desperate for another sight of your flower-like face." ("*Ugh!*") —"Only in dreams does my angel Claribel appear before me. I am losing weight by the stone, and can't eat anything at all. I only want you, my dear one."

"Sounds as if he's a cannibal," Esme murmured just above his breath.

"Oo! Horrible rubbish!" exclaimed the grimacing headmistress, who had not heard Esme's remark.

"Horrible!" groaned Miss Budging, looking just as shocked as she imagined she was expected to look.

"I can't write a long letter, my angel," Mrs. Toy continued reading. (" *Angel! Huh!*") "And I don't expect a long one from you. But I want you to put me out of my misery."

"I'd love to put him out of his misery!" Esme thought grimly.

"I think you've known all along that my intentions were honourable." (*"Honourable! Pha!"*)

"I know I haven't much of a job, but the guv'nor makes me a pretty good allowance. Will you risk it, and run away from that silly old frump of a Toy woman" (*"Wup!"*) "and marry me? I swear I'll make you happy, my fairest one. Let me know soon, I shall neither eat nor sleep until I hear from you. Yours for ever and ever, Cedric Bingham."

"Cedric Bingham!" repeated Miss Budging in an awful voice.

"Cedric Bingham," repeated Mrs. Toy, and shot a sudden suspicious glance at the assistant mistress.

Esme saw that glance and saw Miss Budging's face, and suddenly laughed aloud. He had been wanting to laugh for the past many seconds, for Mrs. Toy's voice and facial expression and explosive comments as she read the note had all been irresistibly funny. But now he laughed for sheer relief, for a path to safety had suddenly opened before his feet. Why, the whole school believed that plain, middle-aged Miss Budging was in love with a youth named Cedric.

Once more Esme's luck was in. On the occasion of his first meeting Cedric in Purlingdon, when he had been compelled to invent a Christian name for Cedric to call him by, he had borrowed Miss Budging's as the first that came into his head. He could be grateful for that now. Why, even Miss Budging thought that note was intended for herself!

Mrs. Toy shot Esme a look full of concentrated scorn and loathing.

"Wretched child!" she cried. " If this proof of your forwardness towards the opposite sex, which I now hold in my hand, can do no more than move you to scurrilous laughter—"

"The whole point is," Esme interrupted, "that my name doesn't happen to be Claribel. That's Miss Budging's name."

The headmistress started violently and stared from one to the other. Partly to her relief and partly to her vexation, Miss Budging was blushing and simpering.

"All the girls have been ragging Miss Budging about somebody named Cedric," Esme continued.

Mrs. Toy knew that this was so. Had she not heard it privately from Miss Chadpole?

"But Caroline said—" she murmured doubtfully.

"Caroline said that she *thought* Cuthbert said the note was for me. She may have been mistaken."

"This must be cleared up!" said the headmistress in a hard, dry voice.

She went to a bell, touched it, and in due time a maid appeared.

"Send Cuthbert up here, will you," she said.

Now was the time! Esme's only chance was to shout at Cuthbert giving him his cue before Mrs. Toy had time to say a word. It might be unseemly and suspicious conduct, but it was his only hope. He thought he might allay the suspicion by affecting a state of irrepressible excitement and indignation.

Cuthbert appeared, as he imagined, for the purpose of being cross-examined and summarily dismissed. He entered the room with that slinking look of dejection one sees in a dog which knows it is about to be bathed. No sooner was he across the threshold than Esme squalled at him: "Cuthbert! That note! Was it for Miss Budging or me? Tell Mrs. Toy."

"Silence, Esme!" shouted the headmistress.

Cuthbert brightened almost visibly. He shot Esme a look full of gratitude. So, he thought, Esme had found a way out for both of them. Lumme, that girl wasn't 'arf a nib!

"Cuthbert," began Mrs. Toy sternly, "you brought a note into the school to-night "

"Yes, mum. For Miss Budging, mum," Cuthbert said with a little gasp.

"It is only right to say," murmured Miss Budging with a simper, "that I think the note probably *was* for me!

Mrs. Toy seemed to take no notice.

"Who gave it to you?" she asked the page boy.

Cuthbert hesitated, looked tentatively at Esme and found the glance intercepted, so he began to search the ceiling for light and guidance.

"A young gen'leman, mum," he said at last.

"Do you know where to find him?"

"Let him be brought here immediately," said Esme dramatically, as a hint to Cuthbert. "I insist!"

His mind was working quickly and clearly now. All would be well if Cedric were sent for, so long as Cuthbert were the messenger. Cuthbert would be able to acquaint him of all that had transpired; and Cedric, if he had a spark of gallantry in his calf-like nature, would come and clear Esme by avowing that he had intended the note for Miss Budging.

"Yes," said Mrs. Toy practically, " we had better clear this up here and now. Go and find him if you can.

Cuthbert, deeply mystified, tried to shoot Esme another questioning glance. It seemed to him sheer madness on Esme's part to insist on being confronted with Cedric, but his knowledge of Esme convinced him that there must be somewhere a method in such madness. It was all in the boot-boy's interests for Cedric to say that the note was for Miss Budging. Cuthbert could hardly be blamed for taking a note to one of the mistresses, whereas he would assuredly be dismissed for acting as unofficial postman between any of the girls and a young man outside.

"All right, mum," he said in a hollow voice. "I'll see if I can find 'im."

Outside, light dawned upon Cuthbert.

"W'y, o' course," he reflected, "directly I tell this 'ere Cedric wot's been 'appenin', 'e'll come 'ere and make it all right by saying as he meant the note for Old Vinegar. W'y, o' course."

But neither Esme nor Cuthbert paused to consider the quality of sacrifice which was thus being demanded of the wretched Cedric.

CHAPTER XXV

After Cuthbert's departure, Esme, confident now of escaping for the third time in one session, felt that another demonstration of injured innocence was required of him.

"Are you *ever* going to stop accusing me of things?" he demanded violently. "I won't stand it! I'll write to my father. I'll write to my Uncle Dick. Can't that old cradle-snatcher have a note sent her without it being put on me? First it gets bad and then it gets worse. I'm only a young and delicate schoolgirl—"

"Esme!" exclaimed Mrs. Toy sharply. She believed in using a downright tone to girls who seemed on the verge of hysterics.

But to her and Miss Budging's consternation Esme suddenly turned his face to the wall, hid his eyes against the sleeves of his serge blouse and began to howl like a wolf. The two women immediately bore down on him.

"Stop that, Esme," said Mrs. Toy, somewhat alarmed. "Don't make yourself so ridiculous."

"Poor dear Esme!" purred Miss Budging softly, and, considering what Esme had just called her, rathfer handsomely. "Never mind, then. There! There!"

"Woo-oo-oo-oo!" howled Esme, louder than ever. "Woo-woo-woo-woo—WOO! Let me alone! Wow- ow-wow-WOW!"

"If you don't make less noise," hissed the palpitating headmistress, "people will be coming in to know what's the matter."

Esme was certainly making no small noise, and his breaking voice lent to it a bloodcurdling weirdness.

"A gug-gug-good job!" he bellowed. "Then you can tell them how you've been tr-tr-treating me."

His shoulders were heaving with artificial sobs, and he dared not pretend to allow himself to be comforted, for his eyes were dry and his face was liable at any moment to slip beyond his control into contortions of unseemly mirth. He was therefore compelled to keep it hidden, but when at last nature was too strong for him and he exploded with a series of guffaws, the two women not unnaturally put these paroxysms down to an attack of hysteria, and fussed around him more insistently than ever. This added to Esme's delight, so that he laughed on until genuine tears rolled down his cheeks, when, having slowly checked his merriment and achieved a woebegone expression, he removed his arms from his eyes and allowed the two harassed women to see the moisture in his eyes.

Mrs. Toy was very puzzled and very worried. To bring three serious accusations against a girl, one upon another, and be unable to maintain them, was to put herself in a difficult position with regard to the girl's people. It might look, on the face of it, like an organised series of trumped-up charges. The headmistress, hating Esme with all the bitterness of her heart, found herself compelled to propitiate that objectionable young person. Esme was just beginning to allow himself to appear mollified when Cuthbert returned with Cedric.

Poor Cedric! He had heard all from Cuthbert and knew what was before him. He was fond of reading books in which the staunch true heroes lied like gentlemen to save the reputations of ladies, and now was the time come for him to play their part. Only it occurred to him that life was most unfairly a burlesque of fiction, for whereas these heroes risked death or ever-lasting disgrace, he was called upon to risk something far less romantic and almost as disagreeable. He could only clear Esme by affecting a deep attachment for Miss Budging, and if Miss Budging should hear of it and take him seriously, he would then be in a dilemma of which suicide was an almost legitimate way out. Yet his mind was made up, and he accompanied Cuthbert with a firm tread. "For her dear sake!" he kept murmuring to himself, and needless to add he did not mean Miss Budging's.

For him, the culminating horror of the situation lay in the fact that Miss Budging was present, lending moral support to Mrs. Toy, and what he had to say must be said in her presence. When he discovered this his resolution almost failed, and he looked around him with the air of a hunted animal. But Esme was there, staring at him with large anxious eyes, and his wavering resolution found strength again.

Mrs. Toy sent Cuthbert about his business, and addressed Cedric in a tone which reminded him that he had made an impolite reference to her in the captured note.

"Mr. Bingham," she said, holding towards him the sheet of paper, "this note fell into my hands this evening. As there was neither name nor address on the envelope I had no other option than to open it. I see it is signed by you. Did you intend it for anybody here?"

The wretched Cedric grimaced and licked his dry lips.

"Yes," he said.

"For this—this young lady?"

Mrs. Toy indicated Esme with a gesture of one of her thin hands, and Cedric shook his head and threw off his chest the gentlemanly lie.

"No."

"Did you intend it for any of the girls here?"

"No."

Mrs. Toy looked hard at him, and turning to Miss Budging, laid the note in her hands.

"This seems to be your property," she said. Turning to Cedric she added: " Should you wish to communicate with Miss Budging in this way again I should be obliged if you would write her name on the envelopes. You must remember that this is a ladies' school, and my duty compels me to open and read any correspondence which falls into my hands unless it is addressed personally to the mistresses. I am sorry to have troubled you to call."

Although Mrs. Toy's manner broadly hinted that he was now free to depart, Cedric made no effort to go, but stood still, making noises in his throat and staring hopelessly in the direction of Esme. Out of the tail of his eye he had seen coy blushes climb and mantle the damask cheek of Miss Budging. He wanted to explain that it was all a joke, but the words would not come.

"You will excuse me, I know," Mrs. Toy continued coldly. "I am very busy this evening. Miss Budging will accompany you to the door."

In vain Cedric looked at Esme for one kind smile which would enable him to bear what was to come. But Esme was not looking at him. It is even to be feared that Esme was hardly grateful to him, having no room in his heart just then for such an emotion as gratitude. Miss Budging preceded him gravely into the hall, and then slipped back and closed the door which he had left open behind him. He had done this purposely in the hope that, with Mrs.

Toy listening, he might escape from the premises with no worse than a formal good night. But Miss Budging was not to be denied one of the great moments of her life.

In silence they crossed the hall to the front door, where Cedric began to fumble desperately with the catch of the lock.

"Good night," said Miss Budging softly.

"Oh—er—good night."

Miss Budging intruded her hand between the wretched youth and the door. He had no option but to take it.

"Good night," he said again. His eyes were averted, and he made an effort to free his hand. But Miss Budging held it with the gentle firmness of a policeman in the act of arresting a criminal who might possibly show fight.

"Good night," murmured Miss Budging in tender mockery of his tone. Her eyelids flickered.

"Are you going to say it like that?"

"How on earth did you expect me to say it?" demanded the stricken youth irritably.

"Oh, Cedric, you silly boy! But it's sweet of you to be so shy. I know just how you feel towards me." In that she was wrong. It would have surprised and shocked her to no small extent to know that Cedric regarded her with much the same emotions as an early Christian may have regarded one of Nero's lions.

"If you're very good," cooed Miss Budging, suddenly assuming a girlish playfulness which seemed to Cedric beyond the border-line of decency, "you may just give me one little kiss."

Then followed the worst moment in Cedric's life, a moment destined to repeat itself in his dreams and thenceforth to become one of his favourite nightmares. On those occasions he was invariably saved by waking, as now he was saved by the emissary of fate who had come not only to rescue him, but to be the final undoing of poor dear Esme.

Miss Budging had bent her cheek to Cedric, whose brains, scattered in a wild chaos of panic, could hardly tell him if it required more courage to take a quick peck at it than to decline to touch it at all, when the knocker on the outside of the door slammed violently.

The concussion occurred within only a few inches of their heads, and they both jumped as if they had been stung. Miss Budging relaxed her grip on Cedric's hand, and Cedric turned and feverishly pulled back the catch and flung open the door.

On the top step stood a little man with a round and rubicund face set in a smile which gave him something of the expression of a good-natured Chinese joss. He was in the act of removing a faded soft felt hat which presently revealed his head to be as bald as a billiard ball. A faint odour, which might have been connected indirectly with a Perthshire distillery, preceded him into the hall.

"*Good* evening," he said very affably. "A lovely evenin' for the time o' the year. Balmy, I calls it. W'y, with the weather lovely and mild like this, you feels you ought to be lookin' forward to the City and Suburban instead o' the beginning o' the jumping season."

"What do you want?" snapped Miss Budging. The man, she supposed, had been drinking, at least he was talking in a language quite unintelligible to her.

Before the strange visitor could answer, something happened which took her breath away for the moment. Cedric plunged across the threshold, cannoned into the affable stranger whom he nearly capsized, plunged down the steps, and ran as if for his life.

The little man recovered his balance and turned to stare after the flying Cedric.

"Blimey!" he remarked. "That's what I calls a flying start. No fear of '*im* ever getting left at the post."

"What do you *want?*" demanded the goaded assistant mistress.

"Oh, I'm sorry if I intrude, lady," replied the little man, returning to an air of grovelling politeness. "You mustn't mind me. I'm rough, but I'm all right. I've got a 'eart of gold, I 'ave. I'm Honest Ole John Cooper. Everybody knows. Honest Ole John Cooper."

"What do you *want?*" Miss Budging repeated hopelessly. She at least had never heard of Honest Old John Cooper.

"I wants to see the 'ead teacher, lady. I know she's a busy lady, wot with teachin' 'istory and jography and doing the caterin' and whatnot. But I needn't keep 'er a minute. It's just a matter of 'andin' over fifty-five shillin's."

"What do you want fifty-five shillings for?"

"Bless you, lady, I don't *want* it. I got to give it to 'er. One o' the teachers 'as struck lucky, and what with that odd-job boy bein' away ill, and not cornin' round to the pub as usual, I thought I'd better come an' pay out to her. I'm Honest Ole John Cooper, I am, and never kept nobody waiting yet for their dough. They all knows Honest Old John Cooper."

If Miss Budging heard all this, very little of it penetrated to her brain. She had not the least idea that the stranger was a bookmaker's agent, a man who took ready-money bets at street comers and in public-houses. She was too much concerned about Cedric's violent departure to pay much heed to the man, but here, she realised, was a *rara avis,* one who, instead of calling to collect money, had actually come to distribute. In the circumstances she surmised that Mrs. Toy might be glad to see him.

"I'll ask Mrs. Toy if she will see you," she said, and crossed the hall once more.

"Excuse me, Mrs. Toy," she said, throwing open the door of the room in which the headmistress was still closeted with Esme. "Somebody wants to see you."

Before Mrs. Toy could reply, Honest Old John Cooper, manoeuvring around Miss Budging, had managed to insinuate his small and dapper person between her and the open door. He never stood on ceremony, for him the conventions had no place in his scheme of life. He wanted to see Mrs. Toy and so took the shortest cut; and now stood bowing like a mandarin and grinning all over his little round good- humoured face. Mrs. Toy, in the act of pouring out a glass of port for Esme—partly by way of compensation and partly as an antidote to hysteria—recoiled from the apparition and nearly dropped the glass. She wore the expression of a confirmed materialist on suddenly being confronted with the family ghost.

"Beg pardon, lady," said Mr. Cooper, twisting his pliable hat and fairly squirming with humility. "I know you, but you don't know me. I wouldn't mind betting you've *heard* of me, though. Everybody in Purlingdon knows about Honest Old John Cooper." To Esme the name conveyed nothing. Cuthbert had certainly mentioned the name to him, but he had forgotten it, deeming it of little importance. So he watched the queer little man without a qualm, save of amusement. Not for a moment did he suspect that this oddity was his accusing angel in disguise. Here, he supposed, was some tipsy fragment from the streets, blown in by an alcoholic whim for the discomfiture of Mrs. Toy and his own delight.

"Wouldn't your friend like my chair?" he asked Mrs. Toy, with a bland courtesy which brought him a vitriolic look from the quivering headmistress.

Honest Old John gave Esme a smile which nearly met at the back of his neck.

"No, thank you, my dear," he said. "I just want a word with your teacher and then I'm going. I couldn't stay, not even if you was all to press me. Thank you all the same, though, my dear."

Turning to Mrs. Toy he continued affably: "Bonny little girl, ain't she? I've got one just like 'er at 'ome. 'Elps in a fried fish shop every evenin'. Won't 'ear of goin' into service— oh dear no! Girls is that 'aughty and stuck-up nowadays, aren't they? But she's a good girl, mind you, and kind to 'er mother, and so—"

It was the way of Honest John to expand liberally on any topic which was mentioned or happened in any other way to occur to him. Mrs. Toy, too limp to interrupt before, now nipped in the bud a narrative which would have undoubtedly embraced most of her visitor's domestic affairs.

"What can I do for you?" she demanded coldly.

"I got some oof to give you, lady," said Honest John, brightly, in no wise resentful at having been interrupted. "It's for one of your teachers."

"We call them mistresses here," said Mrs. Toy in a tone of outrage. "Teachers are—er—persons at the elementary schools. But what is the money for? And who is it for?"

"Here you are, mum. Here's fifty-five bob and here's the chit. Drunk as a Lord."

"You seem to be in a very intemperate condition," the headmistress remarked severely.

"You had better go and take your money with you. I don't think you know what you are saying."

"Bless you, missus," exclaimed Honest John, beaming happily, "I likes a drop o' tiddley, same as wot you do, I dessay." Here he glanced meaningly at the glass of port which Mrs. Toy had poured out. "But I never gets like *that*. Haven't been wot you call soused since my ole uncle's funeral. But bless you, you 'aven't got my meanin'. Drunk as a Lord is the name of a 'orse. One o' your teachers 'ad five bob on with me, and it clicked at ten to one."

"*What*!" gasped the scandalised headmistress. She stared at the little man incredulously and turned pale, but not so pale as Esme had turned. At the mention of that horse he had started violently, and now his quick brain had grasped at the truth of the situation. Smiling happily and little knowing the misery he was inflicting on one of his audience, Honest Old John Cooper proceeded for the further enlightenment of Mrs. Toy and Miss Budging.

"It's like this 'ere. That odd-job boy of yours brought me the bet, and after the 'orse 'ad clicked 'e didn't turn up for the doings. I've 'eard 'e's ill. Well, I'm Honest Old John Cooper, I am, and I always pays out. Promptity's my motter. And I didn't see why as the lucky lady should be kept waitin' for her money. So 'ere I am to pay out. And if you or any of the other ladies ever wants a bit on, I'm always in the pub around the comer at twelve-fifteen prompt. That boy o' yours knows where to find me."

Esme was looking as sick as a dog caught in the act of stealing a joint, and he breathed with difficulty. "Five shillings to win, Drunk as a Lord, Esme Geering." was written in his own hand on the slip of paper which Honest John was trying to thrust upon Mrs. Toy. Miss Budging looked on, pale and immobile and puzzled, with half her mind bent upon what was going on, and the other half in pursuit of Cedric Bingham. Mrs. Toy passed one of her thin hands across her forehead, which had become cold and sticky.

In every well-conducted tale the Bad Boy who backs horses does so to his own undoing. Either the horse loses or the bookmaker reveals himself to be dishonest. But here was a case of a horse winning, and a bookmaker who was honest—"too darned honest," Esme reflected bitterly. But the moral holds good, even in this veracious story. It takes a twist or two, to be sure, but arrives safely at the appropriate disaster as surely as it does in all the prize books recommended by the Sunday School Committee.

"Do you mean," gasped Mrs. Toy, "that one of my assistants has been *betting* with you?" Honest John nodded as sunnily as if he were bringing good news.

"Yes, lady," he said, "and what's more she's clicked. 'Ere you are, lady; fifty-five bob including the stake, and 'ere's the slip."

Mrs. Toy's head was fairly buzzing by now. She was strongly opposed to betting on moral grounds, but prepared to tolerate it because she had heard that titled ladies were addicted to the vice. But to bet with this dreadful little man magnified the offence into a serious crime. And to send the boot-boy into a low public- house to negotiate the nefarious transaction made it partake of the nature of an atrocity. Her trembling hands closed on the two pound-notes, the silver and the betting slip. She looked at the betting slip . . .

The headmistress uttered a short wailing cry, and turned upon Esme a face which would have been worth a fortune to Gustave Dore.

"Oh, wow!" murmured Esme. "Wow-wow! *Two* wow-wows! Now for it!"

CHAPTER XXVI

Bearing in mind that all Mrs. Toy found to say to Esme was entirely impromptu she acquitted herself admirably. She must have been a lady of latent but undeveloped histrionic ability. It was like listening to a tragedienne of the older school reciting some tragic passage from the more blood-thirsty Elizabethan dramatists. It was a revelation even to Miss Budging, whose mouth fell open as she listened. The smile faded from Honest Old John Cooper's face, and he gave ear with the wrapt expression of one enjoying some serious form of entertainment. But suddenly, as he made sense of Mrs. Toy's ravings, the smile returned, but it was one of amazement and admiration.

"Lumme," he gasped, "so it was *you!* Now 'ow did you come to pick that one out, miss?" Mrs. Toy turned and pointed dramatically at the door.

"Go!" she cried.

Humility at once bent Honest John to the shape of a note of interrogation.

"Yes, lady. Certainly, lady. Only don't be too 'ard on 'er. A young lady wot could pick out Drunk as a Lord 'as got a future before 'er. Anybody might be proud of a dear little girl like that. I wish she was mine—straight, I do."

He shambled out, and for a long moment there was silence, although the echoes of Mrs. Toy's outraged tones seemed still to be lingering on the air.

For Esme, the last straw had been laid upon him. He had been successful in wriggling out of every other scrape, but he knew there was no wriggling out of this. It meant expulsion. Mrs. Toy, hating him as she did, and infuriated at his previous escapes from justice, would hardly pass any other sentence. It meant going back to Uncle Dick, and the strain of seeing Tom Geering every day until he sailed, bearing the burden of knowing all the while that Christine was really Geering's daughter. He was desperate, but desperation brought with it that unearthly calm which most doomed people have experienced. Mrs. Toy, too, in that moment's pause, seemed to have recovered complete control of herself.

"Have you anything to say?" she inquired icily.

"Nit," said Esme. "That's slang for nix, you know," he added helpfully.

"Go to your room," said the headmistress in the same arctic tone, "and don't dare to leave it until I send for you. Miss Budging, will you be so kind as to tell Cuthbert I want to see him."

Esme hesitated.

"Don't blame Cuthbert," he said. "He couldn't help it. I bullied him into it."

Mrs. Toy snorted loudly. The idea of a mere schoolgirl bullying a hulking lout struck her as supremely ridiculous.

"I don't want to hear another word from you," she said. "Go!"

Esme went. In his normal attire he would have thrust his hands into his trouser pockets. He felt for them absent-mindedly along the sides of his skirt, and, failing to find them, clasped his hands behind his back and departed, whistling tunelessly.

But he did not go to his room. He went in search of Christine to say good-bye to her. She was not in the playroom, but Caroline was, and the sight of Caroline, never soothing to him, affected him just then as a scarlet cloak is said to affect a bull of uncertain temper. The corners of his upper lip lifted in scorn and loathing.

"Sneak!" he said. "Sneak! Well tried! Only it didn't happen to come off! So sucks!"

The half-dozen or so girls who were sitting about the room looked up sharply from their books and stared from Esme to Caroline. Tale-bearing at St. Mildred's was almost unknown, and it was not a popular accomplishment. Caroline's face flamed red, and she took two quick steps towards Esme. She was angry enough at thus being publicly accused, but it was Esme's telling her that her scheme had failed which really infuriated her.

"Don't you call me that!" she cried, her voice rising to a squeak.

"If you weren't a girl," said Esme, forgetting that he too was supposed to be one, "I'd call you something a darned sight worse. You thought you were going to get me into a row, didn't you?"

"Don't tell lies!" Caroline fumed. "I didn't know—"

"Oh, it doesn't matter," said Esme, with a contempt which sounded like acute weariness.

"You can't help being a sneak, I suppose. The bally leopard can't change its bally spots."

The metaphor was a somewhat unfortunate one in connection with Caroline, although Esme had chosen it without any thought of a double meaning. Caroline's face was always dotted with those blemishes which are said to defy the ingenuity of the leopard. They were caused, according to certain coarse people, by too many chocolates and insufficient ablutions. Just then she had a more than usually fine selection.

"You beast!" howled Caroline. "You beast to say that! You know they're indigestion."

Then before Esme knew what was happening, he had received Caroline's open hand clean across the left side of his face. It was a good hard bat, and it sounded like a gallon of water dropping from a great height on to a concrete floor. Esme staggered back three or four paces and cannoned against the comer of a table. A sensation went about the room like a wind. The spectators, half frightened, stared in amazement at the pair, wondering what Esme would do.

"I'll teach you!" fumed Caroline. "I'll teach you!"

For a moment Esme said nothing. One side of his face was very white and the other deep red. Fortunately for himself he did not look so foolish as he felt. He looked strangely puzzled, as indeed he was. For once in a way he was faced by a situation which he could not meet. There was murder in his heart, but nothing under Heaven would have tempted him to lift his hand against a girl.

"I wouldn't let her hit me like that," said a voice at last.

"It doesn't matter," Esme growled, trying in vain to assume an air of being too proud to fight.

"I know how to behave like a lady, if she doesn't."

There was a general laugh at this, a laugh in which scorn was freely mingled. The popularity which had flowed around Esme's feet ever since the hockey match ebbed all in a moment. "Coward!" snorted Caroline with a malignant laugh, and Margaret Buddery echoed the word.

The colour lingered bright in Esme's smitten cheek, and now the other cheek began to rival it in hue. He was nonplussed, helpless, hopeless, utterly ashamed. He turned on his heel and walked out amidst loud satirical laughter, and was hard put to it to refrain from making his exit more undignified by running.

That was the darkest hour of Esme's life, or rather it would have been if it had lasted an hour. But it so happened that his courage was under suspicion for only a matter of minutes. Behold Esme sneaking out, despised by those whom he despised, having taken a blow and answered it with words. If nature had given him a tail be sure it would have been tucked tightly under him. He felt as if he wanted to go somewhere quiet and cry. Everything was wrong with the world. He had let Uncle Dick down by getting himself expelled, for he could not doubt that such was to be his fate. He was in a position where he must either betray Uncle Dick or do Christine a deep wrong. And now everybody was laughing at him and calling him a coward because he had allowed a girl to strike him without retaliating. He had no idea what he was to do in the immediate future. Just then he was incapable of thinking. More from habit than by design he stole round to the boot-room to see Cuthbert. He reached the boot-room a few moments after Cuthbert's return from his second interview with Mrs. Toy.

Now Esme was sorry for Cuthbert, who had helped to get him out of one scrape that evening. He knew that Cuthbert must have got into dire trouble with Mrs. Toy on his behalf, and was willing to give him some small financial recompense. As a matter of fact, Cuthbert's interview with the headmistress had been, like the popular Sunday afternoon services, brief, bright and brotherly. Cuthbert had been told to finish his work that evening and call on the morrow for a week's salary in lieu of notice. But if Esme refrained from blaming Cuthbert for what had gone amiss, Cuthbert was not so tolerant towards Esme. A thundercloud dwelt on Cuthbert's brow, for the bottom had dropped out of his life. He had lost the pleasant sums he had been making for executing Esme's commissions, likewise the larger sums for carrying notes between Esme and Cedric, and he had lost his job. A cloudy little brain which had never been taught how to reason and which knew nothing of sportsmanship or fair play, attributed all the blame to Esme.

"You get out of 'ere," he snarled, scowling. "You've done enough 'arm, I should think, to a pore 'ard- workin' bloke. I got the sack, I 'ave."

"We've both been unlucky," Esme acknowledged.

"If it wasn't fer you a-comin' and temptin' a pore bloke with yer money—"

"Oh, shut up! " Esme growled. "You got money or taking chances. You knew what you were doing."

"Yes," said Cuthbert, looking very intently into Esme's face, "and I knows wot I'm doin' now. I want ten bob a week out o' you, young lydy. If not I'll tell all yer friends at the school wot I knows." He looked suddenly sly and impudent and ineffably knowing. "'Oo's got a brother in prison, eh?"

With a smile of cunning and satisfaction he saw Esme start violently. Esme indeed remembered the story he had told Cedric, but he had no time to wonder how the boot-boy could have heard it. At this cool attempt at blackmail Esme's temper flamed up.

"You little swine!" he howled.

With one pounce he was on Cuthbert and had him by the scruff of his short thick neck. On the table before him was a large flat tin of damp blacking. Esme picked it up with his left hand and holding Cuthbert's head down with his right proceeded to rub the sticky black substance all over the boot-boy's face. Cuthbert swore, spat and struggled to get free. He aimed a lucky blow at random and caught Esme on the cheekbone, slightly cutting the skin. Esme then dropped the blacking, loosed his hold on Cuthbert, and hit him hard on the nose. Cuthbert had no scruples at all about hitting one whom he supposed to be a girl. It was one of the things which were "done" in his own stratum of society. As he had already been dismissed from St. Mildred's he had nothing to gain by curbing the angry passions which inflated his youthful breast. Also his nose, which spurted blood at both nostrils, hurt him consumedly. So he fought back with spirit.

It was just what Esme wanted. All the forces which had been pent up and repressed in him for weeks now rushed out of him in a riot of freedom, cheering for liberty. He knew nothing of boxing and was not, as far as he knew, a fighter; for, in spite of those full- blooded stories which delay our errand-boys, fights at a public school are comparatively rare. But, with the safety-valve now open, Esme gladly let the steam away, and for some thirty seconds it was as pretty a set-to as anyone could wish to see.

For no more than five of those thirty seconds did Cuthbert hold his own. For the remaining twenty-five Esme knocked the pained and bewildered youth all over the boot-room. It was a highly unscientific display, but not the less effective. In such instances a knowledge of boxing is about as valuable as a knowledge of needlework.

A madness born of pain and terror afflicted the wretched Cuthbert. Surely, his tortured brain insisted, this was no ordinary girl who was using her fists like a riveter on the plates of a battleship. She was super-normal, uncanny; for all he knew she might be a demon. Covering his head with his arms he made a sudden plunge for the boot-room door and bolted.

Then followed a scene which will be told of, with those embellishments which come with tradition, as long as St. Mildred's remains a school. Cuthbert ran blind with terror to the open door and Esme followed, blind with rage. In the passage just inside the house Esme caught him and punched his head twice, blacking one of his eyes. With a yell which only a tom-cat could emulate, Cuthbert broke loose again and ran on blindly.

In the playroom the girls were still laughing and talking of Esme's cowardice, and Caroline was parading her triumph, when alarums and excursions outside the door caused them to hush their voices and stare in amazement. Then, into their midst, crying aloud for sanctuary, rushed the wretched Cuthbert, a strange object now recognisable only by his clothes. His face a mask of blood and blacking; blood from his nose bedewed his waistcoat, and a trail of it followed him across the room. Hot upon his heels came Esme like an avenging angel, and a chorus of shrieks went up.

Howling aloud for help, Cuthbert ran blindly into a corner, and, finding himself at bay, turned and fought back, with the instinct of a trapped rat. Hearing the commotion Miss Chadpole rushed into the room. She was closely followed by Miss Budging, but neither sought to interfere. Like the girls they stood spellbound. To them it was given to see Cuthbert double up after a blow on the solar-plexus, and then Esme hit him left-right, left-right on the jaw until Cuthbert crumpled, fell forward and lay prone on the floor.

"There!" said Esme, with a sigh of satisfaction. "That'll teach the little skunk to blackmail *me!*"

Then, for the first time, he became conscious of his surroundings and looked about him. "Golly!" he said briefly.

He walked slowly towards the door. Neither Miss Budging nor Miss Chadpole attempted to lay a hand on him. Indeed, nobody moved except Caroline, who climbed over two desks to get out of his way. But Esme did not even see her. He walked unmolested to the door and so passed out of St. Mildred's forever. It was a fitting end to a short but somewhat sensational stay under Mrs. Toy's roof. So long as St. Mildred's lasts so long will live the legend of Esme, like some mediaeval tale of a personal visitation of the devil.

He went slowly out into the garden and climbed the high wall thoughtfully and without apparent effort. Mrs. Toy, looking out of her window, saw him go. A feeling of awe stole over her.

"That isn't a girl," she whispered to herself. "It's a fiend!"

Twenty minutes later the cook requested an audience with her, and on the cook's face was written an expression of one who comes with a tale of death and disaster.

"Excuse me, mum," she said. "I don't know 'ow to tell you. My brother's just come from the ' Green Man,' the public just round the comer. He thought as you ought to know. One of the young ladies is in there, wearin' the school colours. And—and she's smoking cigarettes and drinking beer and standing everybody pints."

A moment later footfalls might have been heard rushing up the stairs. They were the footfalls of the faithful Miss Budging, gone to look for the brandy and the smelling salts. For Mrs. Toy was in sore need of them.

CHAPTER XXVII

It was a desperate Esme who flaunted the colours of St. Mildred's in the "Green Man," to the scandal of an unforgetting Purlingdon. His doom, so far as St. Mildred's was concerned, was already sealed. Even if Mrs. Toy had not intended to expel him for his excursion among the pitfalls of horse-racing, his treatment of Cuthbert had been the last straw. Memories and events moved in his mind as through the brain of a fever patient. The possible consequences to himself troubled him not at all; it was the ghastly dilemma in which he was placed which demanded an old head for his young shoulders. If he gave Christine the father she had always wanted, and gave Tom Geering the daughter of his desire, he imperilled Uncle Dick to whom he owed everything. If he saved Uncle Dick he wronged Christine. Was ever a boy of his years in such a hopeless predicament?

A desperate Esme was liable to do all manner of regrettable things, but even a blind man may stumble across the path which will lead him to his door. So it was with Esme. Having shaken the dust of St. Mildred's off his feet, and declared his independence of that institution by drinking a pint of beer and smoking two cigarettes in an adjacent tavern, the problem of the immediate future presented itself before him with almost the vividness of a new poster. He had to go somewhere for the night, and the thought of returning tamely to St. Mildred's—there probably to be locked in until such time as Uncle Dick could be sent for to take him away—he dismissed without consideration. He remembered with pain and regret that Mrs. Toy had clung to the fifty-five shillings, the proceeds of Drunk as a Lord. He had only about nine shillings in his possession, hardly enough to pay for a night at one of the cheap hotels. Besides, if he went to one, there might be inquiries about a schoolgirl of tender years who was unaccompanied.

There was only one course left for him to pursue, namely to go straight up to town and plant himself on Uncle Dick.

Purlingdon is linked to Waterloo by an electric railway, by which it may be reached in half an hour for the modest sum of one and a penny. By ten o'clock Esme was one of a small crowd moving from one of the platforms towards the exit on the suburban side. A line of taxis was drawn up opposite the steps. Esme hailed the foremost, gave the driver Uncle Dick's address in Bloomsbury, and got in. It was while he was crossing Waterloo Bridge that the light of inspiration blazed upon him.

He sat transfixed for a moment as one who sees visions. Then he slapped his thigh, laughed and exclaimed aloud. By a miracle, as it seemed to him, the path lay clear before him. By handling the situation with proper tact and discretion he could yet right Christine and Tom Geering, and still save Uncle Dick from the consequences of his folly. "I've never bucked much about myself," said Esme to his immortal soul, "but I b'lieve I *must* have brains."

The taxi-cab duly deposited Esme outside the house of Uncle Dick's address, and Esme, having paid the driver, found himself confronted by an open door—a common phenomenon in houses inhabited by more than one family.

Uncle Dick had the second floor landing to himself, but the flat was not self-contained. There was no front door to it, no barriers, once in the house he was free to walk straight into Uncle Dick's rooms. He walked upstairs and found the second floor in darkness. Uncle Dick was evidently out. Turning on the electric light in the living-room he found the table laid and the relics of a repast still remaining.

"Gone to a show," thought Esme. "That means he won't be back for at least another hour." Continuing his explorations he wandered into Uncle Dick's bedroom, where, on seeing the parts of a lounge suit and a coloured shirt and collar lying in different parts of the room— Uncle Dick was just about as tidy as a spaniel pup—he deduced that his guardian had put on evening dress.

Esme peeped under the bed and found two trunks.

"I wonder!" he murmured to himself as he hauled them out.

Without ceremony he proceeded to rummage through them, and to his great satisfaction he found his own suits, shirts, collars and ties.

"Oh, cheers, cheers, cheers!" he cried, and proceeded for the last time to divest himself of feminine attire. Within a minute the hated female apparel had joined the litter of Uncle Dick's clothes about the room, and Esme was experiencing the joy of getting into his old comfortable clothes. He made a successful raid on the dressing table for studs, and when he had once more knotted a Wryvern tie and his toilet was complete, there remained only his longish hair to remind him of the brief period of his girlhood.

Having surveyed himself in the glass he marched out of the room, kicking viciously at his old skirt where it lay between him and the door, and went in search of food. Uncle Dick's housekeeping would have appalled most women, but it did not err on the side of stinginess, and there was plenty to eat. He was just finishing some stewed apricots upon which Uncle Dick had hardly made a start, when heavy footfalls sounded on the stairs. Two men were coming up to the second floor, and one of them was Uncle Dick.

Esme recognised his foster-uncle's footfalls, and guessed that his companion was Tom Geering. In that he was right. They had been to a theatre together, and Tom Geering had accompanied Uncle Dick home for a drink before parting from him for the night.

Esme remained seated at the table as Uncle Dick, followed by Tom Geering, entered the room.
At the sight of Esme, Uncle Dick brought himself up abruptly like a man on the edge of a chasm, and a choked exclamation jumped from his lips. Tom Geering echoed it. He was staring not so much at Esme as at Esme's clothes.

"W-what are you doing here?" Uncle Dick faltered.

"Eating," said Esme. "I say, I hope you weren't wanting any supper. Good evening, both. I daresay you're surprised to see me."

"Wretched child!" Geering burst out. "Does this mean that you've been expelled from school?"

"That's a pretty good guess," Esme conceded. "No, I haven't been expelled yet, but I was going to be. So I thought I'd better come straight home and save trouble. How do you like my clothes?"

"She's mad!" cried Geering, with a strange wild lift to his voice. "She's mad!"

"Well, I should have been if I'd stayed at St. Mildred's much longer. Uncle Dick, the time has come for me to break the news and blow the gaff and all the rest of it. Mr. Geering, I'm not your daughter."

Uncle Dick turned the colour of a new coat of paint on a pillar-box.

"Esme!" he cried in horror. "What are you saying?"

"I'm going to tell him everything," Esme pursued relentlessly. "Mr. Geering, I'm not your daughter. I'm not a girl at all. I'm a boy."

Tom Geering nearly drowned Uncle Dick's howl of protest.

"Boy?" he cried stupidly. "Boy? How boy?"

"Boy!" repeated Esme. "Don't you know what a boy is? Trousers—cricket—football—all that sort of thing . . . Shut up, Uncle Dick, I've got to tell him . . . Uncle Dick brought me up in place of your daughter whom he lost. He didn't like to tell you he'd lost her. Thought you might go potty or something. A fat lot you'd have cared, though! And he couldn't refuse to take your allowance without letting you know he had lost her. See?"

Dazedly Tom Geering passed a shaking hand across his forehead.

"What are you saying?" he murmured fainthy. "What are you saying?"

"So when we heard you were coming home we were in a frightful mess. Uncle Dick was afraid you'd have him sent to prison for having taken your money Sill these years, when he'd lost your daughter as a baby. So I dressed up as a girl, and he got me sent to a girls' school so as to see you as little as possible. Got that?"

"Well—"

Uncle Dick interrupted him with a sudden cry of protest.

"Esme! My boy! My boy! I trusted you, and you've ruined me!"

Tom Geering turned upon the bigger man, who shrank from his gaze.

"You infernal scoundrel!" he cried.

Esme sprang up at once. In a moment he was standing between the two men, and staring at Geering with wide-open, flashing eyes.

"You keep a civil tongue!" he cried. "Don't start calling my Uncle Dick names, or you'll be sorry. He's done everything for me, and I'm not going to let him down. He did everything for the best. It didn't seem to him at the time that he wasn't playing the game, in taking your money and not letting you know the truth. It's all right, Uncle Dick. He can't do anything. I've got a hold over him. I'm not letting you down."

Tom Geering stared at the boy in growing bewilderment.

"Are you raving," he asked, "or what?"

Esme laughed aloud.

"You don't think I'd come here and tell you all this unless I could protect Uncle Dick? Not likely! If you do anything to hurt him you shan't have your real daughter."

"My—real—daughter!"

"Uncle Dick doesn't know where she is, but I do. She's about my age, and she was found at a lodging- house in Margate where Uncle Dick lost the real Esme. And if they aren't the same I'll eat my boots."

Uncle Dick swallowed slightly and stared from one to the other. He could hardly realise what he heard. He seemed to be living in some vague unpleasant dream.

Tom Geering laughed satirically.

"I'll call that bluff," he said. "You don't expect me to believe—"

"I don't care what you believe!" Esme shouted. "If I tell you where to find your daughter, and prove she is your daughter, will you swear not to do anything to Uncle Dick?"

"That's a safe promise," Tom Geering said with a dry laugh.

"All right! Well, you know her already. You took to her, I think, and she took to you. She's called Christine Richards, and she's supposed to be Miss Cheville's niece. But Miss Cheville only adopted her. She told me all about herself. That's how I know. And a fine fix it put me into at first!"

There was a noise in the background. It was Uncle Dick diving to the sideboard in search of brandy. He needed it.

For a moment Tom Geering's face lit up. The girl he had felt he wanted for a daughter! Was it possible? Or was this strange boy only spinning yams to gain time?

"Esme!" he cried, almost piteously. "In God's name, is that true?"

Oh!" cried Esme, almost wearily. "Would I be here, giving the whole game away, if it weren't?" Geering turned again to confront Uncle Dick.

"We'll go and see Edith Cheville first thing tomorrow," he said.

Uncle Dick was gulping hard, and he could only nod.

CONCLUSION

In the August of the year following, a happy family party was assembled at Looe in Cornwall, and two of its members sat on a boulder on the beach within a convenient distance of the refreshment hut. Esme and Christine—to call them by their old names which they still retained—had grown a little towards maturity in the intervening months. Christine was prettier than ever, and Esme had sobered down a little. He wore the Wryvern blazer with the dignity of a fellow who had recently made forty-five against the M.C.C.

"What a long time they are!" Christine murmured. "I wonder if they're looking for us." Esme shook his head.

"No, they're still at the ' Ship.' Mr. Cook said he'd commissioned a man to get us some bait, and I expect that's what's holding them up."

Christine sighed and stretched herself in the sun.

"Isn't it lovely to be all living together?" she murmured. "We didn't guess when we first met—did we?—that we were going to be brought up as brother and sister."

"It's all worked out beautifully," Esme murmured contentedly. "Mr. Geering wanted you, but he couldn't take you away from Aunt Edith."

"And Aunt Edith married Uncle Dick," murmured Christine.

"Because," added Esme, grinning, "she said, after the mess he'd made of everything, she thought she'd better come and look after him, after all. I'm awfully glad. They're as happy as two-year-olds."

"So the only thing," laughed Christine, "was for Uncle Dick and Aunt Edith to get a house and go on bringing us up, and for father to come and live with them. It couldn't be better, could it?"

"Everything in the garden," said Esme contentedly, " is—er—horticultural. I say, aren't you glad your father took you away from St. Mildred's? What a hole!"

Christine laughed reminiscently.

"Poor St. Mildred's. Do you ever think of it?"

"When I have bad dreams. I s'pose it's all going on the same as usual. I wonder whether Mrs. Toy suspects what sort of an angel she entertained unawares. She couldn't do much if she did. It wouldn't advertise her school if she made a fuss."

"I heard from Margaret Buddery only a fortnight ago," said Christine. "There isn't much news. Miss Budging got her claws into Cedric, and nearly made him marry her. But she had to let him go because he was under age and his father made such a fuss. Cedric's been seen about a lot with a shop girl lately, so it looks as if there's more trouble brewing."

Esme laughed tolerantly.

"Poor old Cedric! He ought to have been sent up to the 'Varsity, instead of being let loose like that. And that reminds me! Isn't it splendid of your pater to be going to send me up to Oxford. He's no end of a good chap. Isn't it funny how we hit it off together now, when we began by hating each other like poison?"

"All's well that ends well," said Christine.

Esme seized her by the arm.

"People who make trite remarks get their wristesses twisted-ed," he said. "Come on—let's go and get an ice."

A.M. Burrage – A Short Biography

Alfred McLelland Burrage, better known as simply AM Burrage, was born in Hillingdon, Middlesex on July 1st, 1889, to Alfred Sherrington Burrage and Mary E. Burrage. On his Father's side writing already ran in the family's blood as both he and an uncle, Edwin Harcourt Burrage, were writers of the then very popular boys' magazine fiction.

Life in late Victorian times was by no means easy and writing has always been a precarious career for most. For an insight into the young AM and his surroundings it is interesting to see how certain facts were captured in the 1891 census when he was aged one. The family is listed as living at Uxbridge Common in Hillingdon. His father is 40 and his mother 36. In the next census of 1901, and with it the end of the Victorian era, the family has moved to 1 Park Villa, Newbury. In that time his father has aged 17 years his mother 6 years and young AM has disappeared from the records. It's almost a precursor to one of his stories.

There is little documented about his growing up and education. What we can glean though is something about his environment. His neighbours were varied: a tailor's journeyman, a corn porter, a lodging-house keeper and a grocer's assistant. Nothing particularly illustrious, so times cannot have been as rosy as they should, especially in the light of his Father's hard work. Alfred Sherrington wrote for The Boy's World, Our Boys' Paper, The Boys of England, and various others. He also appears to have written under the pseudonym Philander Jackson and edited The Boys' Standard and that one of his more celebrated pieces was a retelling of the story of Sweeney Todd entitled "The String of Peals; or, Passages from the Life of Sweeney Todd, the Demon Barber".

Sadly Alfred Sherrington Burrage died in 1906. There is a biographical note in Lloyd's Magazine, from 1921, which suggests that young Alfred McLelland was studying at St. Augustine's, the Catholic Foundation School in Ramsgate, and most probably away from home at the time.

A.M. Burrage was 16 years old when he had his first story published; the same year as his father's death, in the prestigious boys' paper, Chums. It was a great start to his professional career and whether doors had been opened by his father and family or not the young man's career now had to stand on its own. He was now primary provider for the household and this was the only way he could do it. His Mother, sister and aunt must be provided for.

Magazine fiction was his family's blood and business and for A. M. Burrage, business was good. He established himself as a competent and creative writer and was busy writing stories and articles on a weekly basis for publications such as Boys' Friend Weekly, Boys' Herald, Comic Life, Vanguard, Dreadnought, Triumph Library Cheer Boys Cheer, and Gem, under the pseudonym 'Cooee'.

However, unlike his father and uncle who had remained firmly and easily categorised as boys' writers, he had his sights set on the more well regarded, more lucrative, adult market. Burrage was aided in his early years as a professional writer by Isobel Thorne of the off-Fleet Street publishing firm Shurey's. Her publications have been characterised as "low in price, modest in payments, but whose readers were avid for romance, thrills, sensation, strong characterisation and neat plotting", and this estimation of her publications also fits nicely the description of Burrage's own writing at that time. For a young writer this sort of readership was vital, and the modest wages he received were bolstered by the exposure the publications brought him. Burrage was certainly helped by Thorne's use of young writers.

At the time Burrage was beginning to really establish himself as a writer, the entire magazine fiction scene was benefiting from what we would now see as disruptive influences: new printing techniques, a growing readership with more disposable income and leisure time and other media failing to provide – though obviously movies and such were only in their infancy at the time. The market was lively and commercial, and the readership interested, excitable and willing to pay. P. G. Wodehouse, of Jeeves fame, recalls these years:

We might get turned down by the Strand, but there was always the hope of landing with Nash's, the Story-teller, the London, the Royal, the Red, the Yellow, Cassell's, the New, the Novel, the Grand, the Pall Mall, and the Windsor, not to mention Blackwood's, Cornhill, Chambers's and probably about a dozen more I've forgotten.

With War clouds darkening the skies of Europe in 1914 Burrage was firmly established as a magazine writer, securing publication in London Magazine and The Storyteller, which were both highly prestigious publications. Alongside he had plenty printed in less illustrious publications such as Short Stories Illustrated.

By now Burrage, a young man of twenty-four-year-was eligible for the Armed Services. Under the 'Derby Scheme' he confirmed that he was available for service if called upon in December 1915. Conscription was to follow shortly though, by that time, Burrage had already voluntarily enrolled in the Artists Rifles.

The significance of Burrage's decision to join the Artists Rifles is made clear by the nature of the unit itself. They formed in the middle of the nineteenth century, a group of volunteer artists comprising musicians, writers, painters and engravers. Minerva and Mars were their patrons, one of wisdom, arts, and defence, the other of war. The unit boasted several significant figures as ex-servicemen, including Dante Gabriel Rossetti, Algernon Charles Swinburne and William Morris. It was a popular unit with students and recent postgraduates, and the training was considered and extensive.

In Burrage's vivid, celebrated account of World War I entitled War is War, he insists that he was a volunteer and not a conscript, though as has already been noted, it is quite possible that his decision to join such a respected territorial unit may have been more of an effort to secure himself a more congenial army posting; had he waited for conscription, he would have had little choice over those with whom he was posted. Unlike poets Wilfred Owen or Edward Thomas, Burrage did not achieve a commission, and he suggests in War is War that this may be a result of his extremely unmilitary personality and his shortcomings as a soldier.

Add to this the fact that as the breadwinner for the family he was putting himself in harm's way. If anything were to happen to him the result on the family would be devastating. With the death of
Edwin Harcourt Burrage in 1916 it came even more starkly into focus.

Even though he was now a soldier he was still a writer and writers had to write.   It also helped that it was a distraction from the mindless carnage around him.   He experimented with various genres, excelling in the one that was to prove most lucrative for him; the light romance, in which a male character invariably meets a female character, there is a problem or hurdle to their being together, they overcome it and they live happily ever after. Burrage's talent for this formula was such that he could work seemingly endless minor variations from the same basic storyline and so he was able to keep writing a steady body of easy work.

He gives a fascinating account of the practicalities of writing such fiction during wartime in War is War, in which he remarks on the difficulties of censorship: "the problem of censorship was an acute one to me. It was well enough to write a story, but the difficulty was to get it censored. Officers were shy of tackling five thousand words or so, written in indelible pencil..." After some time he managed to find a chaplain who was willing to undertake the censorship. However, in order to secure this chaplain's favour and thus his services he was obliged to appear to be holy. Though he did so in earnest while he was with the chaplain, his efforts were dashed when the chaplain found him, sprawled on top of a young girl, and realised Burrage's piety to be a fraudulent con. As Burrage had anticipated, the reality of his behaviour ensured that this particular opportunity was swiftly ended. Resourceful to the last, though, he writes of his solution: "there were 'green envelopes' which could be sent away sealed and were liable only to censorship at the base, but these were only sparingly issued... I met an A.S.C. lorry driver who had stolen enough green envelopes to last me for the rest of the war; and since he only wanted two francs for them I was free of the censorship from that day forward."

Although we know that Burrage had his family to support at home as an incentive to keep writing, at times in War is War he reveals a more intimate aspect of his relationship with his work.

"It was a great relief to me to write when it was at all possible – to sit down and lose myself in that pleasant old world I used to know and pretend to myself that there never had been a war. Some of my editors seemed of the opinion that we were not suffering from one now. One used to write to me saying "Couldn't you let me have one of your light, charming love stories of country house life by next Thursday." I would get these letters in the trenches during the usual 'morning hate' when my fingers were too numb to hold a pencil, when I was worn out with work and sleeplessness, and when I was extremely doubtful if there ever would be another Thursday".

Writing is a useful therapy and for Burrage it provided a means to escape if only for a short time to a world that he could control and move at will. With the misery and harsh conditions of the War dragging on he was eventually invalided and so he returned to England.

One of the best insights we have as to the character which Burrage presented on his return from the war is to be found in Lloyd's's 1920 publication of Captain Dorry, one of Burrage's story series. In that publication there was included a brief sketch of Burrage, describing his personality.

A.M. BURRAGE is the type of young man who might very well walk out of one of his own stories. He commenced yarn-spinning as a boy of fifteen at St Augustine's, Ramsgate, writing stories of school life to provide himself with pocket-money. Since then he has won his spurs as one of the most popular of magazine writers. Everything he does has charm and reflects his own romantic spirit – for he is incurably romantic and hopelessly lazy. It is his misfortune, although he would not admit it, that his work finds a too ready market. Nevertheless, his friends hope that one day he will wake up and do justice to himself. Otherwise he may end up as a "best-seller", a fate which doubtless he contemplates with equanimity.

Despite the sketch's fairly accurate but negative summation of Burrage's literary output up to that point, some of his stories seem to exhibit a desire to write about more than just his usual romantic plots. The most immediate change of this nature is in his decision to bring some of his wartime experience into his work, despite being perfectly aware that such writing was not at all what his editors desired, for they feared it would upset and intimidate their readership.

An example of this can be found in "A Town of Memories", published in 1919 in Grand Magazine, in which he uses his well rehearsed romantic story with a slight shift of emphasis to explore his own return from the war and the general reception which soldiers received on their return. Following a young officer as he returns to the town in which he grew up, Burrage portrays an almost hostile environment into which he returns; he is unrecognised, and nobody pays any interest, respect or attention to him or his stories of the war, nor even to his reception of the Distinguished Service Order. Instead, the people of the town have their own interests and priorities with which to concern themselves. Though this contentious portrayal of post-war society certainly marks a slight shift in Burrage's writing, he returns to the romantic convention expected of him by reuniting the officer with a beautiful girl who had admired him throughout school. It would be harsh to not accept that market conditions expected one thing and to ignore them would mean turning his back on publications who still clamoured for his penmanship.

Another of Burrage's alternative directions is to be found in "The Recurring Tragedy", in which a General whose war tactics of attrition had been to the slaughtered cost of his soldiers, and he comes to re-imagine his own past as a Judas figure in a terrible vision. The Strange Career of Captain Dorry became a series for Lloyd's Magazine in 1920 about a gentleman crook and an ex-officer with a Military Cross who, idle in peacetime, meets a mysterious man called Fewgin whose business is in stolen goods and mind reading. Fewgin realises Dorry is a suitable candidate for recruitment into his gang of like-minded ex-military thieves, stealing only from "certain vampires who made money out of the war, and, by keeping up prices, are continuing to make money out of the peace". Again, in this motive, we see a glimpse of Burrage's own feelings on the war, as there is undoubtedly a bitterness towards those profiting from the suffering of others in such a manner. Fewgin justifies himself, saying:

"I help brave men who cannot help themselves. I give them a chance to get back a little of their own from the men who battened and fattened on them, who helped to starve their dependents while they were fighting, who smoked fat cigars in the haunts of their betters, and hoped the war might never end."

Burrage began to see slightly more success in the 1920s, achieving a couple of hard back publications entitled Some Ghost Stories and Poor Dear Esme. The latter, a comedy, concerns a boy who, for various reasons, is forced to disguise himself as a girl. Though these hard cover publications were a notable achievement, and one of which he was proud, the fact was that there was less money in it than in the magazines. In his history of the Strand Magazine, Reginald Pound portrays Burrage around this time, likening him to his equally prolific contemporary Herbert Shaw, considering them "two Bohemian temperaments that suffused and at times confused gifts from which more was expected than come forth. They had a precise knowledge of the popular short story as the product of calculated design. Both privately despised it, though it was their living."

The early 1920s, and with them a boom in prosperity, hope and happiness, now brought with them an increase in demand for war stories. Rather than preferring to ignore the atrocities of the war, which had seemed the general attitude in the immediate post-war years, society became more interested and concerned with the manner in which the war was fought, and the greed and political battles which had necessitated such bloodshed. Burrage answered this demand in 1930 with his own epochal piece, War Is War. He published under the pseudonym 'Ex-Private X', saying "were it otherwise I could not tell the truth about myself", though its publisher, Victor Gollancz, "who published the book and greatly admired it, had to point out that the critics would hardly take the book seriously if it became known that the author earned his living producing two or three slushy love stories a week".

In one of a series of letters he wrote to his contemporary and fellow writer Dorothy Sayers, Burrage bemoans how War is War "promised to be a great success, but was only a moderate one". The book itself was received with reviews on both sides of the spectrum. Cyril Fall's War Books, a survey of post-war writing published in 1930, gives a clear indication as to why the critics were so mixed in reception of the book. He writes:

This book is extremely uneven in quality. The account of the attack at Paschendaele and of conditions at Cambrai after the great German counter-attack are very good indeed; in fact among the best of their kind. But the rest is disfigured by an unreasoned and unpleasant attack on superiors and all troops other than those of the front line, which is all the more astonishing because the author is inclined to harp upon his social position as compared with that of many of the officers with whom he came in contact. He does not use as much bad language as many writers on the War, but his methods of abuse will leave on some of his readers at least a worse impression than the most highly-spiced language.

Dorothy Sayers was the editor at Victor Gollanz for anthologies of ghost and horror stories which included stories by Burrage. She says, in one of her letters of Burrage's story The Waxwork, a piece beyond the nerves of the editors, "what you say about "The Waxwork" sounds very exciting, just the sort of thing I want. Our nerves are stronger than those of the editors of periodicals, and we will publish anything, so long as it does not bring us into conflict with the Home Secretary". Though their correspondence began as strictly business, Burrage's acquaintance with Atherton Fleming, Sayers's husband, allowed their interactions to become less formal and friendlier. Burrage wrote of Fleming "I hope to encounter him soon in one of the Fleet Street tea-shops". 'Tea-shop' being a popular euphemism for the pub, where both Burrage and Fleming could frequently be found, though their alcohol consumption came to damage both their health and their professions, with Burrage coming off the worse.

Happily for Burrage, as a result of being featured in one of Sayers's anthologies, The Waxwork became one of his best-known stories and it would grab the attention of the film companies several times down the years even becoming an episode in the TV series 'Alfred Hitchcock Presents'.

The developing friendship between Burrage and Sayers enabled him to reveal more details of his personal life, admitting to her his "neuritis at both ends (legs and eyes)", and hinting at his troubles with alcohol: "Fleet Street is not a good place for a man who delights in succumbing to temptation, and whose doctor says that even small doses of alcohol are poison to him". Sayers sympathises, replying that Fleming "agrees with you entirely about the temptations of Fleet Street; he has, however, succeeded, through sheer strength of character, in being able to drink soda-water in the face of all his fellow journalists".

In another of Burrage's letters, he apologises for a delay in sending proofs of a story, with the words:

I have had a pretty thin time lately through illness and anxiety. And for days on end haven't had the energy in me to write a letter, and when I had the energy to send a complete set of proofs to you I found I hadn't the postage money (This is when you take out your handkerchief and start sobbing). I owed my late agent over £1000, so I got practically nothing out of War is War. He stuck to it. Well, he is paid off now, and so are my arrears of income tax. All this took a toll of my very small earning capacity, and I have been sold up. This on top of something which promised to be a great success and was only a moderate one, was a bit too much for me. Still, in spite of sickness I am resilient and shall float again. "You can't keep a good man down," as the whale said about Jonah.

For a man who had so many stories in so many magazines, and was gaining pace in Sayers's anthologies as a talented writer of horror stories, his income will have been far higher than the then average wage, and yet as he says, he finds himself short of money.

Several questions are left unanswered about his personal life. It is unclear whether he was still supporting family, or whether he spent the majority of his money on alcohol, or whether he chose to conceal his true fortunes from those around him. Perhaps most incongruous is the apparent absence of a wife; though his death certificate indicates that he had one, listed as H.A. Burrage, he seems never to mention her to Sayers.

He was around forty-two when he wrote that apology letter to Sayers, though in tone and circumstance it seems to be from a man in a far later stage of his life.

Burrage continued writing until his death in 1956, and continued to be prolifically published. Indeed, the Evening News alone published some forty of his stories between 1950-56. His death is recorded at Edgware General Hospital on 18th December, and the causes of his death are recorded as congestive cardiac failure, arteriosclerosis and chronic bronchitis. He was sixty-seven years old, and his last address is listed as 105 Vaughan Road, Harrow.

Though his name is not often remembered in lists of prominent writers of his time, or even it's genres, his ghost stories are highly regarded by critics and fans alike, while his life story tells us much about the trials and stresses placed on authors during and after the war, and on soldiers returning from that war. His reluctant acceptance that the money was in the magazines while the esteem was in the poorly-paying hard covers, and his persistence as a writer, speak of a determined man, doomed to circumstance yet living as best he could.

In ending A.M Burrage wrote a few sentences which best sum up two things. Firstly his love for his son Simon (who sadly passed away in October 2013 and was a great and passionate advocate for his Father's works.) and secondly his succinct reasons for writing.

TO JULIAN SIMON FIELD BURRAGE
who at the moment of writing will
soon achieve the great age of four.
From somebody who loves him.

In War is War I admitted being a professional writer, or in other words one who depends for his bread and cheese and beer on writing, typing or dictating strings of sentences which his masters, the Public, are kind enough to buy and presumably to read.

The book brought me letters from a few old friends and a great many new ones. A large percentage of the new friends, who missed having seen that my identity was rather unkindly betrayed by the Press, wrote and asked (a) who I was and (b) what sort of stories did I write?

The answer to the second question will be found in the following pages. The answer to the first question is 'Nobody Much', worse luck.

Most of these stories were written with the intention of giving the reader a pleasant shudder, in the hope that he will take a lighted candle to bed with him—for candle-makers must be considered in these hard times. Some have already made their bow from the pages of the monthly magazines. The best have, quite naturally, been rejected.